CRITICAL ACCLAIM FOR THE FRED CARVER SERIES BY EDGAR AWARD-WINNING AUTHOR JOHN LUTZ

TROPICAL HEAT

"Smooth, first-rate...A writer who knows how to seize and hold the reader's imagination from the start."
Cleveland Plain Dealer

"Lutz has never written leaner prose...A delight"
USA Today

SCORCHER

"Fast-paced...Superior entertainment"
San Diego Union

"SCORCHER is another reason why John Lutz is one of the best mystery writers of the 1980's, and isn't too far from the best of any other era."
Newport News Press

KISS

"The grip on the reader is relentless until the final, entirely unforeseen shocker... Lutz's best novel so far."
Publishers Weekly

"One of the best private eye series. The proof is in KISS."
Orlando Sentinel

Other Avon Books by
John Lutz

Kiss
Tropical Heat

SCORCHER

JOHN LUTZ

AVON BOOKS ◢ NEW YORK

AVON BOOKS
A division of
The Hearst Corporation
105 Madison Avenue
New York, New York 10016

"A Rinehart Suspense Novel"
Copyright © 1987 by John Lutz
Published by arrangement with Henry Holt and Company, Inc.
Library of Congress Catalog Card Number: 87-221
ISBN: 0-380-70526-5

First Avon Books Printing: July 1988

AVON TRADEMARK REG. U.S. PAT. OFF. AND IN OTHER COUNTRIES, MARCA
REGISTRADA, HECHO EN U.S.A.

Printed in the U.S.A.

K-R 10 9 8 7 6 5 4 3

For Steve, Marcia, and Andrew John

I see the Judge enthroned; the flaming guard:
The volume open'd!—open'd every heart!

—Young,
Night Thoughts

SCORCHER

CHAPTER 1

After about 10:00 A.M. it gets too hot to sit outside during July in central Florida. It was nine o'clock now, and already bright, baking, and humid. Everything warm-blooded and not working on a tan sought the shade.

On the brick veranda of Carver and Edwina's beach house in Del Moray, the umbrella that sprouted from the center of the white metal table was tilted to block the morning sun, which was crawling up the hazy blue-gray sky over the Atlantic like a burning thing, slow in its agony. The upper half of Edwina's face was in the shadow of the umbrella, as if she were wearing a mask. Maybe she sat that way on purpose. Though they'd lived together for almost ten months, here in the house that was actually Edwina's, Carver still didn't know her. There was a part of her that belonged to a past she kept private. He'd kept his ramshackle beach cottage, twenty miles up the coast, because there might be a day when Edwina would want him out of her future as well as her past. She was unpredictable that way; possibly Carver loved her for it.

She sipped grapefruit juice from her tall glass, then said, "How long will your ex and the kids be in Florida?"

Carver looked out at the sun-flecked ocean and shrugged. "Maybe a week. Maybe a little longer. She's going to take Ann and Chipper to Disney World, go with them to the beach, that kind of thing."

"Tourist shit," Edwina said.

Carver nodded. A sea gull arced low over the rise above the beach and screamed, as if it had an urgent need to tell

1

him something, then soared away, all without one flap of its wings.

"Do you think Laura chose Florida for a vacation so she could see you?" Edwina asked.

It surprised Carver that she'd used his former wife's name; usually Laura was simply "she" or "your ex." "I think she wanted to take the kids on vacation, and I've got a court-sanctioned visit coming up, so she decided to combine the two. Nothing devious going on."

"Ah, the proverbial two birds with one stone."

"Sure. No reason to read anything else into it."

Edwina bowed her head slightly and lifted her glass again. The sunlight caught her green-flecked eyes and exposed their intensity before they withdrew again into shadow. She took another sip of grapefruit juice, as if she needed the acidic stuff before phrasing what she meant to say. "I think she's still interested in you."

Carver was sure that wasn't true. "You're assuming a lot about a woman you don't even know."

"I know her through you. Enough about her."

"Laura's probably doing this mainly so I won't show up outside her door in Saint Louis next month and shake up her life."

Edwina absently ran a finger through the moisture left by her glass on the smooth table, creating a wavering pattern. "She didn't waste any time in calling here and letting you know she was in Florida."

"That's so I can't have any excuse for not exercising my visitation rights with the kids while they're here; I won't be able to say I never had an opportunity. She's dictating location."

Carver felt a pang of anticipation at the thought of seeing Ann and Chipper again. It had been autumn when he'd seen them last in Saint Louis, where Laura lived with the man she claimed she was going to marry. Six-year-old Ann had put on weight and was beautifully chubby, while eight-year-old Chipper had grown taller with a suddenness that had left him gangly. Let Laura take them to Disney World, Sea World, Circus World, and all the various other manufactured worlds of central Florida. Carver yearned to take his children for long walks on the beach, to slow down their growing up and talk to them about the real world, the one they were fated to live in.

"When are you planning to see her?" Edwina asked.

"I'm not planning to see her; I'm planning to see Ann and Chipper. But Laura will be there. Tomorrow evening at the Howard Johnson's on the Orange Blossom Trail. Want to come?"

"That would be awkward."

"Not for me. And I'd like you to meet my kids."

"Maybe it'd be awkward for Laura."

"So who cares?"

Carver did, but he could almost convince himself he didn't. His marriage had been a quicksand tragedy, mainly because of him. He didn't want Laura back and she didn't want him, and he didn't fool himself about who carried the blame for the divorce. He didn't hate Laura, didn't even remotely dislike her. And he didn't want to cause her any trouble. She was simply a woman who'd been caught up in the wrong life at the wrong time. His life. After the divorce she'd married again, to a psychologist named Charles Montaigne. Carver had agreed to let them legally adopt the children, though he'd maintained minimal visitation rights; he wanted Chipper and Ann to be part of a family unit even if he wasn't in it. Carver still thought of Chipper, young Fred Montaigne, as Fred Jr.

Carver's inclination these last few days to stereotype Laura as the disdainful and vaguely vengeful former wife was, he knew, a sort of reassuring manifestation of his love for Edwina.

But Edwina wasn't reassured.

"I can't go anyway," she said. "I've got some property to show tonight down the coast." She sold real estate in and around Del Moray and was serious about her work. Ferocious about it.

Carver didn't know whether to believe her.

Edwina cocked her head to the side sharply at the sound of tires crunching on the gravel drive at the front of the house. A car door slammed, and Carver looked toward the front gate, idly toying with his coffee cup.

He'd remember the feel of the cup, the warm curved surface of smooth china, the sharp spur against his knuckle near the base of the arched handle, for the rest of his life. A permanent moment. Because as soon as the tall figure of Alfonso Desoto appeared from behind the palm trees and pushed through the gate, Carver knew in a part of his mind older than he was that something was very wrong.

He knew it by the strained lines of Desoto's handsome Latino face, by the lack of vigor in his walk and the slump of his shoulders. The jacket of Desoto's pale gray lightweight suit was unbuttoned and flapping in the soft ocean breeze. Desoto was a clotheshorse who always automatically buttoned his suitcoat when standing up or climbing out of a car. Like zipping his fly after relieving himself. But not this morning. And the fact that he was here instead of at the Municipal Justice Building in Orlando, where he was a police lieutenant in Homicide, was in itself ominous. Carver had talked to Desoto two days ago, and he knew Desoto was working the day watch and should be behind his desk or out on an important call.

Unless something more important, and personal, had brought him here.

As he approached the table, Desoto flashed his white, dashing smile, but it was obviously mechanical. He was ethnic matinee-idol handsome, with broad, squared shoulders and a lean waist, and with the carved and faintly hawkish features that gave away his Aztec heritage if one looked closely enough to realize that he wasn't Cuban, as many people assumed. Desoto's father had been Mexican, his mother American of Italian descent. The draw of the gene pool had produced in Desoto a man who, had he been an actor, would have been cast by any producer in the role of romantic bullfighter.

Without speaking to Carver, he bent gracefully and kissed Edwina's cheek. Always Desoto gave first and special attention to women. He whispered something in Edwina's ear. She sat back in her chair until her entire face was

concealed by the shadow of the umbrella. Then she stood
up and walked into the house. She was wearing a skimpy
blue bathing suit and her walk was incredibly elegant and
sensual, but Desoto didn't stare after her. Instead he turned
and gazed down at Carver with somber brown eyes and
said, ''Another day almost too hot for crime, eh? It's a
wonder there's work for people like us.''

Small-talk time. As if Edwina had gone inside merely to
cool off.

''Want some juice or coffee?'' Carver asked, letting
Desoto work up to the purpose of his visit in his own
fashion.

''Neither.'' Desoto turned and looked out at the sea and
sky beyond the rise on which the house was built. The land
was graded, so there was a drop to the ocean. From the
veranda you could hear the waves breaking on the rocks the
Army Corps of Engineers had piled there to keep the beach
from eroding. ''You're in the midst of true beauty here,
Carver. Tranquillity. I hope you appreciate your situation.
It could make you stronger.''

Carver started to get up.

''Stay down, *amigo*,'' Desoto said gently.

Carver had heard that sad tone in Desoto's voice before.
He settled back in his sun-heated metal chair and waited.
Desoto sat down across from him, where Edwina had been
sitting.

''This world,'' Desoto said, shaking his head, ''I don't
know what it all means. Two weeks ago, down in Pompano
Beach, a souvenir-store owner was found burned to death
in his shop. There were two tourists at the back of the
place, out of sight. They heard a man argue with the
shopkeeper about some item the man wanted to return. Then
they heard a kind of whoosh and a scream. One of them
looked toward the front of the shop and caught a glimpse
of someone using what looked like a scuba diver's air tank
for a flamethrower. A gelatinlike material, on fire, was all
over the shopkeeper. He leaped over the counter, ran three
steps, and died. He was still burning when the police
arrived. The man with the scuba tank got away without

anyone getting a close enough look at him to give a description. A hell of a thing, *amigo*."

"I read about the case," Carver said edgily. He was growing impatient to get to what he feared. "We subscribe to the papers and watch the news here in Del Moray, just like you folks in Orlando."

"Of course," Desoto said softly, instead of responding to Carver's sarcasm. That scared Carver. Desoto was making conversation about interesting cases instead of telling him something was wrong. That someone was hurt— or worse. Or that Carver's beach cottage had burned down, or the department was cutting off Carver's disability pension for the bad leg.

"I'm tired of twisting on the hook," Carver said.

Desoto expelled a lot of air and smiled sadly. "I don't mean to leave you twisting. I insisted on being the one to come here and tell you, so you're right: I should tell. Last evening in Fort Lauderdale a woman let her son run back into a small restaurant to retrieve her purse, which she'd left behind. When he didn't come out, she went in to find him. The restaurant's only employee on duty was behind the cash register, burned to death and still smoldering. On the floor was the woman's son, in the same condition."

Desoto paused and Carver watched the gulls circling way out at sea. A couple of sailboats lay beyond them, tiny white objects pinned against the brightening water. Far beyond the sailboats, ghostly in the mist of distance, a giant oil tanker, seemingly motionless, was making its ponderous way down the coast. The breeze gained strength, carrying the fresh yet rotted scent of the ocean to Carver and making him realize by its coolness on his face that he was perspiring heavily.

"Get to it," he said.

Desoto swallowed, and for the first time since Carver had known him, his voice broke. "The woman is your former wife, *amigo*. The boy was your son."

The gulls continued to circle. The sailboats and oil tanker remained unmoving. The tireless sea slapped at the rocks below the veranda. The sun hammered down. All the way it had been a moment ago, yet not the same. Nothing could ever again be the same.

From far away, Carver heard Desoto say, "I'm sorry."

CHAPTER 2

"I told you, you didn't have to," Desoto said to Carver. "Sometimes it's like you hate yourself."

They were at Wolfie's on East Sunrise in Fort Lauderdale, where Desoto liked to eat whenever he was in the vicinity. It was a hall-like place with lazy ceiling fans, a hundred tables, and an excellent reputation it deserved. There were about a dozen other diners, seated along the walls. Desoto was helping himself to sweet rolls from the wicker basket on the table. Carver wasn't eating.

"I guess I did have to," Carver said, trying not to think about the blackened thing he'd seen curled on the table at the morgue. But Desoto was right; it had been stupid of Carver to insist on viewing the body and putting himself through the horror. Masochistic. There was little enough left of Chipper to identify other than by dental work. Carver knew how that was done postmortem; he tried not to think about that, either.

"I feel helpless," Desoto said. "I don't like seeing this dumped on you, *amigo,* and there's nothing I can do to change what happened."

"And no way I can change it," Carver said. He ran his hand down his face. His eyes felt dry, his cheeks stiff, as if he'd been crying and had passed beyond tears. Or had screamed himself beyond emotion. He caught sight of his reflection in a wall mirror: average-sized guy, in his forties, gleaming bald on top but with a thick mass of curly gray hair over his ears and in back. Sun-bleached eyebrows; blue eyes like a cat's against a tan, almost swarthy complexion.

Nose long and straight, lips full and stubborn. Features not handsome, but strong, maybe cruel, because of the boyhood scar that gave a slight twist to the right corner of his mouth. No hint in the reflection of what had happened to the inner man. No sign that a universe had shifted.

"Laura seems to be coping okay," Desoto said, spreading butter on a roll. Some of it melted and dripped golden onto his plate.

"She's in shock."

"She's also going to be joined in a few hours by Sam Devine." Devine was the lawyer Laura was living with in Saint Louis. "Maybe you should see her first." Desoto, wise in the ways of women, even women numbed by grief.

"I want to see her," Carver said. He'd spoken to Laura only briefly after Chipper's death, outside Fort Lauderdale police headquarters, and he'd been stunned by how much smaller and older his one-time vital, dark-haired bride had become. She was still beautiful, but in a different way, as a middle-aged woman. Maturity and grace had supplanted the healthy, almost feverish quality that had first attracted Carver. He wondered if grief over Chipper had diminished and aged her overnight, or if it had been the usual gradual process become suddenly visible.

"How do you feel about Laura?" Desoto asked.

"Right now, I feel sorry for her."

"I'd talk with her, comfort her, *amigo,* then I'd leave her with this Sam Devine."

"She'll return to Saint Louis with him anyway," Carver said, "when she has Chipper shipped back there for burial."

"Muumph," Desoto said, around a mouthful of sweet roll. A towering teenage waitress wandered by, noticed the basket on the table needed replenishing, and returned within a few seconds with more rolls. Their aroma was deliciously pungent, but right now it made Carver slightly nauseated. The lanky waitress, who had a name tag lettered *Tanya* pinned to her uniform blouse, poured more coffee for Desoto and then loped away. Tall Tanya.

"What do you have on this guy who burns people?" Carver asked.

"I was worried you might ask."

"Why?"

"You seem as calm as Laura, only in a different way."

"Maybe I'm in shock, too."

"No. Something else. Something that makes me afraid for you."

"Does that mean you're not going to tell me?"

"No, *amigo*, you'd find out anyway. You're as persistent as heat rash. We don't have any reliable witnesses, either at the burning at Pompano Beach or in the restaurant here in Fort Lauderdale. The restaurant is Casey's, over on Northeast Thirteenth Street, off Route One. It's a tiny place that specializes in chicken wings, mostly carry-out orders. Laura decided to stop there because your daughter was complaining about being hungry. They had their meal and left, and in the parking lot Laura realized she'd forgotten her purse inside. She sent Chipper back for it. Five minutes later he hadn't returned, so she went back to the restaurant and . . . found him."

"What kind of flammable substance was used?"

"The lab's trying to analyze it now. It's not like gasoline or alcohol; this sticks and burns, like flaming glue."

"Like napalm," Carver said. He'd been in Vietnam briefly and remembered the scarred civilians who'd suffered through napalm attacks; the grotesque, disfiguring burns. "Flaming glue" was a good description of napalm, and the stuff could be used in flamethrowers, even homemade flamethrowers. It burned hot, it burned long, and it burned through things.

"My guess is, whatever was used was concocted by the maniac who killed your son," Desoto said. "But genuine, industrial-manufactured napalm might mean a military connection, something we'll check out."

"There were witnesses in the Pompano Beach killing, weren't there?"

"In a way. Two. But they saw very little. They heard more. They swear the killer was arguing over returning something he'd bought there, but they don't know what."

"A hell of a motive for a killing," Carver said.

"That depends. The police psychiatrist thinks the murderer might be a schizophrenic with paranoid delusions."

"I'm not surprised. I don't want to hear any psychobabble. It's out of vogue for good reason."

"I'll tell you, I had a cousin like that, Carver. Really thought people were out to get him personally, and saw great danger in it. I saw him fly into a rage and hurl coins into a clerk's face because he got too many pennies in his change. If he'd had a flamethrower, he'd have used it."

"But who walks around carrying a flamethrower?"

"Someone who gets mad, stays mad, and goes back to the source of that anger. He'd give the victim one last chance, according to the psychiatrist, and if the victim wouldn't give him what he wanted, the killer would feel perfectly justified in taking almost any action."

"You're telling me Chipper might have been killed because some mental case wanted revenge for being short-changed and my son was in the way."

"Or something like that. You know the trivial motives for murder, Carver. We've both seen people killed for sport. Thing is, this killer might have feared Chipper as a witness."

It was possible, Carver knew. Maybe probable. Only someone unbalanced would kill in such a bizarre manner. So why shouldn't the motive seem bizarre to everyone but the killer? But it could be a mistake early in a case to put too much stock in what a police psychiatrist theorized. Psychiatrists were mistaken much of the time when they had their subjects sitting in front of them and cooperating.

"Shrinks are more interested in speculation than in justice," Carver said. "They don't seem concerned with right and wrong."

"Or else they know how hard it is sometimes to distinguish one from the other."

"You checking pyromaniac cases on file?" Carver asked.

"We are, but I'm told this doesn't necessarily relate to fascination with flame. More a vengeance thing, a desire to make the antagonist suffer. Maybe a metaphor for hell, eh?"

"A religious crank?" Florida had a surfeit of those.

"Could be," Desoto said. "Legwork's being done." He reached across the table and patted Carver's wrist. "I'm on this, *amigo,* even if it's out of my precise jurisdiction."

"I know you are," Carver said. He got his hard walnut cane from where it was leaning against the wall, set its rubber-encased tip firmly on the floor, and stood up. He managed this smoothly. Carver's left knee had taken a holdup man's bullet that had shattered bone and cartilage. That was what had knocked him off the Orlando police force and given him a knee frozen at a thirty-degree angle for life. He'd undergone physical therapy, and he still swam every day. That, and dragging his lower body around, had lent his upper body a strength that sometimes surprised him.

"Where are you going?" Desoto asked.

"To see Laura. Then I'm going to buy a bottle and take it home with me."

"To be with Edwina?"

"I'm driving up to my cottage."

"You should go to Edwina," Desoto said solemnly.

"No. She'll understand. I have to be alone for a while. That's the way I feel."

"Like after you were shot, eh?"

"No, nothing like that."

"Oh? Like how, then?"

"I'm going to find the bastard," Carver said. "I'm going to kill him."

"That won't work, *amigo.* Won't help you. It can't."

But Desoto didn't know about the thing that lived beneath Carver's calm surface, the beast that goaded as it grew stronger. It made everything else irrelevant. It was huge. It filled the hollowness of grief with purpose. There was no room in Carver for anything other than his hunger for revenge. "I can make it work."

"And afterward?"

"Afterward shit," Carver said.

He limped from the restaurant, dragging his images and his horror and his quest out into the brutal heat.

Desoto followed him to the door and called after him, "You oughta reconsider this, don't you think?"

But Carver hadn't really considered it in the first place. He was just going to do it.

CHAPTER 3

Laura was staying at the Carib Terrace, a small but well-kept motel on Pompano Beach just north of Fort Lauderdale. Carver found her in an upper room that was luxuriously furnished, with a kitchenette, and an angled glass wall that afforded a wide view of the beach and the glimmering ocean beyond. On the counter by the sink were a half-empty coffee cup and a glazed doughnut with one bite out of it— the remains of Laura's abortive attempt at breakfast.

She looked better now, Carver thought, as he settled into a soft chair near the glass doors that led to a balcony. More her old self, a pixie with boundless strength and energy. Though she was subdued, the fierce vitality he remembered in her was reawakening. She had more color in her cheeks and more light in her eyes, and she'd made a pass at arranging her short black hair. The hairdo was flattened in back; she'd been lying down. She was still lean, with traces of the natural athlete's lithe movements; the middle-aged set of her face hadn't entirely caught up with her body. Time was taking her by degrees, toying with her.

She sat down on the edge of the bed, opposite Carver, her knees pressed together beneath her dark skirt. He wondered if she'd viewed Chipper's body at the morgue. He hoped not. His identification, along with the dental-work findings, should be sufficient to establish positive I.D.

She said, "Yesterday I was worried about him growing out of his clothes, and today he's dead."

Carver didn't know what to say to that; he cleared his throat and used the tip of his cane to make quarter-sized

14

depressions in the deep-pile carpet. Then he looked out at the beach. A speedboat towing a water-skier circled in too close to shore, angering a few swimmers who'd ventured beyond the breakers. One of them waved a fist at the boat, which swung wide and made another pass. The drone of its outboard motor, like that of an angry insect, found its way into the room.

"Sam will be here soon," Laura said. "We'll take Chipper back to Saint Louis to be buried."

Carver turned away from the ocean view. "I'll fly up for the funeral. You need help with the arrangements?"

"No." She seemed distant, lost somewhere in her vast grief. Carver wanted to comfort her but didn't know how. He was surprised to find himself angry at the thought of Sam Devine holding her and nursing her through the inevitable eruption of sorrow and tears. It was Carver's son, *their* son, who had died.

"Where's Ann?" Carver asked.

"I put her on a plane this morning. She's with my father."

"She all right?"

"Yeah. So far. She doesn't understand what happened yet."

"I'm going to find out who did this," Carver said. "I'm going to make him pay."

She glanced up at him, held his gaze with her grief-deadened eyes. "Why?"

"Justice," Carver said.

She said, "Revenge."

"Call it whatever suits you."

She sighed and looked out at the sea and the beach, at the glaring sunlit world beyond the dim room. "I was afraid you'd react this way. It'll only make things worse, Fred."

"Worse for the animal who's going around burning children to death. And I'll admit it, I crave revenge. Jesus, I crave it! You can't tell me you don't feel the same way."

"I *feel* that way, Fred. I don't think that way. What I want is to get through this somehow, not live with it any longer than is necessary." She bowed her head; it didn't hide the tic in the delicate flesh beneath her eyes. The light from the glass doors revealed some kind of rash along the left side of her neck and her cheek, a mark of her violent emotion. "What I feel, Fred, is guilt. If I hadn't forgotten my purse, sent Chipper back inside to get it . . ."

Carver was standing before he realized it, leaning on his cane, his free hand on her quaking shoulder. She was about to sob. He didn't want that; he was afraid he wouldn't be able to calm her. And he feared his own reaction; something he didn't understand was drawing him to her. "That's irrational, Laura. There's no guilt involved except for whoever killed Chipper and the poor guy in the restaurant."

"Dammit, I know that! It doesn't help. Your obsession for revenge is irrational, too."

There was a knock on the door, then the knob rattled. Whoever was out there was impatient. Laura sniffled, got up, and trudged to the door and opened it. Carver sat back down.

Sam Devine stepped in, his beefy face contorted with concern. He was a big man, all lawyer. Acres of pinstripe material topped off by mobile, sincere features and a head of thick white hair any politician would have given back graft money to own.

Laura threw herself at him, hugged him, and he encircled her with his thick arms and patted her on the back. She was sobbing now; she'd been waiting for Devine before trusting a release of her pain. She couldn't get close enough to his protective bulk. Her entire body was convulsing, thrusting mindlessly against him in an obscene, unintentional parody of sex.

Who needed to watch this? Carver nodded to Devine and got up out of the chair.

"I'm sorry as hell, Fred," Devine said, holding Laura tighter.

Carver said, "Thanks, Sam. I'd better get going."

"You don't have to, Fred."

"I do," Carver said.

Laura stopped sobbing as Carver stepped near her and Devine on his way to the door. Incredibly, her face became composed and soft. It struck Carver that she might rather be in his arms than Devine's. For an instant he felt like snatching her away from Devine and clutching her desperately, merging their suffering. She drew a deep breath that caught halfway like something fuzzy in her throat, dropping her voice an octave and making it someone else's. "Fred, think about what you said. Don't commit yourself to anything too soon. Please!"

Devine held her away from him and put on a curious expression. She'd left tearstains on his blue pinstripe suit. Then he understood and stared at Carver. "Christ, Fred, don't do anything crazy. I mean, I'm a lawyer and I've seen the results of what you must be considering. Hey, it's natural to think in terms of revenge, but please don't do anything but think it. If you feel like you gotta turn it over in your mind, that's okay; that's legal. Could be it's even some sort of release."

"Listen to him, Fred," Laura said. "Remember what he's telling you."

Devine said, "Some things you should leave alone, Fred. That's just the way it is."

Carver set his cane and stepped around Devine and Laura. "Call me if you need anything," he said.

"You call *us*," Devine said magnanimously, as Carver limped out.

Carver drove north on 100, stopping once, at a grocery store, for a bottle of Johnnie Walker Red Label. Then he put up the canvas top on his rusty Oldsmobile convertible and continued north toward his cottage, driving too fast.

The cottage was isolated on a curve of bright sand. A low finger of land jutted out to the north, and the public beach to the south was seldom occupied by swimmers and sunbathers, never crowded. Carver had bought the place with his disability settlement last year after being shot.

He entered the one-room cottage, sniffed the stale air, and left the door hanging open. The sparse furniture had a dusty, unused look about it, and the viny potted plants that dangled on chains from the frame of the wide front window were dark and dead. Outside, the ocean whispered like a vicious gossip. Damn, the place was depressing!

After prying open a couple of screened side windows, Carver sat at the Formica breakfast counter with the bottle of Scotch in front of him. He didn't feel like uncapping the bottle, wasn't sure why he'd brought it. A fat and glistening blue-black fly touched down exploringly on the counter, and he watched it crawl, wobbling out of sight over the far edge. Story of life.

"Carver."

Edwina was standing in the doorway. He stared glumly at her.

"Great welcome," she said, "but not unexpected."

"I don't feel like Mr. Effervescence," Carver said. "Don't feel like companionship. That's why I came here."

She walked inside and stood near him. He used his cane to shove one of the stools out from the counter for her. Its legs made a loud scraping sound on the plank floor.

Edwina sat down and said, "You came here to grieve and brood about how you're going to avenge your son's death."

"Incisive bitch."

She smiled. "That's me." She stood up, got a glass from the cabinet above the sink, and rinsed it out. Then she poured two fingers of scotch from the bottle and handed the glass to Carver. She sat back down, got a small brown plastic bottle from her purse, and set an incredibly tiny white pill in front of him on the counter.

"What the hell is that?" he asked, staring at the pill.

"It'll help you sleep. It's prescription stuff I've had around the house for about a year. It's still plenty potent, though. I took one last month. It'll have you blotto in no time."

"I don't want to be blotto, God damn it! Don't want to sleep. How'd you know I was here?"

"Desoto told me."

"Figures."

"He's your friend; he knows what's best for you."

"He's a plague."

"You know better."

Carver did. He picked up the pill, popped it into his

"Yeah, that's a point I concede with regret."

"You sent Edwina to me."

"I thought she should be with you."

"Thanks." Carver's voice was flat.

Desoto shot his dashing devil smile, pleased with himself. "After a reasonable period of mourning, Carver, you'll feel differently about things. Naturally it's hard for you to see matters clearly now. Grief clouds our vision but doesn't last forever."

"Spare me the sugar."

"Sure."

"What have the Lauderdale police got on the burnings?"

"Show yourself some mercy, *amigo*."

"You show me some."

Desoto made a helpless throwaway gesture with his right hand, gold ring glinting. "Witnesses at the Pompano Beach murder say only that there was nothing unusual about the man they glimpsed running from the shop. No agreement on hair coloring or clothing. Two different witnesses; could have been two different guys they saw. The word *average* comes up often in the report."

"Not very revealing," Carver said. But he knew eyewitnesses seldom gave accurate descriptions, even when a crime was committed three feet in front of them. Or even against them. He looked out the window where the radio sat; the sky was pale blue and cloudless, as if bleached by the fierceness of the sun.

"It means we're not looking for someone obese, much over six feet tall, or instantly recognizable," Desoto said. "Or with orange, spiked hair. Mr. Average. Not a former presidential candidate. Narrows things down."

"Any fingerprints?"

"Hundreds. The souvenir shop did a brisk business in shells, suntan lotion, and Florida T-shirts. You know the kind of place: Visa-card heaven for tourists."

"How about at the restaurant where Chipper died?"

"Nothing to fix on there, either. Guy walks in with a small scuba diver's air tank; not so unusual that near the ocean. *Whoosh!* and two people are dead. Nobody notices him going in or out from the street, or if they do they don't pay particular attention to him. Except . . .''

Carver felt his heartbeat accelerate; he leaned forward, bracing himself with a hand on his extended stiff leg. He knew Desoto, knew he had something.

"Not a thing on the restaurant killings," Desoto said, "but a couple of people at the murder in Pompano Beach say they saw a car leaving the area about that time, driving fast. A navy blue, late-model Ford with a white roof and a bashed-in right front fender, they think. They're not sure. Nobody's sure of anything yet. Maybe nobody should ever be sure of anything.''

Carver ignored Desoto's musings. At times the lieutenant could be too philosophical for a cop. It grated.

"There might be no connection here, Carver. Coincidence. But then, coincidence is a policeman's friend and enemy.''

"What style Ford?"

"Big. The regular sedan, judging by the scanty description. Nobody noticed its plate numbers.''

Carver sat still and thought about that. From outside the office came the faint staccato undercurrent of a dispatcher's voice directing units to various reported crimes, reminding Carver of when he started on the force as a patrol-car officer. His future had seemed clearly charted then, before his life underwent a series of abrupt and tragic changes of direction. The divorce, the bullet, and now this. A bad stretch, all right.

"What about the lab report on whatever was used as flammable material?" he asked.

"As near as they can tell so far, it was a naphtha cleaning solvent, probably jetted by compressed air or propane. That's a petroleum product, *amigo,* and this one was turned to a thick, sticky consistency with the addition of chemicals.''

"What kind of chemicals?"

Desoto rooted through some papers on his cluttered desk, singled out one, and said, "Aluminum soaps, is what it says here. Added to a liquid hydrocarbon—that's the naphtha.''

"Aluminum soaps. That's what they add to gasoline to make napalm."

"I wouldn't know."

"Nobody sells something like that in a diver's oxygen tank," Carver said. "Or in a propane tank."

"No, but it would be possible to fill part of a reusable tank with the naphtha mixture, then take it somewhere and have the propane pumped in without anyone suspecting. Or somebody with rudimentary knowledge—say, a scuba diver—could transfer the propane or oxygen from another tank to supply the propellant. We figure an ordinary welder's igniter was used to create the spark. The guy could twist the valve, snap the igniter for fire, all in about two seconds. Presto! Flamethrower."

"Christ!" Carver said.

"Scary, eh?" Desoto said. "And sick. We're running checks to find area people with histories of mental illness that might conceivably result in that sort of action."

"How long will that take?"

"Not long. The computer can be a marvelous tool as well as a pain in the ass."

"You'll keep me tuned in on this?"

"I don't want to, Carver, because you're my friend. But I will, because you're my friend. Life is complicated; something for you to remember."

"Sometimes life can be simple," Carver said. "Sometimes knowing what you need to do is easy."

"Or seems that way."

"I need the names of the witnesses in the Pompano Beach souvenir shop," Carver said.

Reluctantly, Desoto jotted the information on a sheet of memo paper and handed it to Carver. "A man and his wife," he said, "Jerry and Margaret Gepman. Vacationing here from Chattanooga. They were upset by what they saw and returned home the day after the murder. They won't help you much, I'm afraid, even if you travel to talk to them."

"They the ones saw the Ford driving away?"

"No, they stumbled on the crime scene right after the

murder. The shock put them in a fog; they won't add to your knowledge."

Carver stuffed the paper into his shirt pocket. It made a crackling sound going in. "As you pointed out, we can't be sure of anything."

Desoto swiveled inches this way and that in his chair, holding up the pen he'd used to write the witnesses' names and staring at it. As if something printed on it intrigued him. "Has Laura returned to Saint Louis with Sam Devine?"

"I don't know. She's going to call me about the funeral."

"You think she loves this Devine?"

"Yeah. A lot."

Desoto dropped the pen on the desk. "Well, that's a good thing for her, maybe."

Carver got his cane, placed its tip on the floor, then folded his hand over the curved handle and levered himself to a standing position. The air-conditioner breeze played coolly over his arms.

"Where to now, vigilante?" Desoto asked.

"Haven't made up my mind."

"Ah, Carver. We both know you're going to check out places that sell or rent diving equipment, hangouts for scuba divers along the beach. You're going to ask about a white-over-blue late-model Ford with a dented fender, and who owns it. Don't you know the police are doing that? Do you think you can do it better?"

"Maybe. I'm more motivated."

"I won't try to stop you," Desoto said. "Or even remind you that interfering in an open case can endanger your investigator's license and your rather precarious way of earning a living."

Carver released a long breath and decided he'd better try not to be such a hardass here in the office. Desoto really was a friend. "I'm sorry if I cause you trouble. I mean that."

Desoto's liquid brown eyes were sympathetic. "I know. But this line of work *is* trouble. And remember our conversation cuts both ways, *amigo;* keep me informed about whatever you learn."

Carver promised that he would and limped to the door.

"As *soon* as you learn it, Carver," Desoto said behind him in a firmer, cautioning tone. "The Fort Lauderdale police, they won't be enthused about your participation in this."

Carver turned at the door and leaned heavily with both hands on his cane, his back stiff and his shoulders slightly shrugged, like a song-and-dance man about to do a number. "Anything else?"

"Yes. Where might I send flowers?"

CHAPTER 5

Carver spent the next two days doing as Desoto had predicted, making the rounds of charterboat docks and shops that specialized in diving equipment, asking about a dark-blue-and-white late-model Ford. He felt like the Ancient Mariner, stopping one in three. Only he didn't want to tell a story; he wanted to hear one.

Many of the people who hung around the marinas and boat owners' haunts had heard about the burnings and sympathized with Carver, but no one knew anything that might help. It was as if salt water eroded memory.

At Scuba Dan's, on Route A1A just south of Fort Lauderdale, Dan Mason, who ran the shop, told Carver that he did recall a young guy who drove a blue-and-white Ford—at least Mason thought it was a Ford—and bought diving and snorkeling equipment now and then. And sure, the car might have had a dented right front fender. It had been awhile since the guy had been in, though, so it was difficult to be hardrock sure of anything.

Scuba Dan's, a mock-driftwood building that was larger and more modern than it appeared from outside, had the facilities in back to recharge diving tanks, and Mason said that the man with the Ford had had a twin tank setup refilled there several times. Bought some flippers once, too. But he hadn't charged them, and Mason had no record of the sale, no receipt that might give Carver a name. He could only describe the customer as young, maybe in his early twenties, with sandy hair and dark eyes, average height and weight but muscular. There was nothing distinctive about the man,

Mason said, and apologized for not being able to help Carver more.

That afternoon Carver phoned Desoto from his cottage and told him what he'd learned.

"We talked to Dan Mason yesterday," Desoto said, rather laconically.

That got Carver irritated; the deal had been to share information. "Why didn't you tell me?"

"Didn't think it was solid enough to pass along. Probably nothing. Mason's uncertain about what he remembers. Don't grab hold of things and twist them into more than they really are, *amigo*. That's the danger of working a case where you're so intimately involved."

"You people who aren't so intimately involved," Carver said, "what are you doing?"

"We're still checking area residents with histories of mental illness, and we're tying that in with the white-over-blue Ford, matching names with auto registrations."

"Looking for the homicidal maniac with the right car."

"Exactly. Which is also what you're doing, *amigo*, only we're going about it more systematically and efficiently. Our wheels grind slowly but very fine."

"What about places that sell the chemicals used to thicken the flammable solvent? Or stores that sell the naphtha itself?"

"We're investigating along those avenues, too, Carver." Desoto suddenly sounded impatient, harried. He pitied Carver, but Carver was being a pest. "The naphtha is sold a lot of places as a household cleaning solvent. The thickening-agent chemicals might provide more of a lead. We're talking to manufacturers and suppliers. Trouble is, a good amateur chemist could fool around in a well-equipped lab and concoct a lot of this stuff himself. And that's something else we're investigating."

"Can some of the chemicals be bought by mail order?"

"Yeah. In small quantities. That makes our job tougher, but not impossible. You know we have the machinery to conduct this kind of investigation, *amigo*, so why don't you try to relax as best you can and let us do the job? Get your tax dollars' worth.''

"This is me relaxing," Carver said, "trying to find the man who killed my son."

"Yeah. I'm sorry for you." Desoto wasn't being sarcastic; he meant it.

Carver hung up the phone, then limped behind the folding screen that divided the sleeping area from the rest of the cottage.

He stood for a moment, feeling a pressure deep within him build until his body shook. It took a while for the trembling to stop. Weeping might be the only way he could find temporary relief from how he felt, and he chose not to weep.

He began packing to go north for his son's funeral.

CHAPTER 6

Chipper's funeral was held on a sunny day in south Saint Louis. Laura had decided Ann was too young to attend. There was a stiff and tearful ceremony at a chapel in Clayton, where most of Laura's family chose not to speak to Carver, then the long drive in the funeral procession to a cemetery scattered with old tombstones and ancient trees. A tall, ornate iron fence bordered the acres of graves, and jays and sparrows cavorted and chattered in the green, overhanging limbs of the spreading elms. Carver liked the cemetery. It was the only thing about the morning that he did like.

After the funeral he said his good-byes, shaking hands and accepting condolences. But he was curiously without emotion, cut off from what was happening. A visitor from another world. His mind had disassociated itself from the pain and would face it little by little, as time passed. For now he'd concentrate on finding the man who burned people.

Laura and Devine invited him to come to the apartment, where some of the relatives were going to gather and have something to eat, but Carver refused. The day felt more like a beginning to him than an end. He had things to do.

He'd arranged a layover in Chattanooga on his way home so he could talk to the Gepmans, the couple who'd witnessed the Pompano Beach murder.

After a connecting flight from Nashville, he found himself in a sputtering rental car in Chattanooga, studying a street guide and trying to find the Gepmans' house on Starlight Lane.

Chattanooga was a clean and compact city huddled at the base of Lookout Mountain, where a Civil War battle had been fought, and few people outside Tennessee remembered which side had won. Said something about battles, Carver thought. He drove away from the looming, misted mountain, following his map.

Starlight Lane was north of the downtown area, a cul-de-sac lined with similar low frame houses. The Gepmans' home was painted lime green, with dark green shutters, and was almost completely hidden behind a large magnolia tree.

Carver parked the car, then made his way up the walk, ducking the tree's branches with their thick, waxy leaves. He used the tip of his cane to ring the doorbell and heard its muffled chimes deep in the house's interior, like the bell of a ship far out at sea.

He'd thought about phoning the Gepmans to make sure someone was home, but he'd rejected the idea. It was better to talk to people cold, without them having a chance to form preconceptions. He was hoping, after the passage of time and a change in locale, that one of the Gepmans might remember something they hadn't told the police in Pompano Beach. Memory was unpredictable; time passed and hidden moments sometimes bobbed to the surface.

Mrs. Gepman opened the door. She was a tanned brunette about thirty, with a full and well-proportioned figure and dark, inquisitive eyes. She was wearing blue shorts and a red blouse with brown stains on it. She smelled like peanut butter. "I'm awful busy," she said with a smile. "So if you're selling something or taking a survey . . ."

"My name's Fred Carver, Mrs. Gepman. I'm not taking a survey, but I'd like to ask some questions. My son was killed in Florida. The way you saw somebody killed."

That found a nerve and the smile twisted into a grimace on her soft, handsome features. "I'm Margaret Gepman, Mr. Carver. C'mon in. You'll have to excuse me, though; I'm feeding the kids right now."

Carver stepped into a small, neat living room with glass-topped end tables and lots of potted plants. Above the sofa was a vast print of a snowy landscape, bought more for size and color coordination than for artistic merit. A Bible lay open on a tall walnut dictionary stand in a corner. The air-conditioning was humming away softly; it was cool in there. "Is your husband home?"

"Jerry? Sure. He's in his royal chamber. This way."

He followed her from the tranquil neatness of the living room into a large den that was a riot of toys and children's books scattered over the floor and furniture. A chunky wooden truck large enough for a small child to ride rested on its side near the sofa. Identical bright blue plastic parts of some kind of construction toy were spread haphazardly over the oval area rug. They were all the diameter of a pencil, about half as long, and had tiny protrusions at each end so they could be linked together at angles. They were mixed in with spilled pieces of what looked like an impossibly difficult jigsaw puzzle.

In the middle of all this, leaning back in kingly repose in a brown vinyl recliner and munching a grilled cheese sandwich, was Jerry Gepman. He was dressed as informally as his wife, in ragged jeans and a plaid, short-sleeved shirt. He had a stomach paunch and a simple, friendly face. He looked like the kind of guy who'd command a Boy Scout troop until he was seventy.

"This is Mr. Fred Carver," Margaret Gepman said. She had dimples not when she smiled but when she talked. "He wants to ask us some more about what happened in Florida. It concerns his son."

"Sure." Around a bite of cheese sandwich.

A shrill scream cut through the house, like a fingernail and blackboard demanding something at high volume.

Margaret Gepman shrugged. "I'm sorry, I gotta go feed the kids or they'll tear the place asunder."

"How many do you have?" Carver asked, wincing as another scream raised the hair on the backs of his hands.

"Three. All under nine years old. We went to Florida thinking we were going to get away from all the stress, left them with their grandparents. And then . . ."

"I been to Vietnam," Jerry Gepman said, "seen me some things. But I tell you, nothing like what was done to that fella in the shop. All blistered and black. Damned piece of bacon overcooked.''

"This is Mr. Fred Carver, *concerning his son*," Margaret Gepman reiterated, as if Gepman were slow-witted. He was the dominant force in the household, but she was a guerrilla who sniped. It was a pattern a lot of marriages fell into. "He's the father of that poor boy that died the same way in Fort Lauderdale.''

"Oh, Lord, sorry," Gepman said leaning forward in his chair. It made a ratchety, grinding sound and conformed to his new position. "I mean, it must be rough.''

"It is," Carver said. "What I want to ask you is, did either of you notice a dark blue Ford with a white top in the area of the shop?''

"Not that I can recall," Margaret Gepman said immediately.

But Gepman wasn't so quick to deny. He rubbed his unshaven chin with obvious pleasure; office worker relishing playing slob during a weekend with the family. "Might have been," he said. "Not a Ford, though. I do recall seeing a big blue Lincoln parked a ways down the street. I remember admiring it before we went into the shop, because it was in such good shape. Except for a dinged right front fender. It might not have stuck in my mind, only restoring cars is my hobby. Working on a 'sixty-five Mustang now.''

Carver felt an excitement coil in him. An older Lincoln and late-model Ford could be mistaken for each other. They shared the same basic body style, squared-off and distinctive. And one in good shape other than the dented fender might be assumed to be newer than it was. "Do you remember what year and model?" he asked.

"Oh, it was a two-door—I remember that. But I honestly didn't pay much attention to the year; they didn't change much for a while there in the late seventies, early eighties, you know. It did have a white vinyl roof; I'd bet on that. I noticed it was starting to peel a little around the rear window. Vehicle was overall in darn fine condition, though.''

Margaret Gepman wanted to stay and listen to the

conversation, but something fell in the kitchen and there was the sound of glass breaking. "Damn!" she said. She hurried from the den, her high, wide hips swaying rhythmically as she ran.

Jerry Gepman shook his head and grinned. His kids would do nothing really wrong, ever. "They keep the wife hopping," he said, as if that were the test of quality in a child. "All boys," he added, beaming.

Carver swallowed.

"Hey, I'm sorry," Gepman said. "I forgot."

"That's okay," Carver said. The thrust of anguish that had sliced into him subsided. The lump in his throat went away. "Was the Lincoln still there when you came out of the shop?"

Gepman thought back, rubbing his bristly chin again. Sunlight glinted off his beard stubble, showing a little gray though he was only in his mid-thirties. "That I can't tell you. I mean, we were too shook up over what happened to notice much of anything. And I was worried about Maggie, the way she was crying and all."

"Is there anything else you can think of that might have slipped your mind down in Florida?"

"No, there isn't. I mean, I hope they catch the crud who did that to your son. We read about it in the papers, and we tried to think of some detail that might help. The first night we were home, me and Maggie prayed. Then we sat at the kitchen table after the kids were in bed and talked over what happened. I mean for hours, since we couldn't sleep anyway."

"Anything you might not have mentioned to the police about the killer's description?"

"No. Listen, I'm sorry, but we really been over this. We just saw what we said we saw and nothing else. The Florida cops were great at helping us remember."

Carver gave Gepman his card and told him to call collect if he or his wife did happen to think of anything new.

"Something jogs my memory," Gepman promised, "I'll call." He slipped the card smoothly into the pocket of his wrinkled plaid sport shirt. Probably it would be forgotten there and run through the wash with miniature socks and jeans.

Carver thanked him for his time. "You've been a help."

"I hope so. You want to stay around, have some supper with us?"

"Thanks," Carver said, "but I've got a plane to catch. Tell your wife I said good-bye."

"Sure will." Gepman got up to show him out, walking slowly as Carver limped to the door. "Some families," he said, "tragedy just haunts them. Won't let up. It's too bad."

Another healthy young scream erupted from the kitchen. Carver understood why the din failed to bother Gepman. For an instant he envied the man almost painfully.

"Too bad," he agreed, and he made his way down the walk and beneath the magnolia tree to his rental car.

CHAPTER 7

When Carver stepped into his cottage, cool, dry air hit him and he knew Edwina was there waiting for him. He wasn't sure how he felt about that.

She was in the chair by the wide window that looked out on the ocean, sitting with her legs crossed. Apparently she'd been showing property or doing floor duty today; she was wearing a pale blue skirt and blazer and what appeared to be a man's black silky bow tie. Her business look. She said, "How was the funeral?"

Carver let the door swing shut behind him and struggled in with his carry-on suitcase. "Grim and too long," he told her. He dropped the suitcase near a wall, where it would be out of the way until he was ready to unpack it, then he limped to the refrigerator behind the counter that separated the tiny kitchen from the main room and got a cold can of Budweiser.

"Are you coming home now?" Edwina asked.

"It wouldn't be a good idea," Carver said. The refrigerator clicked on when he shut its door. He popped the tab on the can, fizzing beer onto the back of his hand, then leaned on the counter and sipped. The beer stung his dry throat but felt good going down. There was a point, in a case like this, where hunter might become hunted. Whoever had burned Chipper might go on the offensive and come looking for Carver, to stop him from closing in, and might find Edwina. Carver didn't want her hurt or killed. He'd made it no secret that he'd moved out of Edwina's home and was staying at the cottage.

35

She knew what he was thinking. "You didn't change your mailing address," she said. She got up, languidly crossed the room on her high heels, and handed him a white envelope.

It was addressed, typewritten, to "Fred Carver, Curious Cat." Carver had a good idea who it was from. A killer who liked to joke.

Though the address was that of Carver's beach cottage, the envelope had been forwarded to Edwina's house. It bore a Fort Lauderdale postmark. "I found it in the mailbox this afternoon," she said. "Right in there with the seed catalogs and offers to virtually steal nylon luggage."

"You tell Desoto about it?"

"No, I wasn't sure you'd want that. I handled it as carefully as I could. Can they get fingerprints off of paper?"

"They can sometimes," Carver said. "They can even lift prints off human flesh now."

"Science," Edwina said, and crossed the room again and sat down. She stared at Carver, waiting for him to open the envelope, not wanting to show too much interest and intrude in what to him was an intensely personal matter. He could share with her what was inside, or he could choose not to, her blasé expression told him.

Carver got a sharp knife from beneath the counter, held the envelope gingerly by the edges, and slit the top open. It was a cheap envelope, dime-store quality, and it parted easily and smoothly with a soft tearing sound.

Inside was a matchbook that read *Casey's Wings and Yummy Things*. There was nothing else. Carver suddenly felt ice in his stomach.

Lifting the matchbook carefully at the edges, lightly between thumb and forefinger, he held it up for Edwina to see.

She squinted at it but didn't rise from her chair. "What is it?"

"A matchbook from the restaurant where Chipper died."

"You think the killer sent it?"

"Yeah. A warning to me to stop asking questions. Or I go the same way."

"What curiosity did to the cat, huh? Subtle but to the point."

"If curiosity killed all cats," Carver said, "dogs would lead dull lives."

"Interesting reasoning. If it's reasoning at all. You going to heed the warning?"

"Think I should?"

An enraged, reckless kind of light glittered for an instant in her gray-green eyes. "No. I'm scared for you, worried, but if it's what you need, I think you should keep at it."

"It's what I need."

"But I think you should give the matchbook and envelope to Desoto, or to the Fort Lauderdale police."

"I will," Carver assured her. He didn't understand why he'd received the matchbook. How did the killer even know Carver was after him?

He replaced the matchbook in the envelope and took a swig of beer. Out the window, beyond the dead potted vines, the sky was beginning to darken as the sun made contact with the horizon behind the cottage. A pelican skimmed gracefully inches above the sea, flying a final search mission for dinner before nightfall. On the beach the surf rolled and foamed in lacy white ribbons, but Carver couldn't hear it because of the hum of the air-conditioner. "Have you eaten?" he asked Edwina.

"No. I've been showing property to a retired couple from New York. They wanted to look at one condo after another."

"They've come to the right state," Carver said. "Florida's got one condo after another."

"You've changed the subject. When are you going to tell the police about that envelope?"

"Morning's soon enough. Let's drive somewhere and get supper."

"How was Laura at the funeral?"

"She held together."

"You see her afterward?"

"No."

"You *do* know I love you?"

"I know. I don't take it lightly. Right now, all I can think about is finding my son's killer. And supper."

"Two kinds of hunger."

Carver stared at her silently.

Edwina started to say something else, then thought better of it. She got up and followed him out to where the Olds sat ticking in the heat.

In the morning Carver drove into Orlando and gave the envelope to Desoto. The lieutenant, sitting behind his desk, manipulated his shoulders so that the sleeves of his elegant dove-gray suitcoat rode up on his arms, out of the way, before he examined the envelope and its sparse contents.

"A murderer not without humor," he said. "Of a kind, anyway."

"Missed my funny bone entirely," Carver told him.

"There are still people who think 'I Love Lucy' is funny."

"Some," Carver said.

"Fort Lauderdale ought to have this. It's their case."

"You've got better lab facilities."

"So true, *amigo*. We're all-round more capable crime fighters here." The radio was on today, playing music softly with a hypnotic Latin beat. Carver thought it was the score from *Evita*, but he wasn't sure. The yellow ribbons on the air-conditioner grille were straight out this morning. The day was already steaming; the unit was on High. "Obviously a warning," Desoto said, studying the envelope and match-book on his desk. "I don't have much hope these'll tell us much, despite the expertise of our lab personnel."

"Give them to Marillo," Carver said. "He'll find something."

"Then they go to Fort Lauderdale," Desoto said. "Professional protocol. Can't have them too pissed off over there."

Carver sat silently while Desoto made an interdepartmental call and a clerk came in, used a tweezers to place the matchbook and envelope in a plastic container, then left for the lab.

"There's a Lieutenant William McGregor in Fort Lauderdale who resents you snooping around over there," Desoto said. "It's his town, his department, he's in charge of the investigation, and he's got this idea that makes it his case."

"My son," Carver said. "Fuck McGregor."

"Hmm," Desoto said. The breeze from the air-conditioner ruffled the dark hair over his left ear. Behind him, on the radio, a woman with a sad voice began singing "Don't Cry for Me, Argentina." "Did you stop over in Chattanooga and talk to the Gepmans?"

"The husband told me he was sure he saw a white-over-blue Lincoln parked near the restaurant the day of the murder."

Desoto seemed interested, but he said nothing and sat there wearing his stoic Latin mask. He'd have looked at home on an Aztec coin.

"An older model," Carver said. "They look like Fords of a later vintage. Gepman restores cars for a hobby, so he knows Lincolns from Fords. He also remembers a dent in the right front fender."

"Could mean nothing, *amigo*."

"It's your optimism I like most about you."

"I can't be optimistic about that envelope and matchbook," Desoto said. "It means you're in danger now. You've stirred the beast in his lair. It also suggests that whoever killed your son is methodical and aggressive, a difficult combination."

Carver held his cane vertically with both hands and absently rotated it between his fingers, its tip revolving on the tile floor like a blunt drill bit. "Why not gasoline or kerosene?" he said. "And why go to the trouble to mix thickener with the naphtha? If our man is careful, wouldn't he have used some more common flammable liquid by itself, something more difficult to trace?"

"I've thought about that," Desoto said. He hesitated. "It could be he wanted something sticky that burned longer so it would cause more suffering." He regretted his words immediately and bit his lower lip with his very white teeth. Then he frowned. "I'm sorry, *amigo*."

"I came to the same conclusion," Carver said softly, trying not to remember his son's blackened body on the morgue table, trying not to picture the yawning grave waiting for the casket after the funeral back in Saint Louis. Yesterday. My God, that had been only yesterday. Time could torture as well as heal.

"The man who did this," Desoto said quietly, "I feel the way you do about him, Carver."

"Yeah, but it's a matter of degree."

"Like most things in life."

"Maybe he isn't warning me with the matchbook," Carver said. "Maybe he doesn't want me to back off. He might be taunting me."

"That's even worse," Desoto said. "Cats do that with mice. Mice usually lose."

"The guy who sent that matchbook thinks I'm a cat."

"You're not, though. He wants you to think that so you'll get confident and careless. Old cat trick. What better way to corner a mouse?"

Carver stopped rotating the cane, shifted his weight over it, and stood up. It was a relief to be out of the straight-backed chair. "I'll check with you this afternoon about the matchbook and envelope."

"And in the meantime you'll drive down to the Fort Lauderdale—Pompano Beach area and continue your search along the shore for the driver of a blue Lincoln, despite this message from a killer."

"That's where I'll be," Carver confirmed.

Desoto sighed. "Mice should learn when to lay low in their holes," he said, "but they don't. They keep finding the cheese irresistible."

CHAPTER 8

Around three in the afternoon it began to rain, as it often did at that time in Florida in midsummer. A squall had drifted in off the sea, churning water and bending palm trees and sending the swimmers and boaters with good sense scurrying for shore.

Carver put up the top on the Olds and raised the windows just enough to keep rain from blowing in. He sat quietly, occasionally switching on the wipers for a couple of swipes so he could maintain a clear view of Scuba Dan's. The rain pattered like fingers drumming impatiently on the canvas top.

He was parked down the road, on the ocean side, near a line of tall palm trees whose long fronds were whipping wildly in the wind like the hair of madwomen tossing their heads. Scuba Dan's hadn't done much business in the past three hours; Carver had seen only half a dozen customers entering and leaving the low building with the roof-mounted air-conditioner and aluminum gutters. Scuba Dan's phony antique wooden sign was swinging lustily now in the storm like that of an eighteenth-century pub's, a pirates' hangout. Even with the car windows rolled halfway up, and parked as he was some distance from the place, Carver could hear the sign creaking as it fought to free itself from its mountings and fly through time back to the days of the Jolly Roger.

A new gray Pontiac swung in ahead of Carver's Oldsmobile and parked on the highway shoulder. A very tall, stooped man got out and trudged back toward the Olds. He wasn't wearing a coat, and his wrinkled tan suit was getting water-spotted from the rain off the ocean. He walked slowly to the driver's side of the Olds, as if it weren't raining on him. He seemed too preoccupied to care about mere moisture.

Carver cranked the window all the way down and felt cool drops on his face.

He wasn't surprised when the man fished a Fort Lauderdale police lieutenant's shield from a pocket and said, "Mind if I come in?"

Carver rolled up the window and leaned over to unlock the passenger-side door. He watched the tall man walk around the front of the car, estimating his height at maybe six-foot-six. Though he was thin, almost skinny, there was an unmistakable strength in the coiled, controlled way he moved. Pro basketball centers moved like that.

"I'm McGregor," the man said, as he lowered himself next to Carver in the Olds and slammed the door closed. He gave off a mingled, musty scent of wet clothing and cheap, perfumy cologne. "You're Fred Carver." He said this as if there might be some doubt in Carver's mind as to his own identity. "Gray day, huh?"

"It just got grayer."

"Still damned hot, though. But I guess that's what you can expect this time of year. And the sun'll be banging down on us again within an hour, I'd bet. Fuckin' steambath!"

Carver wasn't in the mood for diversion. He stared out at the dull gray ocean churned into whitecaps by the wind, then he looked directly over at McGregor. McGregor's name suggested Scottish ancestry, but he looked Swedish. Ruddy, rawboned, lantern-jawed. Straight, lank hair so blond it was almost white. Pale blue eyes, set too close together. He had to bow his head slightly to keep it from bumping the canvas roof. There was something about him that suggested he could be mean. "How did you figure out I was here?" Carver asked.

"Didn't figure. Desoto told me." McGregor felt like getting to the point now himself. "That envelope and matchbook told us nothing except that whoever handled them last wore gloves. Cheap envelope that can't be traced, and addressed with an IBM Selectric typewriter. They're selling a couple of million of those even while we sit here and chat.''

"And maybe right now the guy who killed my son is killing somebody else's.''

"Maybe. But we on the Lauderdale force haven't exactly been standing around with our thumbs up our respective asses.''

"What *have* you been doing?''

"You know the answer to that; you used to be a cop. And a good one, according to Desoto, and he oughta know. He's an old friend of mine. Solid guy.''

"He never mentioned you.''

"I hardly ever mention him.'' McGregor lit a cigarette without asking if Carver minded. The car hazed up with smoke; the windshield fogged near the top. "How long you been sitting here?'' he asked.

"Awhile.''

"Looking for a white-over-blue Lincoln?''

"Yeah. I haven't seen it.''

"You won't. We impounded it last night.''

Carver's stomach knotted and he hit the steering wheel hard with his fist. Pain jolted up his arm and left the heel of his hand tingling. The blow made a dull, reverberating sound. "God damn it, why didn't somebody tell me?''

"Say again?''

"I'm a victim's father! I should have been told!''

"We don't generally run out and notify vigilantes whenever there's a development. That's what you are, Carver, fuckin' John Wayne movie walkin'. You're on a lone-avenger trip, and that's not good. I won't allow it.''

"Desoto told me you were an asshole.''

"Naw. Not my old buddy. You're making that up.'' McGregor cranked down the window all the way and flicked the cigarette away. The rain had stopped. The palm trees that had been whipping around were still now. He left the window down. Warm, fresh air pushed into the car.

"I need to know who owns the Lincoln," Carver said.

McGregor shook his head slowly, patiently. "What you need to know, Carver, what is essential, is that I *am* an asshole. I'm not your usual cop—not by half. Like you, I want to catch the garbage that burned your son. I want him to pay. Not as much as you do, I grant you." The wide jaw set and muscles played in front of McGregor's oversized, protruding ears. "But I want the bastard. Oh, I do!"

"Let me guess," Carver said. "There's a promotion in it if you make the collar on this one? Maybe catapult you all the way to captain?"

"Could be that's part of it. Could be I don't think an animal like that has a right to walk around and breathe in and out like decent citizens. It bothers me, I guess more than it should. I'm just like you, only it doesn't have to be my son. I'm stuck with a strong moral sense; that's why I'm a cop. But it doesn't mean diddly shit to me whether you believe me. The proposition is the same."

"Proposition?"

"The owner of the blue Lincoln is a guy named Paul Kave," McGregor said. "His address is on Route A1A in Hillsboro Beach."

"Millionaire's Mile," Carver said. That was what Floridians called the area.

And suddenly Carver was afraid and angry. The stretch of beach property in Hillsboro was among the most expensive in Florida. Luxury estates and condominiums with water views front and back—the Atlantic to the east, the Intracoastal Waterway to the west. Money was involved here, all right. Major money. The man who'd killed Chipper was rich. Carver knew what that meant. He told himself grimly that no battery of high-priced lawyers was going to save this killer.

"Paul Kave is the son of Adam Kave," McGregor said, as if that meant a great deal and Carver should know it and be impressed.

"Is he one of our U.S. senators?" Carver asked. "Or a

Disney World founding father? I don't keep up on things like that."

"You ever hear of Adam's Inns, one of those rare times something outside your own experience touches you?"

"Sure." The fast-food restaurants, featuring hot dogs served in various fashion, were in practically every shopping mall in the South.

"Adam Kave owns them," McGregor said. "All of them except a few sold off for franchises. Paul Kave is his only son. There was a scuba air tank in the trunk of the Lincoln; it contained traces of naphtha. Paul Kave is an amateur chemist with a lab in his parents' home. And he's a skin-diving enthusiast. The kid has an I.Q. over a hundred and forty, but he's got a history of schizophrenia with paranoid delusions. His mother says he's been under treatment off and on since he was fifteen. He's twenty now. He's also disappeared. Hasn't been home for two days. He fits like a Florsheim shoe, Carver. He killed your son and he's running."

"Is this proposition going to involve me backing off while Kave gives himself up and gets a wrist-slap sentence from a bought judge?"

"No, it involves finding him. Desoto says I can't talk you out of your vendetta, and I believe him. So I'm gonna channel all that hate, Carver. I want you to go to the Kave family, tell them what kind of work you do, and give them some bullshit story about wanting the killing to end, since you lost your own son in a holdup shooting. They won't connect you with your real son's murder because his name appeared in the papers and on television as Montaigne. Tell the family you know how they feel and you sympathize with them, and you want to help find Paul before the police get to him and harm him. You know he's ill. Tell them the odds are good that the police will kill Paul rather than arrest him. They'll buy it and hire you; I sort of laid the ground-work."

Carver sat silently for a while, watching the waves, calmer now, roll in and break in layers of surging foam beyond the palm trees. He could hear the surf pulling on the beach. What McGregor was suggesting, cultivating and then betraying a killer's family, turned the pure white heat of Carver's obsession for revenge into something tainted.

"I don't like it," he said finally. "It doesn't set level. It makes me feel dirty."

"So feel dirty. You want your son's killer, don't you? Any way you can nail him?"

Carver squeezed the steering wheel and stared straight ahead.

"I got my neck stuck out a mile and a half on this," McGregor said. "Taking what you'd call a career gamble."

"Desoto must have told you how good I am," Carver said. "The odds are in your favor."

"You aren't so good I'm gonna let you go mucking around in an active homicide case on your terms. That's impeding justice. I'll fall on you like something very heavy from very high up."

"I know how to stay legal."

"Oh, really? I'm kinda like the Supreme Court, Carver. Sometimes I interpret the law any which way."

"Maybe you oughta just enforce the law instead of trying to turn the screws on me."

"This is the way to get Paul Kave," McGregor said. "Listen, I saw your son at the morgue. Holy Christ, I don't see how you can even sleep nights much less be thinking twice about what I'm proposing. I mean, I'm handing you what you claim you want. I'm fuckin' turning you loose, tough guy."

"I like to work in my own way."

"I thought this *was* your way. Doing what you had to so you could wring out some justice for a change. Not enough goddamned justice in this society and you know it."

"I know it," Carver said.

"And now you back away." McGregor spat dryly, disdainfully, with his upper lip curled over an eyetooth. It was a dandy expression of contempt and one Carver imagined the big man had practiced to make perfect and used in tough interrogations.

McGregor worked the chrome door handle, about to get

out of the car. The musty cologne scent got stronger with his sudden movement.

"Wait a minute," Carver said. "There's one thing we haven't talked about."

Twisting his long body back toward Carver, McGregor arched a blond eyebrow. "What's that?"

"If I find him, I get him. I don't want to see his money make things light for him. You, personally, can have credit for bagging him. But later. When I'm finished with him. I'll fade out of the scene."

"Jesus, Carver, you're asking a lot."

"You've got a lot to gain by giving it to me."

McGregor made a fist with one hand and massaged its massive knuckles with the other. "It's gotta be miles, miles off the record," he said, "like the rest of this conversation. I mean, I never told you any of this."

"How could you? We haven't met."

McGregor smiled. It made his eyes seem tiny and cruel. There was a wide gap between his teeth and his breath smelled sour. Carver didn't like the idea of having him as a co-conspirator, but there it was.

"So we got an agreement," McGregor said. "The kid's yours."

He climbed out of the car and slogged back to the Pontiac, his boat-size shoes sloshing rainwater in his wake.

Carver sat and watched him drive away, then reached forward and twisted the ignition key.

CHAPTER 9

The Kave estate on A1A could barely be seen from the road as a glimpse of bright red tile roof through the trees. Carver waited for a break in the passing Lincolns and Cadillacs, then turned the Olds sharply into the graveled entrance.

McGregor had indeed laid the groundwork for Carver's visit. When he identified himself over the intercom at the gate, a male voice immediately instructed him to drive through.

It wasn't a gate, really; it was a drop barrier of the type used at railroad crossings, only smaller. The black-and-white-striped, tapered length of lumber rose smoothly to allow the Olds to pass, then automatically settled back into place behind it. Made Carver feel like a locomotive engineer.

He tapped the accelerator, and continued up the gently sloping, winding drive toward the red roof and now a section of stark-white stucco wall. The top was down on the Olds and the sun was just beginning to get serious about making misery, and over the rumble of the car's big V-8 engine he could hear the rush and sigh of the ocean beyond the house.

The grounds abruptly became immaculately tended: neatly trimmed hedges; colorful yet controlled explosions of lush bougainvillea; healthy-looking, precisely placed palm trees with symmetrical white stripes about their trunks; deep-green grass of uniform height and at erect attention. A lizard, green as the grass and primitive as the Mesozoic age, struck a travel-poster pose on a nearby tree trunk, as if it had been bribed by the gardener. Carver felt like the only flawed object on the grounds. He paused and let the engine idle as he took in the house. Sat feeling the vibration of the powerful car.

The house was two stories and rambling, all white stucco and black wood trim and fancy wrought iron. Spanish architecture, with rough-hewn cedar arches and decorative rails. Red shutters and red front double doors matched the vivid color of the tile roof. The driveway curved to run beneath a wide portico from the ceiling of which dangled a heavy iron-and-stained-glass Spanish-style light fixture.

To his left, Carver saw a path winding to wooden steps that led down to the beach and blue-white rolling surf and a boathouse and dock. A white-and-brown pleasure boat—a forty-foot Gulfstar with a flying bridge—bobbed gently at the dock. The private beach was wide, and the sand was clean and flawless except where the sea had washed in some globs of oil from passing ships, along with dark tangles of kelp. The place made Carver wish he were rich.

He parked the Olds in the black shade of the portico and struggled out with his cane.

As soon as he slammed the car door one of the tall red front doors opened and a sturdily built man of medium height well into his sixties stepped outside. He was wearing dark slacks and a gray silk short-sleeved shirt buttoned halfway up. Casual but unmistakably expensive. His straight, black but graying hair was brushed back as if he were facing a stiff wind. Silver-rimmed squarish glasses magnified his intense dark eyes and made him look as if he'd never blink, even if you touched his pupil with a pencil point. Around the loosening flesh of his thick neck hung a glinting gold chain that lost itself in the gray mat of hair on his chest. He had prominent cheekbones and very thin lips, and a wide, square jaw that looked capable of cracking walnuts.

"Mr. Carver," he said. There was something mechanical about the way his lips and lower jaw moved, as if there might be a battery pack in him somewhere. He shaped a lower-face smile as he stepped down off the concrete stoop.

"I'm Adam Kave." He extended a hand and Carver shook it. Kave squeezed hard, sensed the unexpected power in Carver's grip, and let up quickly. Not a man to waste time on losing battles.

He led Carver through a large foyer with a terra-cotta floor and some high-priced Spanish-style furnishings, along a hall lined with mirrors and paintings, and into a room spacious enough for indoor polo.

The Spanish touch was here, too. Massive wood beams sectioned off the high ceiling. The walls were rough-textured white stucco, like the house's exterior, with decorative colorful tiles set in them. Except for a massive, gold-framed oil painting of a three-masted battle galleon forging through a wild ocean storm, the ornate tiles were the only wall decorations.

Carver negotiated the floor carefully. It was set with large hexagonal sections of tile or marble, strewn with thick throw rugs. The furniture was black leather and dark, heavy wood. All the tables and a few elaborate wooden chairs had curlicued black iron legs. The room was cool. No need to switch on either of the two large, wicker-bladed paddle fans that extended on slender brass pipes like bizarre gigantic spiders at rest and at watch from the center beam of the lofty ceiling.

"Sit down, please, Mr. Carver," Adam Kave said in his deep, phlegmy voice. He was one of those men who always seemed to need to clear his throat, and who had probably cultivated and disciplined the timbre of his voice to approximate a tone of command.

Carver set the tip of his cane and lowered himself into a black leather sofa that faced a wide window overlooking the beach. The ocean seemed vast from here. A gull touched down nimbly on the pure sand, gazed about, realized it was trespassing, and uneasily took to the air again. It was no stranger to packing orders.

"Something to drink?" Adam Kave asked.

"Thanks, no."

"I'll have a Scotch," he said, as if it were Carver who'd offered. He moved to a dark-stained wood credenza and opened its doors. There was a kind of compact power in the way he swung his arms and carried his shoulders as he walked; he'd probably been physically tough when he was younger, and might have a few good minutes in him even now. Carver caught a glimpse of glittering crystal, a miniature refrigerator, a bright row of bottles.

Kave plunked ice cubes into a glass, doused them with Cutty Sark, then closed the credenza doors and turned again toward Carver. The force of his attention came in waves.

Carver said, "I'm sorry about your son's trouble."

Kave stared into his glass, swishing the Scotch and ice around. The ice made a tiny tinkling sound. Musical. "Not sorry for the victims?"

"Them, too," Carver said. He took a deep breath, plunged. "My own son was killed a few years back in Saint Louis, Mr. Kave. A boy about Paul's age was holding up a convenience store. My son walked in at the wrong time; he wanted a can of root beer and instead he got a bullet through the brain."

Kave was watching him, still swirling the liquid in his glass. More slowly now. Carver couldn't hear the ice.

"At first I wanted the boy who did the shooting tried and executed. Could have easily killed him myself. Without conscience, I thought. Then his sister came to me, told me about him, and eventually, despite myself, I began to feel sorry for my son's murderer. He had a history of mental illness and was married and had a son of his own. He was actually robbing the store for food to feed his wife and child, and he saw my son as a threat and panicked. The clerk testified that he hadn't demanded money; he'd asked for a bag filled with canned goods and ice cream." Carver shifted on the sofa, almost knocking over his cane leaning on the arm. "I know it doesn't make sense, that kind of risk for ice cream and canned vegetables. But the sister convinced me it made sense to her brother. Or it did at the time he walked into that store with a gun."

Kave was staring hard at Carver through the thick-rimmed squarish glasses. His wide jaw was set like a curbstone.

This guy isn't buying it, Carver thought, with a falling

sensation. Not believing me for a second. McGregor's idea was loonier than the story Carver was concocting. He began to sweat; he could feel it in his palms and beneath his arms.

"Go on," Kave urged. Carver wondered why.

"The boy was declared legally insane and is confined for life in a mental institution in Missouri," Carver said. "When I heard the verdict, I was glad. Glad he wasn't executed. And when I read about your son Paul being on the run, and having had his own share of mental problems . . ." He paused, picked up his cane, and ran its tip lightly over the tile floor in a circle, as if trying to describe boundaries for his emotion. "Well, it struck a responsive chord and made me want to help you. Help your son. Empathy, I suppose they call it."

"I'd assumed it was counter to professional ethics for a private investigator to solicit business," Kave said calmly.

"I'm glad you feel that way," Carver said. "Most people don't credit the profession with any ethics at all."

The iron-vise jaws were clenched, but again the thin lips snaked into a slight smile. "I thought Detective McGregor said Chicago."

"Pardon?"

"Chicago. I thought, when he recommended I employ you, he told me your son was killed in Chicago."

"Saint Louis," Carver said. Christ! he thought; what *had* McGregor told Kave? This whole thing should have been worked out more carefully.

Yet Kave seemed to believe. For now.

"Shall we talk about fee, Mr. Carver?"

"Not unless I show you some results." *Something to prove this one is from the heart.*

"That's generous of you," Kave said, "and I'll be generous back if in time you do obtain results."

He walked to the wide window and looked out at his grounds and his beach and his ocean. At his boat berthed at his dock. His, his, his. His business had bought it all, made for him a well-managed world under control. Except for his son. Paul wasn't under control. He was wandering around burning people to death. Carver wondered, was it parental love prompting Adam Kave to try to retrieve his murderous son from pursuit and retribution, or was it something else?

Whatever Kave's motives, Carver had his own. Apparently McGregor had set the stage well enough and Kave was going to hire him. For an instant Carver regretted that. But for no more than an instant. Then his mind flicked up the image of Chipper's blackened body in the morgue. He experienced a deep, dark satisfaction as he smiled and said, "I'm glad you're allowing me to help Paul, Mr. Kave."

A girl who looked to be about twenty flounced into the room, stopped short when she saw Carver, and turned abruptly as if to leave before she became visible and interrupted something.

"Nadine," Adam Kave snapped in his throaty voice of command, "this is Mr. Fred Carver."

The girl returned to the center of the room as if drawn by a string. She was tall and well built, though her hips and thighs beneath her white ankle-length slacks appeared on the heavy side. Her features were strong, with a hint of Adam Kave's wide cheekbones and jaw. She had the Kave straight, black hair and vivid dark eyes. She was attractive but would appear more formidable than alluring if she gained much weight as she aged.

"This is my daughter Nadine," Adam Kave said.

Nadine nodded at Carver and smiled. There was something challenging in her eyes; she hadn't liked him seeing her so meekly obey her father's command. She was her own woman, she was telling Carver, despite her youth and her habit-imposed obedience to her father in small matters. If Carver didn't believe it, just let *him* try to boss her around!

"Get your mother, Nadine," Kave told her. Then to Carver: "It would be best if you met the rest of the family now."

Nadine said, "Elana's sleeping in her room." One of those daughters who referred to her mother by first name.

"Go get her," Adam repeated. "Tell her Mr. Carver's here."

Nadine glared at him, spun neatly on her sandaled heel, and left the room.

"I'm afraid Nadine shows a streak of stubbornness now and then," Kave said. "The rebelliousness of youth. She'll settle down after she's married next spring."

Carver wouldn't have described her actions exactly as stubborn or rebellious, despite what was probably going on in her mind. But then he didn't know Nadine. Certainly there was a flinty spark of defiance in her. As there must have been in Lizzie Borden.

The intimidated yet high-spirited Nadine returned within a few minutes accompanied by a beautiful but faded blond woman in her sixties. Elana. Mrs. Kave. Paul and Nadine's mother. Though age had robbed her of fluidity of motion, she still conveyed a gliding grace and elegance as she crossed the room and smiled. Adam Kave introduced her with possessive pride. She was wearing slippers and a long, pink and lacy robe that swished stylishly around her ankles as she walked, as if being worn by her was a privilege. Maybe the robe had something there.

"I hope you can help Paul," she said, as Carver gently shook her cool and bony hand. Up close, the frailty and a kind of resignation in her were obvious. There was also a precarious tension, a balance maintained with difficulty.

Carver and Adam Kave sat down, Carver on the black sofa, and Kave on an uncomfortable-looking wooden chair with ornate iron legs. The women remained standing, as if both of them secretly longed to flee from the room and the presence of either Carver or Adam.

"I'll have to find Paul to help him," Carver said to Elana.

Her large but dimmed blue eyes took on a sad expression. Something tragic flared then died in them. "We've been given to understand the police probably won't give Paul a reasonable chance to surrender if they find him before you do, Mr. Carver."

"That's a fair statement," Carver told her, "though the police would deny it."

"Detective McGregor doesn't exactly deny it," Adam

said. "He confided to me that Paul wouldn't have a prayer of survival if the law located him and he offered the slightest resistance."

"Would he resist?" Carver asked.

"He'd resist," Nadine said. Her voice vibrated as if she were the one who might be called upon to summon resistance and she were already geared up for it. This one was a fighter, all right.

"Are you fond of your brother?" Carver asked.

"Very." She stared directly at him with her dark eyes, daring him to contradict her, to tell her Paul was no longer worthy of affection. Carver let the challenge slide.

"Nadine is twenty-one," Elana said, "only a year older than Paul." She glanced at her husband. "Growing up together, they developed a truly remarkable closeness."

Carver wondered what exactly she meant by that. He decided to prod. "You think Paul's guilty?" he asked Nadine.

"No!" she snapped, and turned away, her sandal heel making a squeaking sound on the tile floor.

"If Paul is guilty," Elana said evenly, "he wasn't responsible for what he did."

"You're referring to his history of mental problems?"

"Yes." Elana wiped her hands on the laced robe as if they were dirty, holding her fingers stiff as she ran her palms down her hips. Carver again sensed something tightly wired in her. "Paul has long been under treatment for mild schizophrenia, Mr. Carver. Do you know anything about the affliction?"

"Very little."

"Those suffering from it have a distorted sense of reality, and sometimes delusions of persecution. At times, in the advanced stages, they even hear voices, sometimes giving them destructive, bizarre instructions."

"Did Paul hear voices?"

"Only his father's," Nadine said.

Elana ignored her. Adam Kave worked his jaw muscles. He'd wear down his molars in no time like that.

"Paul's been in and out of therapy for years," Elana

went on. "Schizophrenia is still something of a medical mystery, though there's a theory now that it's a physical aberration in the brain, a chemical imbalance. The disease often appears in a victim in his or her teens, then gets progressively worse as the person grows older."

"Was Paul getting worse?"

"No," Adam said, "his medication seemed to be controlling the symptoms."

"Would you describe him as paranoid?" Carver asked, remembering what Desoto had told him about the cousin hurling change in a clerk's face for no reason.

"At times, mildly," Nadine said. "But he never would have killed anyone."

"For God's sake," Adam said, "none of us is a psychiatrist! Let's leave the diagnosis to Dr. Elsing."

"Dr. Elsing?"

"The psychiatrist who treats Paul," Elana said. "His office is in Fort Lauderdale. Paul had improved lately, though. He hasn't seen Dr. Elsing in over six months."

"Before the murders and before he ran away," Carver said, "did Paul say anything that might lead you to believe he was tilting toward violence?"

"The police asked us that," Adam said. "Paul's behavior was better than it had been in years, actually. He's had his minor skirmishes, but he's never been really violent."

Until he set three people on fire. One of them my son. Carver felt his hate for Paul Kave grow to a revulsion he had difficulty hiding.

"The past several years, he'd become enthused about scuba diving," Adam continued. "And of course he liked to work in his lab in the carriage house."

"Lab? Carriage house?"

"The garage, actually," Adam said. "It has a room over it where the chauffeur used to live. We haven't had live-in servants for years. Paul uses the place—used it—for his chemical lab."

"What did he do in his lab?"

"Experiments," Nadine said. "He'd gotten away from actual chemistry in the past several years. He was interested in oceanography, and he used his equipment to study sea life.''

Carver thought about the deadly, flammable naphtha compound. He turned his mind away from a vision of fire and death, screams he couldn't bring himself to imagine when awake yet couldn't exorcise from his dreams. What he was doing here was worth it. He wanted Paul Kave! And McGregor was right; this was the way to get Paul.

"Are there any other family members I haven't met?" he asked.

"Joel," Nadine told him.

"Not yet," Elana said tightly. She was wiping her hands on the robe again, extending her wrinkled, lean fingers rigidly. Her brown-spotted arms and backs of her hands were the clues to her age. Still, she was innately lovely, as if it were her birthright. There were women like that, though Carver had only known a few. What had she been thirty years ago?

"I'm not feeling quite right," she said.

Adam Kave was on his feet instantly. Time to tend to his treasure. "Why don't you go to your room and lie down, Elana?"

She nodded. Her face was suddenly very pale. Her pained, parting glance took in Carver. Without speaking, she turned and hurried out the door.

"My wife's ill," Adam said. He said it in a way that discouraged any further inquiry by Carver. "In the past year she's become more and more reclusive. And now Paul . . .''

Nadine *slip-slapped* to the window in her sandals, turned and padded close to Carver. Challenge time again. "And as you can gather," she said, "my mother's less than enthusiastic about me marrying Joel. Not that it will stop us."

Carver decided not to try to stop them either.

"Joel Dewitt," Adam explained. "He's a car dealer in Fort Lauderdale who's just asked Nadine to marry him." Kave didn't seem to have any strong pro or con opinion about the upcoming nuptials. Maybe he was one of those wise ones who didn't worry about what they couldn't change.

"Why doesn't your mother like Dewitt?" Carver asked Nadine.

"You'd have to ask her, but it wouldn't do you any good. Elana has never come out with a direct answer to that question. Because she doesn't have one."

"So there's Dewitt," Carver said, as if making mental notes. "Not yet a family member, but almost."

"And there's Emmett," Nadine said.

"We don't usually talk of Emmett in this house, Mr. Carver. He's my older brother. I wish he weren't. We haven't gotten along for years."

"But Paul and Emmett got along," Nadine said, "when Paul was younger. I don't think they've seen each other for a while. Emmett lives in Kissimmee." Kissimmee was a small town in central Florida, less than two hundred miles from the Fort Lauderdale area, but only a matter of a few hours or so on Florida's Turnpike, where it seemed everyone drove over seventy.

"Paul have any close friends he might contact?" Carver asked.

"None, I'm afraid," Adam said glumly. "The boy's always played the loner."

"I'd like to see Paul's lab," Carver said, standing up out of the soft leather sofa and leaning on his cane.

"I'll go out to the lab with you," Adam said, standing also. "There are some things I'd like to tell you privately."

He started for a door at the far end of the room, walking fast. Was he doing that deliberately?

Carver limped after him, twisting his body to glance back and catch Nadine's reaction to being shut out of the conversation.

But Nadine was already striding from the room, her thighs and buttocks working powerfully beneath the silky white slacks.

Carver followed Adam Kave out past a veranda and a large, screened swimming pool, along a path lined with junglelike foliage and the perfumed scent of blossoms, toward a garage the size of an average house.

The rolling surf sighed louder as they made their way in the direction of the sea. A gull screamed and a private helicopter thrashed its way across the blue sky above the sun-touched ocean. In the shade of the palm fronds, Carver felt sheltered and temporarily at peace.

He wondered what it would be like to grow up in a place like this. His own childhood had been lower middle class, with a father probably not much more sensitive to his youth and yearnings than Adam seemed to have been toward Paul's. What had it been like here for Paul? It would help Carver to get a feel for that, to learn how to think like Paul—if such a thing was possible.

"This is a rough time for us," Adam Kave said in his gravelly voice. "I can't tell you how much we appreciate your kindness and help, Mr. Carver. Are you a religious man?"

"No, there's too much of that in Florida."

"Well, I go to church regularly, and somehow God seems to supply what's needed in crises like this."

Carver didn't answer as he followed Kave along the winding stone path toward bright sunlight and blue sky and ocean.

For an uneasy moment he felt like the serpent in the Garden of Eden. Putting another one over on Adam.

CHAPTER 10

A steep exterior flight of white steel stairs rose like a prehistoric, fleshless spinal column in a museum, to a landing and the top floor of the gray stucco carriage house. Carver could think of the carriage house only as a garage with a room over it. His plebeian background showing. The stucco was cracked and sloppily patched here and there, and grasping green vines had made it halfway up the wall beneath the stairs. He supposed whoever tended the grounds regarded the vines as ornamental; long nails had been driven into the stucco to aid the green tendrils on their upward quest. The nails were rusty, the higher ones waiting patiently for the vines to reach them before metal crumbled in the salt sea air.

Adam Kave stood aside and let Carver take the steps first with the cane. Carver could feel the presence of Kave close behind him as he climbed, as if Adam were telling him he wished they could go faster. The hard walnut cane made hollow clanking sounds on the steel.

On the landing, Adam edged around Carver, unlocked a heavy wooden door, and pushed it open. Heat and silence rolled out. Carver limped inside the lab.

It was dim; only minimal light filtered in through curtains pulled closed over narrow windows. Dust swirled in diffused sunbeams. A fly droned through the dappled light. Carver expected the acrid scent of chemicals, but the air was stale and musty and smelled like attics everywhere. He remembered the heat and buzzing beneath the eaves of his father's house, decades ago.

He heard the click of a wall switch, and an overhead fluorescent fixture sent out intermittent signals of pale, flickering light, then fought its way to steadiness.

Adam examined his hand as if the switch might have soiled his forefinger. "Paul wasn't one to keep this place clean," he said, "and he'd never let the maid from town come in here. It was his refuge from his problems, I suppose."

Partitioning walls had been removed so that the area above the garage was one large room. The floor was unfinished plank. The plumbing that had served bath and kitchenette was extended in copper pipe to the dry-walled ceiling and run to the east wall, then down to a long sink and workbench. Brown-tinted vials lined a shelf above the workbench. A crudely drawn skull-and-crossbones poison warning on lined notepaper was taped to the edge of the shelf. On the bench sat a Bunsen burner, an expensive and elaborate microscope, a series of glass beakers and slides, and an opened and apparently empty Pepsi can. There was a cot against the opposite wall, and near it a bentwood chair on which was piled diving equipment: swim fins, a snorkel, and what looked like the wadded top of a black rubber wetsuit. The only other evidence of Paul's interest in the ocean was a large aquarium tank, empty, with colored pebbles and a miniature chambered castle on the bottom. There seemed to be dust over everything, as if no one had been in the place for a while, but that could be deceptive. An ancient air-conditioner was mounted in one of the windows. The sloping ceiling was insulated, but it was getting uncomfortable in the crude lab, and Carver felt like limping over and switching on the unit.

"The police spent considerable time up here," Adam said. "They removed a few items. I'm not sure what."

Carver nodded. He thumped across the floor with his cane and examined the chemical vials on the long shelf. He discerned nothing from the polysyllabic Latin labels. A brilliant teen-age boy might have learned to concoct anything from explosives to aphrodisiacs with the stuff. "Did Paul spend a lot of time here?"

"I don't think he did in the past year or so," Adam said,

"though I couldn't swear to it. He was increasingly fond of swimming, of the ocean and the creatures in it, and that took up most of his time. Now and then he'd come up here to closely examine something he'd found in the sea, but he wouldn't spend days at a stretch here alone as he did when he was a boy."

"He ever share the things he found? I mean, talk about them with friends or family?"

"No."

"Not even Nadine?"

"Possibly Nadine."

Carver looked at the cot, with its light blanket and sheet folded at its foot. "Looks as if he slept up here sometimes."

"Maybe he did. I never kept that close a watch on his activities. Though Adam's Inns has a national vice-president as well as district managers, I oversee my business from here, from an office in the house, Mr. Carver. I spend a great deal of time on the phone. If you accused me of neglecting Paul, I wouldn't deny it. At the same time, the boy's gone out of his way to cause quite a bit of trouble."

Adam was talking as if burning people were merely another of his son's boyhood peccadilloes. And maybe he figured to use his influence so the resultant punishment turned out to be on a par with the consequences of wrecking one of the family Porsches. It was easy to forget, standing here in the stifling garage laboratory, the extent of Kave's wealth and power. What was a little thing like homicide between friends with money and clout? Carver had seen it before; it made him nauseated. He felt that way now, standing there in the heat.

"I'd like to see Paul's room," he said.

"Sure." Adam stepped aside again so Carver could cross to the door and negotiate the steel landing and stairs first.

The outside air felt cool to Carver, though the temperature was pushing ninety. He heard the light switch click off as he balanced himself between cane and handrail and started down the steep steps.

At the bottom of the stairs, he glanced in a window as

he waited for Adam to finish locking up and join him. No Porsches. The garage had several windows, so there was enough light to see a late-model gray Cadillac, a low-slung red Datsun sports car, and a white Chevrolet sedan. There was plenty of room for more cars. Or a tea or a coming-out party.

"The police impounded Paul's Lincoln," Adam said, clanging down the stairs on his two good legs and noticing Carver's interest in the garage's interior.

"Yeah, I was told." Carver probed with the tip of his cane until he found a hard spot in the sandy earth and moved away from the window.

"Do you know Lieutenant McGregor well?"

"We're old friends," Carver said, and walked ahead of Adam back along the winding stone path to the house. The sweet scent of the flowers was cloying and added to his nausea.

Paul might not be the model of neatness in his lab, but his room looked like the executive suite of a plush hotel just before check-in time. The king-size bed was made up with the spread tucked in at the corners. Other than some ocean-ography magazines neatly fanned on a low table, there were no incidental objects on the dresser or writing desk. On the wall by the desk hung a large, framed, underwater color photo of what looked like a manta ray lurking among grace-fully swaying, colorful undersea foliage while a school of small, bright fish swam past. There was something distinctly ominous about the enlarged print.

"Did Paul do underwater photography?" Carver asked.

Adam shrugged his blocky shoulders in an I-don't-know gesture. Paul hadn't been of much concern to him until lately. He didn't know much about his son the murderer.

Carver snooped around but found no camera. He limped over to the closet, lifting the cane high between steps in the deep-pile blue carpet. He slid open one of the heavy mirrored doors. It glided smoothly and made a politely soft rumble on its rollers.

There were more clothes in there than Carver had owned in the past ten years. Most of them were casual: blue jeans

and pullover shirts. Dozens of shoes of all kinds. The
jackets, slacks, and suits were light-colored and conserva-
tive. Paul's taste ran to blues and grays. On the closet's top
shelf were two stacks of more oceanography magazines,
bound tightly with thick dark twine.

"He take any clothes with him when he disappeared?"
Carver asked.

"We're not sure. If he did take time to pack, he left
much of his wardrobe behind."

"What about money?"

"Paul had his own bank account. As you no doubt know
from the police, he withdrew several thousand dollars from
his savings the day of his disappearance."

Carver hadn't known; he'd have to check with McGregor
about things like that, remind the lieutenant that knowledge
about Paul Kave was supposed to flow both ways.

"Paul left in his own Lincoln," Carver said, and paused
for confirmation or denial.

"Yes. Paul was in love with that car. It's a beauty. The
police found it abandoned in Fort Lauderdale. I don't
imagine we'll see it for a while, the police being what they
are. I suppose Paul had no choice but to leave it
somewhere, under the circumstances." Adam seemed almost
more upset over the temporary loss of the Lincoln than the
likely permanent loss of Paul. Priorities. It was Paul who
concerned Carver, though not in the way Adam Kave had
been led to believe.

"Anyone see him leave?"

"No. Nadine must have been out with Joel Dewitt. I was
engrossed in business most of that evening—our new
barbecue-sauerkraut hot dog."

Yee-uk! Carver thought.

"And Elana was in her room as usual," Adam went on.
He set his jaw muscles quivering and stared hard at Carver
with his intense magnified dark eyes. "There's, uh,
something you should know about Elana, Carver. It will
make you realize why I'm hiring you, and why she
shouldn't be burdened with any . . . negative information
you uncover."

Carver leaned with both hands on his cane and waited.

"My wife is terminally ill with cancer of the spleen. She won't live more than another year. The strain of what's happened might cut short even that small amount of time she has left. That's why I want this situation resolved and left behind us as quickly as possible. I want every precious, irreplaceable moment of life for her—for us. I want Paul found."

"I do too, Mr. Kave. I'm sorry about your wife."

Adam squared his shoulders in a manner that somehow made him appear helpless. He was facing a tragedy his money couldn't buy him or Elana out of, and his iron will might as well be cardboard; it was frustrating. Carver did pity him, as well as the fragile, reclusive woman upstairs. "Do Paul and Nadine know?"

"No. Only I and Elana and the doctors."

"Maybe it would be best if you took your wife somewhere she's always wanted to go," Carver said, "until this is over."

"I suggested that," Adam said. "She told me she wanted our lives to continue as they normally would for as long as possible. At her request, we don't even talk about her illness."

There was a lot this family didn't talk about, Carver thought. He looked around again at the sterile, expensively furnished room, half expecting to see a complimentary mint on the pillow, hotel stationery on the bare desk. He glanced once more at the batlike manta ray hovering menacingly among the underwater plant life and unsuspecting fish. Management would take down the print and put up one of flowers in a vase, or of colorful food to stimulate guests' appetites and requests for room service.

"Not much to see," Adam said. "Just an ordinary room."

But not that of an ordinary man, Carver thought. The Kave family itself hardly seemed ordinary. Or was there such a thing as an ordinary family?

"Do you have a good photo of Paul I can have?"

Adam nodded. He pulled a snapshot from his shirt pocket and handed it to Carver. "I anticipated your request."

Carver studied the likeness of a young blond man who had oddly dreamy eyes and a trace of the strong Kave jaw, wearing jeans and a light jacket and standing hands-on-hips near a large, round boulder. He tried to fathom the meaning in those eyes and the set of the features, as if he might sense the mechanism of thought from nothing but a photograph. Then he gave up. He thanked Adam and slipped the snapshot into his own pocket.

"He's a good-looking boy," Adam said. "Better-looking than in those fuzzy old newspaper photos."

The *Del Moray Gazette-Dispatch* had run a copy of Paul's high-school yearbook photograph. It had indeed been so fuzzy that Carver had stared at it and decided it might be of any high-school student. It hadn't looked much like the face in the current snapshot. "I can see family resemblance," Carver said, thinking he should comment. Polite thing to do.

As they were leaving Paul's room, Carver said, "Why does your wife object so strongly to Nadine's marriage to this Joel Dewitt?"

"She seems unwilling to pinpoint her reasons," Adam answered. "My guess is she thinks Joel's dishonest."

"Why would she? There are honest car dealers."

"Oh, I don't think it's his profession she objects to. She gets feelings about people. Has instincts."

"Accurate instincts?"

"Usually."

"Maybe you should ask her about the barbecue-sauerkraut hot dog," Carver said. "That sounds awful."

Adam smiled. "You'd be surprised."

Carver decided not to dispute the point. Adam Kave was the last man on earth to argue with about wieners. Like taking on the Colonel or his heirs about chickens.

He saw Carver out. They didn't shake hands when they parted.

Waiting for the zebra-striped barrier to lift and release the rumbling Olds back onto the highway, Carver wondered what Elana Kave's instincts had told her about him.

CHAPTER 11

After leaving the Kaves, Carver stopped at a pay phone just outside Pompano Beach and called Fort Lauderdale police headquarters. He gave his name. McGregor was in but was busy, he was told. Did he care to wait? He cared to.

He tried not to touch any part of the sunbaked metal booth as he marked time till McGregor came to the phone. Cars hissed past twenty feet away on A1A, most of them with their windows cranked up and the people inside coolly ensconced in air-conditioning. Carver watched station wagons, vans, big luxury cars, miniature foreign cars—all to be found here on the edge of the sea in summer. A busy combination of fun and commerce. A gigantic, dusty tractor-trailer roared past, its tires singing. Its exhaust fumes drifted over to Carver in its hot wake of low, rolling air. Commerce.

"Carver," McGregor's voice finally said over the line, "I'm up to my ass in work here. You got something important to say?" Polite bastard.

"Better put what you're doing aside for a minute," Carver said, "pay attention to your big career gamble."

"Hell, that's why I'm taking time out and talking to you. But I'd rather be doing some listening."

"The Kave family hired me."

"Told you. This is all gonna go like grease through a goose, Carver. We'll both get what we're after, which really is the same thing even if we're operating for slightly different reasons."

"Why didn't you tell me Paul Kave drew several

67

thousand dollars from his bank account before he disappeared?''

''What? Who the fuck told you that?''

''Adam Kave.''

''Well, it's something he forgot to tell us. I guess I'm gonna have to go out and see the old man again.'' McGregor sounded miffed. Carver knew he was lying, putting on a nice act. If he could somehow collar Paul Kave before Carver caught up with Paul, so much the better. Commendations, publicity, promotion; up and up. All the way to chief someday, by God, and why stop there?

''We need to get on the same wavelength,'' Carver said. *On the same planet.*

''We're on it already,'' McGregor said, ''homed in on Paul Kave. But I sure as hell didn't know the son of a bitch was running with cash. That changes things.''

A listing old Ford station wagon loaded with a cargo of squirming, yelling kids shot past on the highway. A blond boy about ten staring calmly out the back window saw Carver and extended a middle finger. Carver idly wondered what would happen if the station wagon stopped and the driver backed up to use the phone. The barrier broken down by speed-going-away would be removed. He guessed that no one in the wagon would seem more innocent than the blond boy. He'd seen the same characteristic in adults. What was it about people?

''Anything you *do* know that you neglected to tell me?'' Carver asked.

''Nope. Every card in this hand's faceup, Carver. I advise you to play it that way with me, you wanna keep your ass out of a sling.''

Carver didn't like even being in the same game with McGregor. There was no way to know where he stood. He told McGregor the story he'd fed Adam Kave, then asked if that dovetailed with what McGregor had told Adam to set up the family to hire Carver.

''It all tallies,'' McGregor said. ''Adam Kave's mistaken; I did say your son had been killed in Saint Louis, not Chicago. I figure he was testing you. Old bastard didn't sell all them wienies and become a multitrillionaire by taking things for granted.''

"How do you read his relationship with his son?"

"Easy. They didn't get along."

"And with his wife?"

"He loves her. A lot."

"Nadine?"

"The young cunt? She's around, that's all. Guy like that, wrapped up in his business and his own high-powered life, his kids are just there, like furniture."

That was all pretty much the way Carver had sensed the scheme of relationships in the Kave household. Yet there were undercurrents. Thinking in stereotypes and forming snap judgments could lead a few degrees off course in the beginning of a case, and miles from the right destination at the end. Like navigating at sea.

"You know anything about Nadine's fiancé, this Joel Dewitt?" Carver asked.

"Yeah, we checked on him. Got himself a used-car and Honda motorcycle dealership here in Fort Lauderdale."

"Elana's against the marriage. She thinks Dewitt's a crook."

"I knew a car dealer once wasn't a crook," McGregor said. "He's dead now; I think he's stuffed and in a museum somewhere. Now he's gone, there ain't a one won't sell you a car knowing it'll turn wheels-up the last day of the warranty. Sure Dewitt's a crook. All legal, though. He doesn't have a record. Tell you something, Carver, I didn't know the wife objected to the marriage. See, you're paying dividends already. Fucking wealth of information. You make me feel smart I made arrangements with you. You wanna feel smart?"

"It'd be a welcome change."

"I bet. Anyway, the lab says the accelerant used to torch your son and the restaurant guy was the same as what was in a can found in Paul Kave's makeshift lab."

"You're building a heavy case," Carver said.

"All we need is the neck to hang it on."

"I'm working on that, McGregor."

"I gotta go, Carver. But listen, you cover your ass. This Paul Kave is a dangerous punk, and he's supposed to be smart as well as nuts. He knows you're after him and might decide to do something about it, double around on you and have himself another barbecue."

Carver saw his son's curled and blackened body again. Clenched his eyes shut. Thought about a barbecue-sauerkraut hot dog. *Oh, Jesus!*

"Carver?"

"I'm here." Barely. He was feeling dizzy. He braced himself with the cane. The smell of exhaust from the highway came at him again. Heat seemed to crawl up his pants legs.

"You go careful, now. I wouldn't want to lose my man on the inside." A low chuckle. "Other hand, I wouldn't want *you* to lose your *determination*."

"You don't know what determination is," Carver said, "till you know me."

"You're wrong there, old buddy," McGregor said. He hung up the phone.

Carver stood for a moment watching the highway waver like an undulating ribbon in the bright sun. He considered McGregor's warning about Paul Kave doubling around on him. Tigers did that, he'd read somewhere, circled around behind whoever was stalking them. Stalked the hunter. As if they were pissed off anyone would dare try to track them, and they wanted to teach whoever was after them a deadly lesson. Tigers were supposed to be a bitch to hunt.

The heat from the concrete was seeping up through the soles of Carver's shoes. He limped back to the Olds, lowered himself behind the steering wheel, and drove north and then west toward Kissimmee.

The car's top was up but all the windows were down. Carver took the outside lane and passed slower vehicles as if they were crippled stragglers. The wind blasting through the windows and ballooning the canvas top smelled fresh and cleared his head.

He hadn't mentioned Emmett Kave to McGregor. If McGregor didn't know about Adam's brother, let him find out some other way.

CHAPTER 12

Carver was surprised when he saw Emmett Kave's house on Jupiter Avenue in Kissimmee. Obviously it was Adam who had all the family money, and he didn't share it with Emmett. As he parked at the curb in the dappled shade of an insect-riddled sugar oak, Carver remembered Adam saying he wished Emmett weren't his brother. There had been a great deal of force behind the words despite their offhand delivery.

As he straightened up out of the Olds, his view unobstructed by the tree's lower limbs, Carver took a closer look at the house. It was narrow and long and in serious disrepair. The frame siding had been white but was now a mottled gray, showing large areas of bare, rotted wood. The sloping roof wasn't shingled but was covered with green sheet-roofing that was patched near the peak with tar that glistened black and soft in the fierce sun. One of the wooden shutters was dangling crazily from a front window, and the gutter above the small porch sagged as if the sad weight of years bore down on it.

Behind the house and off to the side, at the end of a dirt-and-gravel driveway, sat a garage in equally bad condition. It had wooden doors that needed paint, and the roof was sway-backed. Not sagging in the manner of the porch roof, but as if it had been struck a sharp and powerful karate chop with the edge of a giant hand. Carver noticed a nearby tree and guessed that a falling limb had snapped the roof's center beam.

He looked around at the street of similar houses. This was

a rough section of Kissimmee, but only a few houses were as run-down as Emmett Kave's. All of them were set on stone foundations and seemed to have basements, which were relatively rare even here in central Florida, far from the ocean. The homes must have been constructed by the same builder within a short time of each other, and years ago probably made a modest but pleasant neighborhood. Economics and urban evolution had changed all that.

Emmett's yard, which was mostly sandy earth, was by far the barest one on this side of Jupiter Avenue. A goat couldn't have found a blade of grass inside the rusty wire fence that bordered most of the property. Emmett wouldn't hurt himself cutting the lawn.

The walk leading from the street to the front porch was tilted and cracked. Carver found it easiest to make his way to the door by keeping to the side of the ruined concrete and setting the tip of his cane against sun-hardened earth. His stark shadow angled into puzzle pieces, parting and rejoining, as it passed over the jagged sections of walk.

He made it to the porch and stood still for a moment in the shade. Somebody was home. An old blue box fan vibrated and growled in one of the front windows, causing a few high, scraggly weeds to bend and sway in the sunlight in silent protest. There was a wasps' nest tucked neatly in a corner of the porch ceiling, and one of the warlike insects was droning around Carver as if warning him not to try anything funny. Carver leaned on a supporting post and used the tip of his cane to press an almost invisible, painted-over button.

A buzzer rasped to urgent life inside the house, as if there were a huge version of the pesky wasp in there, communicating with the lookout on the porch. The inane thought made Carver uneasy.

After about half a minute, the door opened and a strong smell of frying bacon drifted outside. Carver squinted through the dark screen door into the house.

A man moved closer to the screen and changed from hazy outline to individual. He was almost exactly the size and build of Adam Kave, but his nose was larger, his gray eyebrows much bushier. He had the square, powerful Kave jaw, and that and the eyebrows lent his face a cragginess that looked good on a man well into his late sixties. There was about him the same energy that seemed to emanate from brother Adam, but tinged with the desperation of near-poverty. Like the last-chance, wild hope that flares just before total resignation.

"Emmett Kave," Carver said.

Emmett looked at him down the length of his body, up again to the face. "You say my name like we know each other." The voice was deep, but not as deep as Adam's, and it had none of the gravelly quality. "We met?"

"No. My name's Carver. I've met your brother. The family resemblance is unmistakable."

"Hm. Up to a point, I s'pose."

"The Kaves have hired me to try to find their son Paul."

"Police are trying to do that."

"They'd like me to find him before the police do."

"Yeah," Emmett said after a pause, "I can understand why. What are you, a private detective?"

"That's what I am." Carver got his I.D. from his back pocket and held it up to the screen.

"Don't mean shit to me," Emmett said. "Got nothing to compare it with for genuineness." He aimed a thick finger like the barrel of a weapon at Carver, as if about to warn him off his property. But instead he used the finger to unhook the screen-door latch and then melted back into shadow, like a man retreating into a protective, gloomy cave. "C'mon in, Carver."

Carver limped into a small living room that was neater than he would have guessed from the outside of the house. The furniture was dark and old and threadbare, but it seemed clean and was symmetrically arranged. A potted plant cowered in a dim corner as if awaiting execution. The floor was waxed hardwood, covered in the middle by a very worn, obviously imitation Oriental rug with uneven fringe around the edges. Through a far door Carver could see into the kitchen: green linoleum, chrome table leg, rounded corner of old-fashioned refrigerator. The bacon smell

seemed stronger when he just looked in that direction. The
senses being mischievous.

"Fixing myself a BLT," Emmett said. "Want one?"

"No, thanks." The box fan didn't help much; it was hot
inside the house. Too hot for Carver even to think about
eating. "You go ahead, though. Don't let me make you
burn the bacon."

Emmett commanded Carver to have a seat on the sofa,
then he strode into the kitchen out of sight. He had the same
purposeful walk as his brother, only it was slower. Maybe
because he was conditioned to existing in smaller spaces.
Neither brother moved like men in their sixties; there was
plenty of spring in their legs.

Carver heard the clatter of silverware in the kitchen.
Something dropped to the floor, bounced, and rolled. He
glimpsed the refrigerator door opening and closing. "Get
you a beer?" Emmett called.

Carver was tempted but called back, "Not now, thanks."

"Why not?" Emmett asked, coming back into the living
room carrying a can of beer of a brand Carver had never
heard of, and a thick BLT-on-toast on a paper towel. The
can was yellow and had what looked like an American
Indian emblazoned on it. Mayonnaise-smeared lettuce
draped from a corner of the sandwich; one of the crisp
bacon slices crumbled, and a tiny charred piece dropped
onto the Oriental rug. Emmett either didn't notice it or
ignored it. Maybe the maid was on her way. "You private
cops can drink on duty."

"But we don't if we don't want a beer," Carver said.

Emmett grinned and sat down in the chair opposite
Carver. It had dark wood arms and its upholstery matched
the sofa's: a maroon flower design embossed on beige,
made browner by the years. He chomped into his BLT. The
splintering toast and bacon made a crackling sound, softer
as Emmett chewed. He looked at Carver's cane, swallowed,
and said, "How'd you get your leg messed up?"

"Shot."

"As a cop or in combat?"

"When I was with the Orlando police."

"Oh. Thought you mighta been a vet," Emmett said. He took another big bite of sandwich and talked around it as he chewed. "You got the look of a man who's seen combat."

"Only for a little while in Vietnam," Carver said. He'd been in Nam for seven weeks and two days, until a superficial wound had brought him home and led to a transfer and then discharge, but he suddenly saw again the victims of napalm attack. He refused to ride the vision into the more recent past.

"Hmph!" Emmett said, as if he might not count Vietnam when he totaled up meaningful wars. "You figure the cops find Paul they'll kill him before he gets a chance to give up?"

"No. But it's a possibility. Emotions are high. And from what I've heard about Paul, he might not try to give up, might not be thinking straight."

"Hah! Boy thinks straighter than they give him credit for."

"How long's it been since you've seen him?"

"He hasn't come around here since he's been on the run, if that's what you mean."

"I was getting around to that," Carver said, "but what I meant to ask was how long it's been since you've talked with Paul." There was an edge to his voice. *Don't anticipate my questions, old fella.*

"I know. I ain't thick." Another bite of sandwich. The bacon smell got stronger. The box fan whirred steadily, stirring the hot air in the corners of the room. Emmett seemed to be thinking. He swallowed hard, as if it hurt his throat, then took a long slug of beer and set the can back down. "About six months. I like the boy; we get along. He'd drive over here and we'd sit and talk every once in a while."

"Oh? What about?"

"Lotsa things, but most often about how that jackass of a father was treating him."

"He has animosity toward his father?"

"Just hates him, is all. I tried to tell him Adam acted the

way he did out of greed and ignorance, not because he didn't love Paul. But I tell you, Carver, I don't think Adam Kave gives a gnat's ass about anything but himself and that god-awful wiener business he runs. Neither of them kids of his had much guidance growing up.''

"You see Nadine now and then, too?"

"Naw. Not that one. Too busy for an old crank like me. Tennis and goin' out with the boys is her games, what I hear. Kinda wild sometimes, but not a bad girl, you know what I mean.''

"I get the impression Adam loves his wife," Carver said, "if not his kids."

Emmett lowered the sandwich and glared at him for an instant with Adam's intense dark eyes. "Love, shit!" he said. "I suspect that poor, sick wife of his is just something else he owns and likes to parade in front of them he figures is his inferiors.''

"You know she's dying?"

Emmett nodded. "I heard. Paul told me; boy's too smart to keep something like that from him.'' He finished the sandwich in one last huge bite.

Carver waited until the old man had chewed and then washed down the last of the brittle BLT with a pull of beer. Emmett's gray caterpillar eyebrows writhed in something like pain as he belched softly and patted his chest. There was a sandwich that hadn't been worth the effort.

"What's his reaction to that knowledge?"

"Seems to accept it."

"What did Paul say about his father?"

"What was the facts," Emmett said. "That Adam didn't understand him and didn't care about him. Kinda hard to ease the boy's mind and steer him away from thinking what was so obviously true.''

"How often do you see your brother?" Carver asked.

"I ain't seen Adam in fifteen, twenty years, when he was in this part of the state on business, and that ain't long enough for me.''

"For either of you," Carver suggested.

"Fine," Emmett said. "Just goddamned fine."

Carver decided to fish. "Guess I can't blame you for feeling somewhat that way." He glanced around the shabby room. "I mean, it's for sure Adam doesn't believe in spreading the wealth through the family."

"I don't want any of that shithead's money." The deep voice wasn't very convincing. Carver suspected dollars might salve if not cure the wounds of the brothers' relationship.

"You think Paul burned those people?" he asked.

Emmett crimped the beer can back and forth in his thick hand, clacking the metal. It was a sound that wouldn't take long to get on Carver's nerves. "My feeling is the boy's not violent, despite a few adolescent fights he got into. Murder? Naw. Wouldn't surprise me if he killed Adam, but then I'd say it wouldn't surprise anybody who knew how Adam criticized the boy when he was young. The things Paul's told me'd curl your ear hairs, Carver."

"So curl a few," Carver said.

Emmett ran his tongue around the insides of his cheeks, as if seeking words between his molars. Found them. "Goddamned Adam! Always assuming the boy'd come out the loser no matter what or how hard he tried. Self-fulfilling prophecy. Paul went out for the tennis team his junior year at high school. Adam used to play like a champ, and he offered to train Paul. His training consisted of whacking serves and returns the boy couldn't touch with his racket. Finally slammed a ball off the side of Paul's head. On purpose. Adam is what you might call competitive; he's gotta show his superiority like that. Can't let up till he humiliates people. Paul didn't make the team. Never played tennis again. Adam said he wasn't surprised Paul stunk up the place in sports. Said he spent too much time alone in his laboratory or reading, and it was no wonder he was a little loony."

Rough treatment, Carver thought. But Paul Kave wasn't the only kid who had to grow up in a house with a super-critical father. Carver's own childhood had been similar to Paul's in that respect.

"Paul's gone haywire a few times in the past couple of

years and broke up some things. Threw a stool through an ice-cream-shop window over in Cocoa Beach. Kicked in the side of a car when its driver stole his parking space. After times like that, I'd see his shiny old Lincoln drive up afore long, and he'd come in to see me and we'd talk over what happened. We'd have a few beers, and he'd say it was just this pressure that built up in him and needed release, but that folks really did pick on him sometimes. But he never hurt people, Carver, only things."

Or maybe to Paul Kave people *are* things, Carver thought. And it was only a question of time before his outbursts of violence included flesh and blood. "Did he tell you he was a diagnosed schizophrenic and was seeing a psychiatrist?"

"Sure," Emmett said. "Paul and I have the same opinion of shrinks: bunch of phonies getting rich off other people's misery. Paul only went to that doctor because he had no choice. Hell, he's smarter'n any shrink."

"Then he didn't think his therapy was helping him?"

"Course not. Didn't think he needed it in the first place. Despite all his mental mix-up and occasional bouts of aggression," Emmett Kave said firmly, "Paul's a fine young man. Can't say for certain he wouldn't hurt somebody, but I sure don't see him setting folks on fire."

Carver glanced through a side window and noticed an orange tree not far from the house. It was brightly dotted with fruit, and darkened oranges littered the ground beneath it, rotting. "Does Paul talk much about Nadine?" he asked.

"No, sir. But from what little he has told me, she's got pretty much the same problems he has. I get the idea she's a rebel, though, and I wouldn't describe Paul as that. I guess she's gone on the offense, and Paul fights defensively."

Up until a few weeks ago, Carver thought.

He said, "If Paul does contact you, will you call me?" He drew a business card from his pocket and stretched to hand it to Emmett.

"If you want me to be honest," Emmett said, taking the

card and laying it in a puddle next to the beer can, "that'd depend on what Paul has to say about them killings."

"Whatever he has to say, it'll be easier for him if I find him before the police do. I want to help him, Emmett. And he's not the type to give himself up easily, is he?"

"No, he's not that. He'd be scared and angry and get himself hurt or killed—or maybe even kill somebody else out of fear. In his way, he's gut-deep stubborn. All us Kaves are."

Carver had gathered that. "Thanks for your help," he said, and stood up. "Can we talk again about Paul sometime?"

"Sure thing." Emmett got up and walked with him to the door. "You do me and Paul a favor and don't mention to Adam that Paul's dropped by here now and then the past several years. Paul was always scared Adam'd find out. I figure Paul's innocent, and when all this trouble dies down, I don't want him thinking I ratted on him and got him in deep shit with old Adam."

Carver almost refused. After all, Adam Kave was his client and he had a professional obligation of loyalty.

But that was ridiculous, an automatic twinge of obligation and nothing more. An illusion of professionalism. He was already deceiving his client, using him. And under the circumstances his behavior was justified. *An eye for an eye, a son for a son.*

"Okay, Emmett. Our secret."

Emmett held out a bacon-scented hand and they shook on the deal, leaving Carver's fingers greasy. The screen door creaked shut, and Emmett faded into interior dimness.

As Carver made his way across the desert of the yard and back to his car, he was sure the old man was grinning behind the dark screen.

Emmett got off on sharing secrets his brother didn't know.

CHAPTER 13

The next day dawned red and mean, as if Mother Nature bore a grudge against mankind. Well, maybe she did. Carver looked out the car window at the rows of expensive homes and high-rise condominiums cluttering the majestic shore and supposed she had reason enough.

He found the Kave family eating breakfast on a screened-in veranda overlooking the ocean. A rust-colored awning had been rolled out overhead to block the sun. The screen was silver, unlike the dark mesh of Emmett's front door, and the view through it somehow made the Atlantic seem brighter and more shot with sun. Occasionally a hot breeze would kick up off the ocean, causing the awning to flap like a sail. The air that morning was thick and felt silky on Carver's bare arms and face.

Adam sat at the head of the rectangular glass-topped table, Elana at the opposite end. Nadine had answered Carver's ring and, after leading him to the veranda, took her seat again before a partly eaten half-grapefruit with a sprinkling of sugar over it. Carver tried to imagine Paul seated opposite his sister but couldn't.

"Care for some breakfast, Carver?" Adam Kave asked. He was wearing a white-on-white shirt and blue-striped tie today, as if he might be going somewhere or was prepared to meet someone. The breeze tried to ruffle his slicked-back graying hair but couldn't manage; a victory for Brylcreem.

Carver declined the offer of breakfast, but he sat down at the table, where Paul might have sat had he been there. The proximity of his quarry in space if not time felt eerie. "I've been to see Emmett," he said.

Elana dabbed nervously at her lips with her pink cloth napkin. She had on the same delicately laced robe she'd worn yesterday. Adam sipped his coffee from a dainty cup that looked lost and imperiled in his big hand, and peered at Carver over the rim. There was a pink flowery design on the cup, traversed by a hairline crack. Carver for some reason remembered vaguely a line from an Auden poem memorized in school, something about a crack in the side of a teacup being a lane to the land of the dead.

"Guess you had to go there," Adam said. "I don't like Emmett involved in family matters, though."

"Sometimes it can't be helped," Nadine said. "There's no changing the fact he's your brother."

"Stay out of this," Adam said casually but with unmistakable authority.

Carver thought Nadine might snap an answer at her father, but three beautifully pitched, melancholy chimes sounded from nearby. The doorbell. End of this round.

Nadine glared at Adam, then rose and left the veranda. She was wearing a white tennis outfit with shorts, and her tanned legs were thick but surprisingly shapely. Calf muscles rippled above her soft-soled court shoes, and the firm flesh of her thighs danced with each step. She would probably be strong at sports, Carver thought. Strong at a number of things.

Adam said, "I suppose Emmett asked you not to tell me Paul's been in the habit of driving over to Kissimmee and seeing him."

Carver was surprised. His face must have shown it.

Adam smiled and took another nibble of coffee from the dainty cup. "I won't put you on the spot and ask if you promised him you wouldn't mention it. Maybe you traded that promise for some useful information."

"I traded it for Emmett's further cooperation," Carver said. "If what he says is true—and you seem to confirm it— Paul might well contact him for help. Emmett promised to call me if that happened."

"Emmett's promises are about as solid as that sand," Adam said, sweeping a backhand motion toward the ocean breaking on the beach below. A large, errant night moth, lost and dazzled by the light, pinged off the screen twice, then flitted away across the bright green lawn toward an uncertain future.

Elana stood up and smiled at Carver. The smile was out of context, as if she hadn't been present during Carver and her husband's conversation. Maybe people looking squarely at death did so from their own intensely personal and narrowed worlds.

"I'm feeling the heat somewhat, Mr. Carver," she said. "I'm afraid you'll have to excuse me while I take myself upstairs."

Adam stood up hastily, causing his pink napkin to slide from his lap onto the floor. Carver stood with him and they watched Elana walk into the house. She moved with her apparently customary slowness, but so gracefully Carver thought there was a dreamlike quality to her. A breeze rose and the canvas cracked overhead, a reminder of reality.

"It isn't the heat," Adam said. "She gets tired faster now." There was the slightest catch in his gravelly voice.

Carver wondered if Adam realized Emmett knew about Elana's illness. Or did it matter? "How did you find out about Paul going to see Emmett?" he asked.

"Played detective," Adam said in a self-congratulatory tone, sitting back down. He poured some more coffee for himself and then held out the elegant silver-and-glass carafe toward Carver, who had also sat down again. "Sure you don't want some?"

"I'm sure," Carver said.

Adam placed the carafe back in its stand, above a wavering candle flame. "Last year, somebody I know in Kissimmee mentioned seeing Paul's car in Emmett's neighborhood. That old Lincoln's pretty distinctive, so I thought there might be something to it, even though Paul lied and told me he was someplace else when I asked him about driving to Kissimmee. So what I did was drive to Emmett's house and back, keeping track of the mileage. And now and then I'd check the odometer in Paul's Lincoln after he'd been gone awhile. Several times the mileage on his odometer matched exactly the mileage to Emmett's house and back here, sometimes down to the tenth of a mile.''

No wonder Paul felt constricted, Carver thought. It wouldn't be difficult to become paranoid with a father like Adam Kave.

Nadine came back onto the veranda, flanked by two men. The one on her right had his arm lightly around her waist. He was about six feet tall and built lean, with straight brown razor-styled hair, a neatly trimmed mustache, and bright blue eyes full of chips of light; the sort of guy who'd look great in any kind of uniform.

The man on Nadine's left looked like a troll that had crawled out from under a bridge. He was not more than five and a half feet tall, and his neck swelled into shoulders bunched with muscle. His hair was a dark, Medusalike mass of ropy curls. The backs of his gnarled hands were sooted with black hair, and Carver imagined the stocky little man had hair matted over most of his body. His face was swarthy and wide, with a pushed-in nose and protruding brown eyes. He reminded Carver of a Pekingese pup; yet, strangely enough, there was a crude kind of confidence and vitality about him of the sort Carver had seen appeal to women. A beast not quite tamed.

Both men and Nadine were smiling broadly, as if they'd shared a bawdy joke on the walk through the house to the veranda.

The tall one with his arm around Nadine she introduced as her fiancé, Joel Dewitt. The troll was Nick Fanning, CEO of Adam's Inns.

Nadine, Dewitt, and Fanning sat down at the table, and Nadine poured them coffee from the fancy carafe. Carver had to refuse another cup of the stuff.

Fanning seemed very much at home here. "These two tell me the wedding's set for April," he said.

Adam shrugged. "That's what they tell me, too, Nick."

Fanning looked around abruptly, as if a slight noise had attracted his attention. The smile was still a shadow on his broad face. As he rotated his head, the cords on his muscular neck jumped like taut cables straining to escape from beneath his flesh. "Where's Elana?"

"Not feeling well this morning," Adam told him.

"Sorry to hear," Fanning said. He added cream to his coffee. He kind of jabbed the marbled liquid with his spoon and swirled it around a few times, then rested the spoon on his saucer with a single faint click. Casual.

Silence moved onto the veranda, stayed, and got heavy. Nobody wanted that.

"Some hot morning," Joel Dewitt remarked.

"Summer," Adam said, explaining it neatly.

"Summer in hell," Fanning said.

"How's the car business?" Carver asked Joel Dewitt.

Dewitt gave him a sharp glance; somebody had been talking about him to Carver. "Booming. I sell Honda cycles, too. New ones. Say, you look like the motorcycle type, Fred."

"Not me," Carver said.

"You driving the Olds convertible out front?"

Carver nodded. "My style. My price range."

Dewitt smiled. "Don't be so sure. Come on in and see me and I'll convince you otherwise. Put you on a cycle and show you what you been missing."

Adam stood up. Fanning took the cue and stood also.

"Well, Nick and I've got a ton of work to do," Adam said. He looked at Carver. "Be in touch soon, eh?"

Carver said he would.

"Bring your coffee, Nick," Adam said, and he and Fanning disappeared into the cool dimness of the house, Adam leading the way. They were reminiscent of Dr. Frankenstein and his assistant Igor.

"They're going to talk for hours about goddamn wieners," Nadine said. "One time they had a four-hour nationwide conference call about how many sesame seeds should be on the bun of something called the Ali-Baba Dog."

"I've tried that one," Dewitt said. "It's not bad. Probably made lots of money for your dad, too."

A large pleasure boat veered in toward shore, moving at

a fast clip just outside the breakers and tooting its air horn, as if it knew the Kaves and was saying hello. Carver watched it continue close to the beach, then angle into the waves seaward, spreading a trough of white foam and unsettled water in its wake. *Fantasy* was lettered on its stern. Neighbors, maybe. The boat was similar to the one moored down at Adam Kave's private dock. Nadine gave no indication that she'd noticed it.

"Any news on Paul?" Dewitt asked her. Carver found it odd that he'd ask Nadine that in front of him.

"Not much," she said. "He's still missing. Mr. Carver's trying to locate him."

Dewitt shot Carver an appraising, cold blue look. "Any way I can help . . ." he said. His words trailed to silence as he caught sight of the figure to his left.

Elana was standing in the doorway to the house. "Nadine, Mel Bingham is here to see you." She didn't acknowledge Dewitt's presence—a queen enduring the company of a fool.

Nadine flushed slightly and squeezed Dewitt's hand. "I won't be long," she said in a tight voice. She got up and followed her mother into the house. Dewitt twisted in his chair and watched them. Maybe he was looking at Nadine's legs. Carver was.

"How well do you know Paul?" Carver asked.

Dewitt swiveled back to face the table, then idly nudged around a bowl with a squashed half-grapefruit in it. He was nervous; possibly he didn't like Nadine talking to Mel Bingham, whoever Bingham might be.

"Paul and I got along okay," Dewitt said. "He's kinda odd, but not a bad kid. It's rough seeing this happen to him."

"Think he's guilty?"

"Don't really know." Dewitt touched the ruined grapefruit with his forefinger, then pressed the fingertip to his tongue, as if to ascertain that the taste was sour. He grimaced slightly. Genuine grapefruit, all right. "The police seem to think Paul's the one."

"You know this Mel Bingham?" Carver asked.

Dewitt's ears reddened. "He's some asshole pesters Nadine, is all. Thinks she should go for him. Elana's all for the idea, I can tell. What are you, a private detective or something? I mean, if the family hired you to find Paul, that's what you must be. Right?"

"That's it," Carver said. "That doesn't mean you have to answer my questions. I'm not the police, just a guy making conversation."

"Hey, I know. Listen, I'd like to help Paul, if for no other reason than he's Nadine's brother. Fact is, Fred, I didn't see him all that much when I came around. The mother, Elana, she isn't so hot on this marriage. So it's uncomfortable for Nadine and me here. We generally don't hang around. Paul never did either. So, you see, our schedules didn't overlap much."

"Why do you think Elana's against the marriage?"

Dewitt turned his hands palms up and raised them a few inches in a helpless gesture, or as if he might be trying to levitate the table. "She doesn't like me. Hell, I don't know why. Chemistry, maybe. Or maybe she's got this idea car dealers are all swindlers. You'd be surprised the kind of prejudice there is against some occupations. Or maybe you wouldn't, being a private detective."

Carver hadn't been off the force and in private practice very long, but he'd already been called a keyhole peeper, a sleaze bag, and assorted things even less nice. Joel Dewitt had a point. But Elana didn't seem the sort to tag people that way. There was a sadness and wisdom to her that suggested understanding gained the hard way and not forgotten.

He gave Dewitt one of his cards and asked him to call if he had anything to say about Paul Kave. Dewitt handed Carver a card with a Fort Lauderdale address and told him he should come in and see if maybe he really *was* the cycle type. "Never too old," he said. Carver didn't care for that, but what the hell, Dewitt might still be in his twenties. Go-getter making it in his youth and about to marry into more of it. Full throttle, kid.

"Tell Nadine I said good-bye," Carver said. He leaned

on his cane and straightened up. The cane had been beneath the table, so Dewitt had to be seeing it for the first time, but there was no change of expression in his eyes. "I'll go out this way and walk around the side of the house." Carver limped toward a door in the aluminum screen.

"Remember what I said about that motorcycle," Dewitt said behind him. "Cane don't make any difference."

"Might even be a good thing to use on sharp corners," Carver said, and went out. The screen door clicked solidly closed behind him; it didn't slam and reverberate like the one on Carver's beach cottage. The fit and finish of big money.

When he'd almost reached the Olds, he heard a spat-out oath and saw a lanky young man stalking toward a mud-spattered red Jeep parked in the shade of the portico. His elongated face was creased with anger and his white jogging shoes seemed to want to pause of their own accord and kick pebbles and bits of bark, causing him to lurch. Forces he couldn't comprehend had control of him.

He spotted Carver and glared; might have been able to burn a hole in paper with that look. "Fuckin' Dewitt!" he said. "When you see him, you tell him I know he's a crook!"

This must be Mel Bingham, and he must be connecting Carver and Dewitt because Carver was standing near the car parked next to the Olds, a new, deep blue Jaguar sedan with tinted windows. Bingham probably thought Carver was waiting for Dewitt.

"I might not see him again," Carver said. "I just met him. You better tell him yourself."

"Oh, I've told him before," Bingham said. He had flame-red hair to match his temper and his splotchy, freckled complexion. He was wearing jeans and a gray T-shirt with *Have a Shitty Day* lettered in black across the front. His caved-in chest was trembling and his hands were white-knuckled fists that seemed to want to strike and burrow and pluck out vital organs. He'd followed the advice on his T-shirt and he was mad.

"I'd like to talk to you for a minute," Carver said,

wondering if Bingham could calm down enough for coherent conversation.

Carver wasn't going to find out today.

"Later!" Bingham snarled. He swung his long body up into the Jeep, fired up the engine, and probably got a lot of satisfaction from the screeching of the knobby tires on the driveway.

Carver watched the Jeep two-wheel it around a corner and out of sight behind some palm trees. He wondered if the automatic barrier at the base of the drive would be triggered soon enough to rise before the Jeep reached it. Bingham was furious enough to drive through the barrier. Through brick walls, maybe.

The Rejected Suitor Blues, Carver figured.

He got into the Olds and started the engine. The vinyl upholstery was searingly hot, and he put the car in Drive immediately to get out of there and enjoy the breeze of motion.

Carver thought he glimpsed Elana's pale features floating behind a front window as he pulled sharply out onto the driveway and coasted toward the highway. He hoped he wouldn't see Mel Bingham's red Jeep twisted around a tree on the way.

Nadine was crazy to prefer Dewitt, he thought. Bingham belonged in this family.

CHAPTER 14

Carver found Dr. Roland Elsing's office easily. Paul Kave's psychiatrist was listed in the phone directory, the detective's friend. There was more information in phone books than most people thought; they were short-form encyclopedias of cities, revealing economic standing, status, neighborhood, entertainment and industrial trends—the stage setting in which the detective had to play out his or her role.

Elsing's address meant he was expensive; most of his patients would be affluent if not downright obscenely rich like the Kaves. Carver remembered Emmett's scathing opinion of psychiatrists, apparently shared by Paul.

The doctor's office was on the second floor of a newish glass and pale-stone building on Commercial, in the heart of town. Architecturally, it looked a lot like a crypt with a view. Next to Elsing's office was a broker who dealt in "pre-owned" yachts. There was a glassed-in corkboard in the hall, plastered with photographs and typed information on various boats, some of them big enough to be called ships. Carver looked at a few of the photographs, a few of the prices. Looked away.

He buttoned his powder blue sportcoat, which felt comfortable in the coolly air-conditioned tomb of a building, and pushed through a brass-lettered oak door into Dr. Elsing's office.

The reception area was carpeted in deep green. The walls were pale green. Most of the Danish furniture was dark green or beige, and the long, curved receptionist's desk had a greenish tint to its gray wood. Must be true about green being the calming color, Carver thought.

He set sail across the sea of green carpet. It wasn't easy
to stay on his feet, but the softness sure felt good beneath
and around his soles. His cane dragged in the plush pile.

The receptionist herself wasn't green, though she wore a
light brown dress with an off-white collar, and went with
the decor very nicely. She was attractive in an intellectual
way, with probing gray eyes behind round-rimmed glasses,
and a prim, lipsticked mouth that looked as if it had never
done anything unnatural. Though she was sitting down, it
was apparent that she was trim and shapely. There were no
sleeves to her dress, and her biceps were firm and smooth:
an athlete. Maybe racquetball or Nautilus training on
weekends. Body and mind as one, Carver thought. And here
was a woman—Beverly, according to her desk plaque—who
didn't look as if she'd neglected either. Could she stay with
Nadine at tennis?

There was no one other than Carver and Beverly in the
reception room. He approached the desk and she smiled up
at him. Great teeth. Was there no flaw in this person? He
said, "Does it always smell like spearmint in here?"

"It's probably my sugarless gum," she said, holding her
perfect smile. "May I help you?"

"I'm a private investigator. I'd like to talk with Dr.
Elsing concerning one of his patients."

Beverly stopped smiling and stared inquisitively at him
through her round glasses. Maybe she didn't believe he was
really a private detective even if he did. Could be a common
delusion. This was, after all, a psychiatrist's office. Some
of the people who came here probably acted crazy, maybe
thought they were Marlowe or Spenser or other dead English
poets.

Carver showed her his identification. "Lighten up, Bev.
I'm who and what I say."

She nodded and leaned back in her chair, crossing her
creamy arms and thinking about Carver's request. It was
part of her job to protect Dr. Elsing from the sort of people
who might wander into a psychiatrist's office unannounced
to sell medical supplies or malpractice insurance. Or to look
for trouble instead of help.

"I don't have a salesman's sample case with me," Carver said. "And I sometimes think I might be going mad, so I must be sane."

"Uh-hm. Which patient did you want to discuss with the doctor?"

"Paul Kave. I've been hired by his family to try to locate him. I really could use Dr. Elsing's help."

At the mention of Paul she uncrossed her arms and sat forward. The Kave name was magic in places where money changed hands. Dr. Elsing wouldn't like it if Beverly pissed off Adam Kave, even indirectly.

She lifted her pale green phone delicately, as if it might be coated with something that would burn her fingers. Then she pecked out a number with a long pencil to protect her painted nail, and explained the situation briefly to Dr. Elsing.

"He's with a patient now," she said to Carver, replacing the receiver. "He'll talk to you in about twenty minutes, if you'd like to wait."

"I'd like," Carver said.

He limped across the soft green carpet and sat down in a leather Danish chair that sighed as it took the brunt of his weight. Beverly glanced with disinterest at his cane, then got busy with paperwork. The maimed were the maimed, physically or mentally. Infirmities were all the same to her, whether she could or couldn't see them.

Ten minutes later an unbelievably obese girl in her teens wedged herself through the reception-room door and said hello to Beverly. Beverly smiled and said hello back, calling the girl Marie. Marie had a face that was all flesh-padded sweetness. She said a shy "hi" to Carver and sat down as far away from him as possible. The chair popped and groaned beneath her. Then she picked up a *Seventeen* magazine and started leafing through it, and Carver ceased to exist.

Some seventeen it must be for Marie, he thought. Grossly overweight and seeing a psychiatrist. Fate was a sadist.

Then it occurred to him that Chipper would never see any kind of seventeen, and he felt less pity for Marie. He looked at the four-color, glossy ad for skin cream on the back cover of the magazine, then looked at Beverly, who was engrossed again in making entries in a large ledger book with pages that crinkled as she leafed through them.

"We can talk in about five minutes, Marie," a man's voice said. It was a soothing voice that came down softly on the crisp consonants. If voices had color, this one would be green.

Dr. Roland Elsing was standing by a light-oak door that had just opened. He was a medium-height man in his late forties, with a balding pate and a moon-shaped face that had deeply etched lines, like bloodless incisions, running symmetrically from the sides of his nose to the corners of his thin lips to form a sort of triangle. They were the kind of lines people with poorly fitted dentures developed. He wasn't dressed the way Carver imagined psychiatrists clothed themselves; he had on a windowpane check sportcoat, wrinkled charcoal slacks, and brown shoes with thick and wavy gum-rubber soles and heels. Practical shoes, made more for comfort and hiking than for impressing wealthy clients who wandered in with phobias and fat wallets. Emmett might be wrong about this guy.

"Mr. Carver?"

Carver leaned on the cane and stood up.

"Come in, please." No flicker of eye movement to the cane. Elsing opened the door wider to make room for Carver to pass.

The soft green decor was carried into the office. There were tall, glass-lined bookcases along one green wall, with books and papers stuffed into the shelves in a jumble. The doctor's desk was dark mahogany. The thick brown drapes behind it were closed. A pale ceramic bust of someone who looked like Beethoven sat on top of one of the bookcases, gazing down on the scene with blank eyes. There was a tiny beige sofa in the room, a love seat. Also a comfortable-looking chocolate brown easy chair. Though it was afternoon, a brass gooseneck lamp with a green-tinted shade glowed on Elsing's desk. It was a restful room, unnaturally quiet. Almost made you wish you had mental anguish so you could come here now and then and pass the time. It was impossible to hear the street sounds down on Commercial.

Elsing smelled like tobacco. He motioned for Carver to sit in the comfortable chocolate brown chair, then sat down behind his desk heavily, as if his feet had been hurting. That might explain the sloppy, comfortable shoes. The pipe rack holding half a dozen well-used wood pipes explained the tobacco smell. The doctor bowed his head, then looked up and smiled expectantly. Carver figured in another couple of years the crown of Elsing's head would be as bald as his own. Tough shit.

"You wanted to talk about Paul Kave?" Elsing said. Right to business; time was something not to be wasted, and the way not to waste it was to take control of the conversation immediately.

"That Beethoven?" Carver asked, pointing to the ceramic bust.

"Uh, yes it is."

"I wondered."

"Mr. Carver—"

"Paul's family's hired me to try to find him before the police do," Carver said.

"Paul's my patient, Mr. Carver. Naturally I respect the confidential nature of that relationship. There isn't much I can, or will, tell you about him."

"Have the police talked to you?"

"Yes. I told them no more than was necessary."

Carver felt himself getting irritated despite all the greenness. "Doesn't the Hippocratic oath take a backseat to murder?"

"Of course. And I cooperated with the police. But I don't think Paul killed anyone. This entire affair is some sort of tragic confluence of circumstance, and I don't want to add to the misdirection."

Carver felt like giving the good doctor a lesson in admissible evidence, but he didn't want to lose him. "Then we'll speak only in generalities, Dr. Elsing. Tell me about schizophrenia. The kind Paul Kave suffers from."

Elsing's lips curved into a momentary smile. The lines swooping from the sides of his nose deepened. "You make it seem so easily categorized," he said in his soft, soft voice. "There's a lot not known about schizophrenia, Mr. Carver. It usually strikes its victims when they're young, between the ages of fifteen and twenty-five, and it lasts for decades. It gets progressively worse if not controlled. Seldom better. It's still one of medicine's most elusive mysteries. And an illness that's prompted a great many public misconceptions. Read the papers about the search for Paul Kave and you'll see what I mean. Schizophrenia isn't at all as most of the media assume."

"What causes it?"

"That we don't understand precisely. One theory is that it has to do with dopamine, a chemical that passes between nerve endings in the brain. In a so-called normal person, stress causes the dopamine levels to drop. This lessens the intensity of the signals that pass between nerves. Not so with schizophrenics. Their brain activity is heightened tremendously by stress. The chemical imbalance causes various symptoms, among them imaginary voices, irrational thoughts. The world can seem like an ominous madhouse to an advanced schizophrenic."

"So it's really a physical illness that causes mental problems."

Elsing shook his head slowly, as if to say it was impossible to give Carver a course in psychiatric medicine in five minutes. "The chemical imbalance triggers certain reactions, Mr. Carver. And as I said, this is one of several theories. We do know that three million people, more than one percent of the population, will at some time suffer from the disease during their lives. It would behoove us to learn much, much more about it."

"What sort of treatment was Paul's?"

"Analysis and, when he was entering a bad period, medication."

"What kind of medication?" Carver asked. He saw Elsing notice his piqued interest and wasn't sure if the doctor would answer. The muted ringing of a phone filtered in from the outer office; Beverly caught it on the third ring.

"Chlorpromazine. It regulates dopamine levels and lessens the patient's delusions."

"Does it regulate paranoia?"

"Yes, you might say that. And as you surmise, paranoia is one of the disease's symptoms." Dr. Elsing was pressing on the desk with his fingertips. "Are you assuming Paul killed those people in a fit of paranoia, Mr. Carver?" His fingertips were white, not green.

"It's a possibility."

"Not at all likely. Paul could get paranoid at times, even mildly aggressive. But I don't believe he's a killer." He shook his head slowly and looked glum. "Few of the misconceptions about schizophrenia make life easier for the disease's victims."

"A police psychiatrist thinks it's possible that Paul was extremely paranoid and killed his victims to avenge some slight or imagined wrong done to him."

"That chain of thought is consistent with Paul's potential behavior, except for the degree of paranoia and the killing part. Maybe he'd insult or even punch someone for this imagined wrong, but taking human life is a different matter. I doubt he'd react with anything near that intensity."

Carver persisted. "The police psychiatrist says it's possible."

Elsing looked as if he had a bad taste in his mouth. He didn't want to call the police psychiatrist a fool, but that was what he thought. That's how it was with inexact sciences. "Possible? Sure, Mr. Carver. But the odds and the illness suggest it isn't probable. I know. Paul Kave is my patient, not the patient of some . . . police employee who's never even met him."

"Or grown to like him."

Elsing smiled again. It was a kind of male Mona Lisa smile, not giving away much. "You're something of a psychoanalyst yourself, Mr. Carver."

"That's what keeps me working. Were some of Paul's problems caused by his relationship with his father?"

Elsing chewed on the inside of his jaw for a moment, then said, "I don't think I'll answer that."

"How often was Paul receiving medication?"

"Once a day. Capsules." Elsing anticipated Carver's next question. "He has enough medication to last another few days."

"And when he runs out?"

Elsing tugged at a button on his coat sleeve. "I don't know. Paul's a brilliant and resourceful boy, but there's no way for him to obtain the drug without a prescription."

"Would Paul recognize the effects of his illness setting in once he's off medication?"

"At first he would. But after a while delusion would seem consistently real to him. It's something like being an alcoholic, Mr. Carver. After the first few drinks an alcoholic thinks he's sober and able to thread needles or drive a car or work calculus. Everything is altered, and a private reality takes charge."

Carver handed out his second business card of the morning. "If Paul contacts you for more capsules, will you phone me?"

"The police have already requested that."

"I'd like you to call me before the police, Dr. Elsing. For Paul. After all, we both want to help him."

Elsing nodded ever so slightly. He wasn't dumb enough to agree concretely, but Carver suspected the doctor would phone. He was obviously fond of Paul Kave. He stood up. "I'm sorry, but I've got a patient waiting, Mr. Carver."

"I noticed her in the outer room. Marie."

"I specialize in helping young people."

"It must be difficult to keep your objectivity," Carver said, "and not feel for them too deeply."

"Every analyst has to learn to cope with that prospect, Mr. Carver. The way to relieve a patient's anguish isn't to become part of the problem."

Carver decided he liked Dr. Elsing. A practical man doing battle with shadows. Carver knew how that felt. He sank his cane into the carpet, braced on it, and levered himself up out of the deep, comfortable chair. "If Paul took this medication long enough, would it possibly cure him?"

"I thought I'd made it clear," Elsing said. "There is at this time no cure for schizophrenia."

"You also made it clear that stress intensifies the symptoms. And Paul Kave's under plenty of stress."

"Paul's got a pisspot full of trouble," Elsing said, momentarily dropping his air of professionalism and surprising Carver with his profanity. "That doesn't mean he's a killer."

Carver didn't see it that way. Not in the face of the evidence.

"Can you tell me that, in your expert judgment, Paul couldn't kill another human being?"

"No," Elsing said, with a sigh almost too soft to hear. "But that's an unfair question. I can't state that about anyone. Including you, Mr. Carver."

Carver said nothing as he limped through the reception room, past Beverly and Marie and the cool spearmint scent, out into the hall with its bulletin board advertising millionaires' floating toys. He was sweating when he reached the elevator.

Seated in the heat in his car, he tried to reconcile Dr. Elsing's apparent affection and belief in Paul Kave with his own unrelenting anger. There were times when that rage for revenge slackened, when Paul Kave was humanized and seemed almost sympathetic. Almost.

Deliberately this time, Carver called up the nightmare, blackened ruin of his son. His namesake. Flesh of his flesh. Burned flesh. Tortured flesh. Black twisted hole of a mouth, tendons drawn tight by blast-furnace heat to curl the limbs into a praying posture. Face like that of a darkened, shrunken head bobbing on a cannibal's hip. A wizened trophy no longer a person except to those who'd loved him. In this case, Paul Kave's grotesque trophy. What had the moment been like when Chipper saw the flames? Felt their first paralyzing licks? How long had that instant lasted in human, clockless time?

Carver started the engine and slammed the Olds into

Drive. People on the sidewalk stared as the big car roared out of its parking space.

Paul wasn't as Elsing or his family saw him.

Carver felt like screaming into the hot, booming wind that Paul Kave was a killer.

A monster.

One that breathed fire.

CHAPTER 15

What to do when confronted with a smooth surface and no handhold? Carver wasn't sure, but the way things were going, he might have to find out. His visit with Dr. Elsing hadn't exactly sprung open doors to fresh vistas of knowledge.

He didn't know how long he'd be in the Fort Lauderdale area. That depended on Paul Kave. But it was here, near where Paul disappeared, that Carver had to seek the beginning of the trail, where he'd find something to grasp and build on and follow to ultimate revenge. Always there had to be at least some thin indication of direction. People changed the world as they moved through it, even as it changed them.

He drove north the short distance to Pompano Beach and registered where Laura had stayed, at the Carib Terrace Motel on Ocean Boulevard. He was given a ground-floor unit, and he sat for a while on the edge of the bed and gazed through the sliding glass doors at the beach.

It was essentially the same view as the one from the unit upstairs, where he'd visited Laura after Chipper's murder. Probably some of the same sunbathers lounged out there on the pale sand, and some of the same children ran and kicked through the surf. Down where the beach was darkened from high washes of foam, an elderly man with his pants rolled into doughnuts just below his knees was walking slowly with his head down, squatting occasionally on spindly legs to examine seashells, none of which was apparently worthy of his collection. Not far from the glass doors, a potbellied

man in violent tropical-print swimming trunks was trying
earnestly to fold or unfold a bulky redwood lounge chair,
wrestling with it as if it were his conscience.

After a while the glare outside caused Carver's eyes to
ache. He got up and pulled the drapes closed. Light and
sound were instantly muted, and he suddenly felt isolated
and lonely. Remotely afraid of something he couldn't
identify.

He phoned Adam Kave and told him where he could be
reached if there was any news on Paul. Then he walked
down the street to a Chinese restaurant and had a lunch of
crab Rangoon appetizers, Hunan beef and broccoli, and two
Budweisers. East meets West.

As soon as he returned, the motel owner's wife stopped
him as he passed the office door and told him he had two
messages. He was supposed to call Nick Fanning sometime
that afternoon or evening. And a Lieutenant Desoto had
phoned from Orlando and wanted Carver to call back as
soon as possible.

The youngish, pretty woman handed him a slip of lined
paper with the phone numbers written on it. She yelled
"Don't run—walk!" at a skinny tan kid by the motel pool,
then stepped back into the air-conditioned office. Sometimes
good advice, Carver thought, sometimes not.

He glanced at Fanning's number but didn't recognize it.
He did recognize the other number: Desoto's extension at
police headquarters in Orlando. The times of the calls to
Carver were scrawled next to the numbers. Fanning had
called half an hour before Desoto. Carver bore down on his
cane and walked, didn't run, away from the lapping blue
pool and the acrid scent of chlorine and went into his room.

The phone was ringing. He lifted the receiver and said
hello, expecting to hear Fanning or Desoto.

A man's unfamiliar voice said, "Her tits swelled up and
sort of split open when they burned, then they shriveled up.
Hey, it was something to see. And hear. I'll always think
of her as my old flame."

Carver sat on the edge of the bed, dragged the phone to

him, and rested the base unit in his lap. His good leg was trembling. "Who is this?"

"You know who I am, Carver. And I know who you are. Yeah, I know."

"Paul? . . ."

Click. Buzz.

The connection had been gently but abruptly broken. Carver sat listening to the hum of the dial tone for a long time. It seemed as if the buzzing might be in his head, the sound of fury and futility. It was a frantic, wavering drone that made his pulse race and his hands clench. *Don't run, walk!*

He made himself calm down and tried to memorize every nuance of the young male voice that had casually projected such horror in him. There was nothing distinctive about the voice. A nice normal voice; that was what had been so chilling about the words it had spoken.

He slowly pressed down on the cradle button, let it up, and pecked out Nick Fanning's number. How had Fanning known where to phone him and leave a message? But Carver realized anyone might have followed him from the Kave estate and found out where he was staying, and then told anyone else.

"I was with Adam Kave when you called to let him know where to reach you," Fanning said, after answering on the second ring and exchanging hellos. "I noticed the name of your motel when he jotted it down on his desk pad." Very pat.

But it didn't explain why Fanning had called. "Do you know something about Paul, Mr. Fanning?"

"More to the point," Fanning said, "I think there's something you oughta know. Whatever Paul's problems, they aren't entirely Adam Kave's fault."

"I didn't suppose so."

"You're going to talk to people," Fanning said, "and they're going to give Adam a bad rap. Or is that the case already?"

"Adam Kave hasn't rated glowing reports as a father," Carver admitted.

"And it's true he *hasn't* been a good father to Paul, but probably not so true as some of the people you've talked to would have you believe. I'm in a position to know. I've watched their relationship, and even tried to intercede a few times. While Adam certainly is too critical of Paul, it's also true that he loves Paul very much."

"So why are you telling me this, Mr. Fanning?"

"Call me Nick. And I'm butting in because I owe a lot to Adam Kave, at least enough to set the record straight about him and Paul. Adam's an exceptional man, Carver, a man who was driven by something in his youth that demanded unequivocal success, and still drives and demands. He's not like the rest of us. He created a multi-million-dollar empire from nothing but an idea." Fanning's voice had taken on a lilt that was almost evangelical. *He's not like the rest of us.*

"And now it's the seventh day and he's resting?"

"No, now he rules his kingdom. That's the real stuff of his life. Exercising the unbendable will that enabled him to succeed spectacularly in business in the first place."

"The Kave stubborn streak."

"Sure. You can call it that if you want to simplify it. While Adam's equipped to found and control business empires, he isn't well equipped to be a father. He doesn't know how and he never took the time to learn. But I've seen him try. It's the only thing I've seen him try at and fail. And he fails as big as he succeeds. It's painful to observe. He doesn't know how to talk to Paul, even how to take a pass at it."

"He still try?"

"The last few years he's tried. But maybe it's too late. There are emotions there he doesn't seem able to handle; he grapples with them and loses and can't figure out why. The thing for you to remember, Carver, is that at the base of all their troubles, Adam loves Paul even if Paul doesn't know it."

"And vice versa?" Carver asked.

"Yes," Fanning said after a pause. "Paul would, deep

down, like nothing more than to please his father. To earn
the symbolic stamp of approval. Can you understand that?''

Carver thought back to his own childhood and felt a pang
of resentment. He understood.

''Apparently approval can be earned,'' he said. ''Adam's
satisfied with your performance.''

''Yeah, but I'm not his son.''

''I'll keep what you said in mind, Nick. Incidentally, did
you mention this phone number to anyone?''

''No, of course not. Why?''

''Nothing. I only wondered.''

''When you find Paul, Carver, tell him his father loves
him. God knows, Adam can't do it himself. Fatherly love
has made him mute when it comes to Paul.''

''I'll tell him,'' Carver said. ''The idea is for me to help
Paul, remember. To save him.''

''I know. Maybe only somebody from outside the family
can do that. Don't give up on the job.''

''I intend to keep at it,'' Carver said.

He hung up the phone. You weren't supposed to feel full
thirty minutes after Oriental food, but the spicy Hunan beef
rested in his stomach like a stone from the Great Wall of
China. Carver closed his eyes for a minute, seeing only
swimming fragments of golden sun that had followed him
into his room. He didn't feel good about what he'd just told
Nick Fanning. Or about what Fanning had said about Adam
actually being fond of Paul.

Somebody loved even Hitler, he told himself, and picked
up the phone again and played the numbers to reach Desoto,
oddly comforted by the thought.

''Somebody loved even Hitler,'' he said, when Desoto
had answered the phone and identified himself.

''Plenty of people would still love him, *amigo*, if
Germany had won the war.''

''A measure of how fucked-up the world is,'' Carver
said. ''How'd you know where to reach me?''

''I called McGregor and he told me.''

''How did he know?''

''He didn't say. He's the kind that hoards information like

a squirrel hoards nuts. Knowledge is power, McGregor figures, and he'd just as soon not share it.''

"Not share anything."

"Except blame, *amigo*. He's good at passing that around. He's one sneaky *bastardo*, a watcher who plans before he moves."

He's watching me. Having me shadowed. Carver automatically glanced at the sliding glass doors to outside, as if expecting to see McGregor or one of his men hunkered down and staring in through the crack in the drapes, like a peeping Tom.

"I'm sorry, *amigo*, but I've got something to tell you that will only worsen that fucked-up condition you mentioned. A woman here in Orlando burned to death in her shop a few hours ago. We're still putting things together, but there's not much doubt it's just like the other killings."

The knot in Carver's stomach got heavier; his heart moved higher in his chest and fluttered. "Fifteen minutes ago I got a phone call." He told Desoto what the caller had said. How the man had graphically described a woman burning.

"She was burned that way," Desoto said quietly.

"Christ! . . ."

"Paul Kave's taunting you," Desoto said. "Making it a game. Showing he can take the play away from you and be the hunter."

For an instant Carver saw a tiger. "Why?"

"Amusement, *amigo*. Twisted kind of sex thing, maybe. We've both seen it. This time it's mixed up with burning people to death. Know what?—I'm afraid for you."

"I'm afraid for me, too."

"Ah, but you feel something more potent than fear. And that's what worries me, Carver."

"I'll worry enough for both of us."

"I sincerely hope."

"Any witnesses to the last murder?"

"None. What was left of the victim was discovered by customers when they walked into her dress shop over on Orange Avenue."

"Orange in downtown Orlando?"

"Yeah. Not all that far from police headquarters. You want details by phone, or are you driving here?"

"I'll check out now and get there soon as possible."

"I oughta be in my office till late evening," Desoto said. "Should have an autopsy prelim by the time you get here."

"That's fast."

"There isn't much left to autopsy," Desoto said sadly. "This was a thorough job. Not an inch of her wasn't burned. *Sacra Madre!*" Soft hissing on the line was the only sound Carver heard for a while. Desoto breathing into the receiver? Carver waited. He knew Desoto was thinking about the dead woman, reliving fresh and vivid impressions. Homicide cops were bedeviled creatures.

"*Amigo*, you think even Hitler ever did anything like this? I mean, personally?"

"If he didn't," Carver said, "I bet he could have worked up to it."

It was something he thought about most of the way into Orlando, whether a murderer of historic proportion and bureaucratic distance like Hitler was actually as evil as Paul Kave, who stood face-to-face with his victims and watched their blazing agony and death throes. Worked painlessly inside their tortured flesh as an observer and enjoyed. The nature of evil was elusive. Like the truth.

When he reached the Bee Line Expressway on the outskirts of Orlando, he wondered if the white Ford rental behind him was the one that had haunted his rearview mirror all the way up from Pompano Beach.

CHAPTER 16

Desoto asked Carver, "You wanna see the body?"

"No."

"I don't blame you."

They were in Desoto's office in the Municipal Justice Building. The air-conditioner behind Desoto's desk was toiling away, humming up its miniature windstorm and elevating the yellow ribbons tied to its grille. It had its work cut out for it; though it was late evening, the temperature outside was ninety-two and the humidity was thick enough to swim in.

Desoto, in his vanilla-colored suit, white shirt, and pale mauve tie, appeared cool as always. He never perspired; maybe he didn't have pores. But he must have felt the heat. "It's the boiling tropics in this part of the country, *amigo,* despite all those Disney World commercials the tourists see on TV."

"It's lots of things despite Disney World," Carver said. "And that's a shame."

"You're not missing much, not viewing the body," Desoto told him. "Just something charred that used to be a woman. It was the fire she died from; she was alive when she was torched. Like the others."

"What about the accelerant?"

"The lab says it appears to be the same concoction that was used in the Fort Lauderdale and Pompano Beach murders. You surprised?"

"No. But where would Paul Kave get that kind of flammable mixture while he's on the run?"

106

Desoto shrugged, an exquisite gesture; elegant man in an elegant suit. "Maybe he took a supply with him. He might think that way. That's why head-case killers are especially dangerous; no way to know how or what they're thinking. Not for sure, anyway."

"Sometimes, if you understand how they tick, they can be the most predictable."

"That what you been doing?" Desoto asked. "Learning about Paul Kave's clockwork?"

"Been trying." Carver watched the yellow ribbons for a moment. "What else do you know about this killing?"

Desoto ran a manicured hand over his dark hair in a gesture of unconscious vanity. Someone not knowing him well would never guess he was a tough cop. They'd see him as a threat to vulnerable females, and nothing more. Carver knew he was much more. Desoto fixed his somber brown eyes on Carver as he spoke: "Adelaide Finney—that's the victim—was alone in Rags and Riches—that's the dress shop. She was forty-seven, single, Caucasian. It's a cubby-hole of a place, *amigo*, racks of clothes, couple of changing rooms with mirrors. One of the Finney woman's regular customers went in to buy something and right away sniffed what it smells like after a person's burned. Some of the dresses were charred, and she saw flames. The sprinkler system started spraying water all over the place, but the fire department hadn't responded yet to an alarm network the shop's hooked into. So the customer, a Missie Jeffries who lives out in Longwood, must have got there minutes after the murder. She ran out and phoned the police and fire department. When we got there, we found the remains of Adelaide Finney where she'd crawled under a dress rack. Her family said she was a big woman, but you'd never have guessed it by what was left."

Carver resisted mental images and concentrated on the facts. "What was Paul Kave doing in a dress shop?"

"I'm afraid that's obvious, *amigo*. It was a small shop with a woman alone. Nice and safe. He did this killing just for you, to warn you and to show you his power. That's why he phoned you about it, to let you know how easy it is for him, how simple it'd be if he decided to make you his next victim."

"Think he's trying to get me to back off?"

"No, no, my friend. He knows you can't back off this one. He wants you to understand what kind of game you're in, and that eventually you're going to lose. You're his plaything. That scare you?"

"Yeah, but not enough."

"See then, he's right about you. You're much better than competent at what you do, *amigo*, but in this instance you've got a perilous blind spot. A kind of Achilles' heel."

"Achilles didn't see with his feet."

"Better for him if he could have, though, eh?" Desoto flashed a sad, white smile.

The air-conditioner's thermostat clicked off, then immediately back on. The tone of the unit's hum didn't change, and the yellow ribbons remained horizontal. The heat outside didn't seem to notice that the sun had set. Carver gazed out at the blackness that crowded flat against the windowpanes. "How do you think he found out I'd been tracking him?"

"Could have happened a lot of ways. You've been flitting all over Florida like a dazed June bug, asking questions. The Kave kid is supposed to be brilliant. It probably took him about a minute to get on to you. Probably he simply caught mention of your name in the paper; guys like that sometimes enjoy reading about themselves. However he found out, I'm sure this last performance was all for you."

"Wait a minute. It was in the news that the family hired me?"

"On back pages. But not that you're the father of one of the victims. You didn't know?"

"No. McGregor must have leaked it."

"Most likely. He wants you waiting in the wings in case something goes wrong and a sacrificial goat is needed. His style. He might also be trying to spook Paul Kave, get him jumpy enough to screw up."

"And Adelaide Finney dies as a result."

"That's how it is, *amigo*."

Clutching his cane, Carver watched the blood recede from his knuckles. He didn't like the notion that he was indirectly responsible for Adelaide Finney's death, but he realized Desoto was probably right. First the matchbook, and now this. His involvement in the case might have led to the murder. Desoto knew what he was thinking but could offer no comfort.

"A shitty business we're in, *amigo*. Could it be we should be selling insurance?"

"That's a shitty business too."

"Something else," Desoto said. He opened a desk drawer, reached in, and drew out a patent-leather black belt with a silver buckle shaped like a sunflower. The end of the belt was charred. There was a price tag dangling on a string from the buckle. Carver could see "12.99" penned on the tag.

"This was on the shop counter near the register," Desoto said, "as if the killer was going to buy it right before the murder. And this was on the floor nearby." He reached into the drawer again, then dropped a bent piece of plastic on the desk alongside the belt.

"What is it?" Carver asked.

"A partially melted credit card," Desoto said. "Look closely and you can read Paul Kave's name."

Carver got up and leaned on his cane, hovering over the desk lamp. He could make out the first name and the letter *K* on the mangled, blackened plastic that had once been a Visa card.

"The account number makes it his, too," Desoto said. "This places him at the scene."

"You check with the credit company records?"

"Of course. Paul Kave hasn't charged anything on the card for six months. Paid cash for most everything, apparently."

"Then why didn't he pretend he was paying cash for the belt?"

"My guess is he's running low on money. But there's another possibility. He might have left this card behind deliberately, so you'd know for sure who burned the Finney woman.''

"Jesus!" Carver said. "Bragging. About that."

"Looks that way, *amigo*. It's the kind of thing you stir up when you get involved in a vendetta instead of your job. What you're doing is dangerous, maybe more dangerous than you can see through your clouded judgment."

Carver remained standing. He said nothing.

"How about we go out somewhere?" Desoto said. "I can get away from here for a while. We could have a late-night snack and talk about this. Talk about whatever you want. It could be we'd solve many of the world's problems."

"No. I'm going to Edwina's. To have a few beers and try to chase the last couple of days away, at least for a while."

"You getting along with McGregor?"

"He's an asshole," Carver said.

"Since I've known him. Your son's murder is his case, though. Something you need to remember."

"But the Finney case is yours."

Desoto smiled. Ivory teeth against tanned flesh. Crow's-feet at the corners of knowing brown eyes. Handsome matador, ready to slay a bull or a heart. "That allows some latitude," he admitted. He knew what was coming next and waited patiently, not speaking.

"I'm asking," Carver said. "I've got to."

"Or think you do. But all right; what there is to know about the investigation, *amigo*, will be passed on to you. So long as you must continue with your insanity."

Carver shifted his weight to his stiff leg for a moment, balancing with the cane. "I appreciate it."

"Something, though," Desoto said. "It's you all by yourself out on a thin limb; I can't help you if it breaks. Nobody can. I'm warning you to back away and let the law do its work. In fact, I'm telling you."

"I'm not listening."

"If I could, I'd put you in jail in protective custody. Protect you from yourself." Desoto did suddenly look angry. "The law's gonna come down outa nowhere on you one of these days, you and your 'man's-gotta-do-what-he's-gotta-do' delusion. Don't you know the families of most murder victims feel exactly the way you do?''

"I guess that's so,'' Carver said.

"Ah, go to Edwina. And have more than a few beers. While you're being appreciative, appreciate her.''

"I do,'' Carver said, limping toward the door. "You'd be surprised how much. Sometimes it surprises me.''

CHAPTER 17

By the time Carver reached Del Moray, Edwina wasn't home. Real-estate agents kept hours almost as irregular as detectives, though generally they weren't involved with killers.

Carver called Quill Realty and the syrup-voiced evening receptionist promised to put him in touch with Edwina. He thanked her and sat down. He absently rubbed his stiff knee; it ached a little today for some reason.

Within minutes the phone rang. Edwina.

She was showing beachfront property at the only time her prospective buyers could keep an appointment, but she told Carver she'd be with him in about an hour. She'd sagely advise the buyers to examine the property by daylight. Looking out for their best interests, even though she actually represented the seller. Full of saleswoman shmaltz, was Edwina.

She was home in forty-five minutes.

Within another ten minutes they went to bed and made love. Carver was gentle with her yet intense, clinging to her at times as if she were life in the midst of death. Shelter from fear. His salvation. It was all self-delusion, he knew, but he didn't want to release it, or release himself into her. *Not yet. Not yyyet!*

Edwina sensed the unusual intensity in him and caught it. Matched it. The padded blue headboard began slamming against the wall, repeating and then dictating rhythm like a muffled metronome; heartbeat and hypnotism.

When he finally climaxed, Carver heard a trailing low moan. From his lips or Edwina's? He couldn't be sure.

She muttered something he didn't understand, her breath a warm, light touch on his face. Whatever she'd said, he was sure it didn't require an answer.

He rolled to the side, aware of the hot, stale scent of their coupling, the sweat rolling down his bare ribs. The sheet was damp beneath him and wrinkled in hard ridges. In the corner of his vision he saw Edwina run her fingertips up over her thighs and stomach, as if checking to see if he'd hurt her. Maybe he had.

"All right?" he asked.

"Uh-huh."

Brief conversation as old as time.

He lay on his back and listened to the rush of the waves and felt his metabolism gradually work its way back to normal. After a while, he told her everything.

Like an ancient sin eater she absorbed his pain and fear. He wondered, though, if now he'd burdened her more than he should have.

What he didn't want to share with her was the danger he was in. So he showered and dressed, then told her he was driving to his cottage.

Edwina objected, but not for long. She could read Carver's determination, and sense when not to push. She didn't like love having its limitations. He didn't blame her, but he couldn't do much about the situation. Life seldom fell into place like a late-night movie. That was why people watched late-night movies.

"Lock your door," he cautioned her.

She shrugged. "You'll leave anyway."

He left her sitting on the veranda, staring out over the moonlit ocean and sipping a tall Tom Collins, her thoughts as inaccessible to him as distant clouds.

The phone was jangling when Carver walked into the stuffy heat of the cottage. He had no way of knowing how long it had been ringing and suspected he wouldn't reach it before the caller hung up. But he clomped with his cane across the hard floor, groped for the phone in the dimness, and lifted the receiver.

"This Carver?" a voice asked. A familiar voice but he couldn't quite place it.

"It's Carver."

"Emmett Kave here. Paul called me. He's here! Well, he ain't *here* exactly. But he's in Orlando."

Carver waited, suddenly aware of the internal sounds and movements of his body, his hammering heart, the coursing of hunter's blood through his veins. His teeth ached; he was clenching his jaw. It reminded him of how he'd felt the first time he'd fired live rounds through a handgun. *The real thing!* "Where in Orlando?"

"What you gonna do if I tell you how to get to him?" Emmett asked.

"Talk to him," Carver said. "Try to get him to go with me and a lawyer to surrender to the police."

"And if he don't want to?"

"I'll try to talk him into going back to his family, let them decide what's best."

Emmett's laugh was like a hard object grating over a washboard. "Not much chance he'll listen to that kinda bullshit, Carver. He's scared, but he ain't that scared."

"I want to help him," Carver said. His voice was level, but he felt like driving to Emmett's house in Kissimmee and shaking the old man until dentures and information flew.

"He said something bad happened in Orlando, Carver. Was it that woman on the news got herself burned to death?"

"Yes. Paul did it," Carver said. "He's gotta be stopped, Emmett. For him and for anybody else he might kill. He's mixed up and almost beyond help. Jesus, you must understand that!"

"Guess I do," Emmett said in a tired voice. "Guess I got no alternative. He's at the Mermaid Motel on the Orange Blossom Trail, just outside town. Room one hundred. You promise me he won't get hurt, Carver?"

"You know better, Emmett. I'll promise you I'll do what I can."

"That'll have to be good enough. Not much choice in this

crazy world. Not much at all.'' Emmett hung up, leaving
an echo of betrayal.

Carver limped to his dresser and slid the top drawer all
the way out and laid it on the bed. The dresser's wood back
had been removed, leaving room for the old Colt .38
automatic that was in its holster tacked to the back of the
drawer.

He removed the gun, checked its action, and stuck it
inside his belt. It felt cool and heavy and important. Then
he replaced the drawer and put on a loose-fitting dark shirt
with squared tails that he left untucked. The gun wasn't
noticeable beneath the shirt.

He went outside and got in the Olds. The big car was
still gurgling and ticking in the night heat after the drive
from Del Moray. Telling Carver it was ready to go again.

Carver started the engine and switched on the headlights.
As he jockeyed the Olds onto the road to the highway, he
heard sand and gravel patter against the insides of the
fenders. The obsolete dinosaur of a motor roared like
thunder from an ancient past, something civilization and
Japanese imports could never tame.

He bent forward over the steering wheel, like a jockey
urging a horse to greater speed down the stretch. He could
hardly wait to reach Orlando and the Mermaid Motel.

CHAPTER 18

Carver slowed the car when he saw a neon mermaid with a tail that flitted jerkily back and forth in rhythmic spasms of light. Beneath the dizzying, blinking white neon was lettered in blue: MERMAID MOTEL. SLEEP, EAT, CHEAP. Brief but to the point.

He pulled the Olds onto the canted shoulder, braked to a halt, and let traffic swish past while he looked over the motel.

It was small, no more than thirty rooms built in a low U-shape around a swimming pool. The construction looked like cinder block painted dull tan. A dark brown or black iron railing ran along the catwalk fronting the upper rooms. The doors were all the same color as the railing. No one was in the swimming pool. The water appeared greenish and coated with algae. There was a metal sign on the chain link fence surrounding the pool, probably informing guests that the pool was out of order, no swimming. The pool looked like a great place to meet alligators.

Like many of the surrounding businesses, the motel was seedy-looking and had an air of resigned despair about it. This was a stretch of the Orange Blossom Trail outside Orlando that was lined with bars, used-car lots, service stations, topless joints, and a few porn bookstores and massage parlors. Not the central Florida the Tourist Bureau bragged about. Maybe Desoto was right in speculating that Paul Kave was running short of money.

Carver U-turned, then parked in the gravel lot of a closed service station and climbed out of the Olds. Hot, humid air enveloped him, holding the smell of rot and of grease and oil that had seeped below the gravel. A cat, or perhaps a large rat, skittered off the lot into the dark brush, running hunkered low. Or was it something he'd imagined? Carver dragged his bare arm across his perspiring forehead.

He walked up the road several hundred feet to the motel, skirted the office, and located room 100. It was an end room on the lower of the motel's two levels. He made his way down a corridor, past an ice machine, and beyond a hulking trash dumpster overflowing with cardboard and reeking of overripe garbage. After testing the ground with his cane, he edged off the pavement and behind some bushes growing parallel to the back wall of the motel.

It was dark there; he clenched his eyes shut and then opened them, trying to adjust his sight well enough not to trip over anything or turn an ankle. Night vision wasn't his strong suit. He moved tentatively, feeling ahead with the cane like a blind man, because the ground was soft beneath the grass, as if it had just been watered. The sweet garbage stench of the dumpster faded as he limped the length of the motel. About half the rooms had lights burning in them.

Opposite the rear of room 100, he found a shadowed area and stood leaning against the trunk of a palm tree. Above him the long fronds rattled softly in the hot night breeze, like clacking dice about to be loosed from a gambler's hand.

Lights were on in Paul Kave's room. The drapes were drawn over the rear sliding glass doors but there was a gap in them, widening toward the bottom. Carver remembered his uneasy vision of someone peering through a similar gap in his motel room in Pompano Beach. Nervous speculation. If Paul Kave saw him looking into the room, Paul would freeze for a moment, wondering if it were *his* nerves, his guilt and fear, causing him to see things that weren't there. In that vital moment of inaction, he'd be a target. And Carver would need a portion of that suspended time to be sure the room's occupant was actually Paul Kave. The thought of killing the wrong man made his stomach twist in on itself.

He drew the gun from beneath his shirt and limped toward the small pool of light outside the gapped drapes.

He'd considered simply knocking on the door of room 100, but Paul would be put on guard, perhaps even try to escape out the back. And the shot would make noise; other guests and the management would be alerted. Better this way, Carver decided. He could squeeze off a couple of well-aimed rounds and quickly disappear back into the night, like the fleeting dark animal he'd glimpsed near where he'd parked his car. He could then make his way to the Olds without being seen. By the time the alarm and confusion subsided at the Mermaid Motel, he'd be miles down the highway. A sound and simple plan. The kind that worked.

He could see faint shadowed movement inside the room. Paul Kave pacing. Trying to walk away his fear so he could remain cooped up and temporarily safe while his instincts screamed for him to run, cried for distance. Or did someone with Paul's warped and murderous mentality think that way? Possibly he felt safe most of the time. Secure. Carver hoped so.

A cloud glided sedately across the moon, fading the earth to black and then returning it to less than total darkness. As if that were some sort of signal, cicadas began their ratchety shrieking in the surrounding fields. There was something desperate in their high-pitched, ongoing scream.

Outside the glass doors, Carver braced himself with the cane, extended his stiff leg awkwardly out to the side, and stooped down. He wouldn't be able to stay in that position long, but while he was there he could hold the gun steady enough. He wouldn't have much time to get off a volley of shots.

He held the automatic ready, aimed through the glass, his gaze fixed on the small portion of the room visible through the gap in the drapes. His mouth was dry and his nerves were singing. He waited for Paul Kave to cross that vulnerable, tiny slice of room 100. The lane to the land of the dead.

Carver controlled his breathing and remained motionless. He could sense that Paul was still moving around inside the room, pacing with restless energy, but not across the deadly area before the gunsight. Carver was one with his prey now, inside Paul's head as only a dedicated hunter could be, as if his own nerve endings were picking up echoes of Paul's deranged thoughts; as if he could influence him, urge him to that part of the room that meant death. *You want to die, want to end it, I know you do.*

The gun's steel bulk grew heavier in Carver's grip. He'd need a steady hand when the time came, so he rested the butt of the automatic against his good knee. He could raise it again in half a second and have Paul in his sights. End this thing for both of them.

After a while, Carver's bent leg began to ache and his thigh muscles started to quiver. He'd have to stand up soon, he knew, or he might not be able to straighten his body after firing into the room. He also feared a muscle cramp that might hinder him in his getaway. He decided to give Paul until the count of thirty before averting the gun's aim and standing up.

No, make it the count of fifty.

At twenty, a figure finally appeared inside room 100. Carver's heart bucked and raced.

It was Paul Kave, looking thinner than Carver imagined, and frightened and young. So young. His blond hair was mussed into greasy spikes. Was that a shadow beneath his nose, or was he trying vainly to grow a mustache? A naïve attempt at disguise?

Carver had the automatic sighted in on target. He felt tension in his trigger finger. He controlled it so he wouldn't pull up on the gun and spoil his aim.

There was a faint sizzling sound, off to his right.

He jerked his head in that direction and saw a short, paunchy man in bermuda shorts and a white sleeveless undershirt, standing outside the glass doors two or three rooms down. The man had stepped out to smoke a cigar, and he was holding a burning match to its tip and causing the flame to dance and flare brightly as he puffed his cheeks in and out like a bellows. He was facing Carver. As soon as the match went out he'd notice him. He'd *have* to!

The man flicked the match away, removed the cigar from his mouth, and started to gaze at its glowing ember with a stogie smoker's satisfaction. Then he spotted Carver, did a show-business double take, and said, ''Hey!''

Without thinking, Carver swung the gun to aim at the man. The cicadas had stopped their ratchety screaming, figuring something was going down and they wanted no part of it. The night was silent except for the distant rush of passing traffic on the far side of the motel.

''Whoa, Christ!'' the man said. He hurled the cigar into the black sky, where it arced like a meteor as he ducked back into his room. For a little fat guy he could really hustle.

Carver was up and limping as fast as possible into the shadows. He plowed through thick shrubbery. His cane skipped on an uneven slick surface and he almost fell, saved a tumble by grabbing a branch, feeling thorns slice into his palm as he held himself erect. Thin branches or vines clutched at his ankles, slowing him down. Nightmare running. The cane snagged and he almost dropped it from his slippery grasp. Behind him he heard male voices yelling. Words he couldn't understand. Then a woman's voice: ''. . . Man with a gun!''

He remembered the automatic and realized he'd unconsciously tucked it back in his belt when he fled. It was a cool, hard lump against his stomach.

Then he was free of the shrubbery, still in darkness so thick he could feel it on him like black oil, and hobbling fast toward his car. He could see headlights on the Orange Blossom Trail; the road curved ahead. He had to be close to where the Olds was parked. His speed surprised him; fear was a powerful motivator. *This was the kind of terror Paul Kave must feel every minute.*

Carver was sucking air in hard, rasping breaths. More voices behind him. He couldn't tell how close—wasn't sure whether he was being pursued. Guy with the cigar wouldn't be chasing him; he'd scared hell out of that one, maybe cured him of smoking altogether. Saved the bastard's life!

The cane started to slide beneath his weight. A grating

sound. Gravel. He was on the parking lot, only twenty feet from the car!

He clambered into the Olds and started the engine, glad he'd thought to leave the key in the ignition switch. Quiet, he cautioned himself. *Quiet!* You're just someone in the area, passing through. Pulled off the road to look at a map or empty the ashtray. On your way to Disney World. Innocent as all hell.

Careful not to spin the tires and send gravel flying, he let the Olds roll toward the highway. He braked, waited for a tanker truck to howl past, then eased onto the pavement and accelerated. Leaned back in the seat.

Jesus, the wind felt grand!

Not too fast! He didn't want to draw attention to himself. His toe tapped the brake pedal. He drove past the Mermaid Motel at the speed limit exactly. There was no sign of activity there, but he knew there would soon be plenty. He also didn't doubt that Paul Kave was right now getting clear of the motel as quickly as possible, and would be lost again to the police and to Carver.

Half a mile down the highway, a patrol car approached him going in the other direction, siren yodeling wildly and roofbar lights flashing red and blue glare. The driver swerved to avoid a station wagon slow in pulling to the side. In a hurry, all right. Too late, pal, Carver thought as the cruiser zipped past. He watched the light show recede in his rearview mirror.

The pulsing lump in his throat receded and his breathing evened out. He was away clean. The cigar smoker had barely glanced at him and probably hadn't noticed the cane, scared as he was. Probably busy fouling his underwear and saw nothing but the gun swinging his way. And Carver had hobbled into the black night before anyone else had a chance to see him.

Near the expressway he parked the Olds on the shoulder and sat for a while, feeling the low drumbeat of the idling engine through his buttocks and thighs. He was sweating hard and his hands were shaking. Something in his stomach wanted out. He wasn't sure he could drive.

What he was experiencing was more than simply delayed reaction to stress. He'd felt that before and knew it well enough to recognize it. This was something else, at a deeper level.

If he hadn't been interrupted, he would have squeezed the trigger and sent bullets smashing through glass, and then the flesh and bone of Paul Kave. Killed the scared kid with the phantom mustache. No doubt at all.

The thing about it, Carver wasn't sure how he would have felt afterward. And for the first time since his son's death, afterward mattered.

CHAPTER 19

Her phone rang twelve times before she answered, even though it was right beside her bed. He wasn't surprised. She slept deeply.

She cleared her throat. "'Lo."

"Edwina, this is Carver."

"Four inna morning. Whassa matter?"

"I'm not sure. I'm sorry; I wanted to hear your voice."

"S'okay. You know it is."

"I almost shot Paul Kave last night."

She paused one, two, three beats. "Why didn't you?" As awake now as she could be at 4:00 A.M.

"I was seen and had to get away."

"Will anyone be able to identify you?"

"I don't think so."

She was quiet for a while, then she said, "You still want to kill him?"

He reached far back into the mysteries of his mind before he answered. "Yes."

"Sure?"

"Yeah."

"You okay now?"

"Okay."

"Sure?"

"Yeah."

"Go to sleep then, baby. Go to sleep."

"Edwina?"

"You rather talk awhile? It's fine, if that's what you want."

123

"No, I guess not. No."

"Go to sleep, baby."

"All right."

She waited for him to hang up first.

He was finally able to sleep, but not without dreams or fear.

It was nine that morning when Carver knocked on Emmett Kave's door. The sun was already glaring hot and harsh, angling in beneath the sagging gutters to cast brilliant rectangular patterns on the concrete porch. The porch floor had been painted gray long ago, but nothing of the color remained except for a stubborn peppering that had penetrated the concrete too deeply to be dislodged by weather. A large palmetto bug, brown and glistening and ugly, dragged itself across a sharp corner of sunlight and then disappeared beneath the wall near the edge of the porch, seeking darkness.

Carver had a headache; he wanted out of the sun, like the bug.

Emmett opened the inner door and peered through the patched screen at him. The old man was wearing a green, limp terrycloth robe that had gone through the wash too many times. When he swung the screen door open, Carver saw that the robe hung to his knobby knees, and his thin, hairless ankles disappeared into old leather slippers with dark stains on the toes, as if oil had dripped on them long ago. He said, "Don't you look like something the cat crapped out this morning."

"I didn't get much sleep," Carver said.

"Here to tell me about last night?" Emmett asked, shuffling backward so Carver could enter. The slippers made soft sighing sounds on the floor.

As the door slapped shut behind Carver, he noticed that the house smelled like frying bacon again. He wondered if it always smelled like bacon. Possibly that was all Emmett Kave ate. Maybe the preservatives kept him alive.

Emmett slouched down on the dark old sofa and motioned for Carver to take a chair. Carver declined. He didn't feel like sitting. He leaned on his cane and looked around. Sunlight was trying hard to break in but hadn't made it yet; the house was warm and gloomy. He wished Emmett would switch on the blue box fan that was wedged in the front window.

"Coffee?" Emmett asked.

"Nothing," Carver said. "I missed Paul last night at the Mermaid Motel." He was immediately aware of the irony of his words. Another few seconds and he wouldn't have missed Paul; he'd have shot him dead-center through the heart.

"Television news said somebody with a gun was scared away at the Mermaid late last night. Didn't say what room he was creeping around. Didn't say much of anything, really. That's TV news, ain't it? Them fashion-plate fuckheads is so busy chatting and smiling at each other they don't tell you beans in the way of details."

"I don't think it was Paul," Carver said.

"Me neither. But it might've had something to do with him. Might've caused him to run, when all them police arrived and the commotion started."

"Could be."

"You know anything about what happened there?" Emmett asked.

Carver put on his best liar's face, feeling the flesh beneath his eyes stiffen. "It happened before I got there. No one was in room one hundred when I arrived."

Emmett's bushy brows lowered and he looked appraisingly at Carver. He had the injured, shrewd eyes of a lifelong victim; a man not easily fooled even though distracted by demons. "You and me's the only ones know Paul was at that motel last night, Carver, or the police'd be making a bigger hubbub about what happened."

Carver stood waiting. He shifted position with the cane. Emmett suspected something, sensed an undercurrent. Carver would have to handle this carefully. The old guy was sharp enough to shave paper.

"Sure you don't know anything about that man with the gun?" Emmett asked. "Seems awful coincidental, something like that happening when Paul was staying there."

"Could have been a cop free-lancing," Carver said. "Maybe he'd traced Paul there and was planning to take him alone, get all the credit. It's rare, but it happens in cases like this that get a lot of publicity and can make careers."

"You shittin' me?"

Carver shrugged, wishing he'd come up with a better story. "Hell, I don't know. I've got no idea what went on at the Mermaid before I got there. All I do know is that Paul was gone when I arrived."

Emmett seemed to mull over this explanation, absently rubbing the sole of one of his slippers on the blackened toe of the other; a habit that explained the stains. "If what you said about a cop acting alone is true, the law would keep it quiet, I guess."

"Sure. He'd be disciplined within the department, probably suspended. Things like that happen. Not often, but they happen. And the public never knows."

"Humph! Police! Bureaucratic bastards!"

Carver was getting uncomfortable standing in one spot, but he didn't want to sit down. He limped around slowly for a moment, then stopped and looked at a collection of old, framed photographs arranged on the faded wallpaper. The sun had found its way around a shade and illuminated that wall, and the photos were well lighted. One was of a young, square-jawed man standing alongside a short, somber woman with hair piled high on her head. Both wore dark clothes of almost Edwardian style. It was a crack-checked, very old photograph. Another photo was of a cluster of men or teen-age boys, snapped from a distance and out of focus, so that their features were indistinguishable. Behind them was a round lake with a fountain in the middle. There were some shots of a small, pale youth with unruly, very blond hair—possibly Paul as a schoolboy, though this child looked almost albino. Below these hung a group photo of some battle-grimy marines. The soldier on the end, grinning with his helmet tilted well back on his head, was unmistakably the young Emmett Kave. Every man in the photo appeared exhausted and was grinning. There was something about the scene that disturbed Carver, but he couldn't define it. Or maybe it was the shot of the square-jawed man and his young, sad wife that had touched some sensitivity in the depths of Carver's mind.

"Nice family photos," he said. Down the block a power mower sputtered to life and began a monotonous drone; a conscientious homeowner getting in lawn work before the hottest part of the day. There was a smart-ass in every neighborhood.

"The old folks is my mother and father back in New Jersey," Emmett said proudly. "That motley bunch of young marines is from my unit in Korea. Them were some wild days."

"The young blond boy," Carver said, "is that Paul?"

"When he was ten," Emmett said. "Liked to raise hell back then, from what I hear. Didn't get withdrawn until just before his teens. Paul give me that photo himself."

"He has darker hair now."

"Hair changed," Emmett said. "I had blond hair myself at that age. Even into my late teens, like Paul. Something about the Kave blood; we get darker as we get older." He absently ran his hand over his hair, which had gone almost completely gray. "Till we get old old," he added, somewhat remorsefully. For an instant his face was much like that of the woman in the photograph, whose brooding likeness had been captured on a bright day almost a century ago. Certain moments survived time.

"When I find Paul," Carver said, "maybe he can explain what happened at the motel last night."

"You sound confident you are going to find him."

"If he contacted you once," Carver said, "he probably will again."

"Unless that gun business spooked him." Emmett hooked his thumbs in the pockets of his robe and tugged at the well-worn material. Carver thought he heard thread pop. "You found out anything?" Emmett asked. "I mean, how's it look for Paul, after that latest burning in Orlando? Lord, poor woman!"

"The police think Paul did it," Carver said.

"Yeah, but what do you think?"

"I don't know. The evidence points to Paul."

"Evidence lies sometimes."

"And sometimes," Carver said, "the police get more interested in where it points than whether it lies."

Emmett shifted on the old sofa and sat up straighter. "Yeah, I know what you mean and it scares me. I'd at least like to see Paul have his say in court. That's one thing Adam and I agree on. Maybe the only thing in this ass-backward world."

Carver thought Emmett might ask how his brother was, but he didn't.

"Adam always put too much stock in money," he said, "had an exaggerated idea of what it could buy. Bet I'm happier here in this ramshackle hovel, living like a hermit with my simple pleasures, than he is in that palace by the ocean."

"Right now you are," Carver said, looking around and not seeing much evidence of even simple pleasures. Well, there was television. Maybe Emmett was a soap-opera fan, involved in that alternate, manageable world that could be relegated to nonexistence at the punch of a remote-control button.

"Some fucked-up family, eh?" Emmett said, staring at the threadbare carpet. Sunlight was lying across it now in an elaborate pattern that almost reached his slippers.

"It works out that way sometimes," Carver said.

Emmett didn't answer. After a while Carver realized he was going to remain silent, as if his well of words had gone dry.

He left the old man on the sofa, still staring down into his past, perhaps wondering what the man and woman in the ancient photograph would think if they could somehow know the success and agony of what they'd set in motion so long ago in their marriage bed.

Outside, the morning was already unbearably hot. Carver

drove away thinking about the photograph arrangement on Emmett's faded wall, trying to figure out what there was about it that acted like a tiny burr on his mind.

By the time he was out of the depressing neighborhood he was concentrating on Paul Kave again, trying to analyze his feelings about the boy. Paul had lived in his own hell, Carver realized, long before he'd murdered Chipper. And Carver thought that maybe what bothered him about the grouping of family photographs in the old house was that he would never see a similar collection of photos that included Chipper past the age of eight. Looking at the photos had brought home to Carver that *his* family, such as it was, had been cruelly deprived of its future as it should have unfolded.

He stoked his rage with the relentless sun pounding through the windshield. He was still determined to make Paul Kave's hell permanent.

CHAPTER 20

Carver had parked the Olds in front of his cottage and was climbing out when the bullet thunked into the left front fender.

It took him a second to recognize the sound. But there was no mistaking the gouged round hole, silver-rimmed with raw steel, plowed into the fender. Air was still hissing from the punctured front left tire as Carver dropped to his stomach and rolled beneath the car. Pebbles dug into his back and bare arms. Fear pressed in on him.

He waited for a follow-up shot, but none came. Dust gritted between his teeth. He swiveled his head and spat. Stretching his right arm, he reached his cane. Then he used his good leg and arms to scoot backward, hooked the crook of the cane over the opposite side of the car, and push-pulled his way on his back beneath the wide vehicle. The car's undercarriage smelled like fresh earth and old grease, and the exhaust system still breathed hot. It was like freeing himself from a stifling cave when at last he emerged on the other side.

He struggled up on one knee, his stiff leg extended with his foot braced against the Olds's rear tire. Oil from the underside of the car streaked his arms and shirtfront. Something sharp had left a long, curved scrape on his wrist; the salt of his perspiration made it sting.

He peered along the shore to the south; the beach was deserted. The strip of pale sand was isolated and rocky and wouldn't be occupied until the searing heat of afternoon drove people to the sea.

The shot had come from the slope north of the cottage, where there was high brush and a few wind-bent palm trees. Carver reached for the Colt automatic tucked in his belt but it was gone. It had fallen out as he'd wriggled beneath the car.

He bowed his head as low as possible, feeling tight strain in his back and neck, and saw the gun on the ground directly beneath the center of the Olds's undercarriage. It was about three feet from where he crouched. It looked like ten feet.

He carefully poked his cane beneath the car and moved it in short, sweeping motions. It bumped the gun a few times. Finally it snagged the Colt near the trigger guard, and he pulled it to him. The cane was coming in handy for more than walking.

If he kept the protective bulk of the car between him and where the shot must have come from, he could reach shelter behind the cottage.

If he moved fast enough.

If the gunman hadn't changed position for a better angle.

Carver swallowed the old-metal taste of fear, gripped the cane halfway up the shaft, and made himself move.

Muscles knotted in his back as he tensed for the rip of a bullet. Fear had settled icy and hard in his bowels, trying to make him weak. Careful to stay in line with the car, leaning hard on the cane, he half crawled, half duckwalked toward the corner of the cottage. His feet and the tip of the cane dug into the soft ground and shot dust and sand behind him as he scrambled for cover. He was sure he looked ridiculous. He'd think about that later. He hoped.

Then he was around the corner.

Safe.

He leaned back against the sun-warmed clapboard wall and took deep breaths. Anger grew alongside his fear, then gained dominance. It was time to go on the offensive.

Staying low, calculating angles so he wouldn't be seen, he made his way toward the thick brush on the slope behind the cottage. He intended to reach the coast highway, stay in cover on this side of the shoulder, and try to work in behind his assailant. Whoever had taken the shot at Carver might be surprised by the fact that his target was armed and ready to return fire; a tiger that had turned around.

Carver backed away from the cottage and into the cover of the low brush. He fought his way up the slope toward the highway, using the cane almost in the way a gondolier powers a boat with a pole along a Venetian canal, setting its tip deep in the soil ahead of him, and pulling then pushing with both arms and his chest muscles as he dug the edge of his good right foot into the loose earth for leverage and propelled his body forward. He was working up a thick sweat, attracting mosquitoes and sand fleas. Something small flitted around one of his nostrils. He ignored it. The soft hushing sound of the surf cautioned him to be as quiet as possible; danger here. The knowing ocean.

As he neared the highway shoulder, he thought he heard a car spin its tires on the baked, dusty ground and drive away. But he wasn't sure. By now it was probably unnerving to the gunman not to be certain of Carver's location. If whoever had taken a shot at him hadn't immediately fled.

Making better time now, getting the knack, he made his way along the road shoulder toward the point where he was reasonably sure the shot had been fired. As he got close, he drew the Colt from his belt and moved silently. On the hunt now. Better than being shot at.

After a moment he paused, forcing himself to breathe evenly.

From where he was crouched he could see the Olds several hundred feet away. In the bright morning light the silver-rimmed bullet hole near the flat left front tire was barely visible. From this distance, the gunman had probably used a rifle. Not with a telescopic sight, or the shot would have been more accurate.

Unless it had been fired by a scared young killer on the run. One used to another murder method. Paul Kave, trying to take out two generations of Carvers.

There was a slight sound, like a long sigh, directly in front of Carver. He aimed the gun in that direction and tried to crouch lower, feeling pain in his hip above the stiff knee. A lump formed in his throat; he swallowed it.

His flesh tingled and he waited.

Waited.

Foliage rattled, and a man with a revolver emerged from the brush and trudged toward the road.

He wasn't Paul Kave. He was a big man in saggy Levi's and a yellow T-shirt with an orange setting sun printed on it and stretched tight across his meaty chest and stomach. He was in his late thirties and had a dark beard and perpetually arched eyebrows, and a hooked nose that was much too large for his round face. Carver thought he looked like an Arab terrorist. The man moved as if tired, letting the revolver brush at his thigh as he swung his long arms. It was a bulky, large-caliber gun, maybe a .357 Magnum.

Carver let him take a few more steps toward the highway and then said, "I can pop three holes through you before you can turn around."

The man stopped and his body stiffened. "Not 'freeze'?" he said. He sounded scared, but not scared enough. Something didn't fit here.

Carver leaned on the cane and stood up. His good leg was shaky, the knee rubbery. "Toss the gun away, then turn around and face me or I'll show you what I meant about those three holes."

"This thing's expensive," the man said. "I don't wanna get sand in the action, you don't mind." He stooped slowly and placed the revolver lovingly on the ground, then straightened up and turned toward Carver in one gradual motion. He was smiling now, so cooperative. "Guy who shot at you got away," he said. "Drove off a few minutes ago."

"Or maybe he didn't. Maybe he's right here lying his ass off."

"That piece didn't put the bullet in your car," the man said, nodding toward the revolver at his feet. "Hasn't been fired, in fact." He moved two slow steps to the side. "Pick it up and give it a sniff."

"Smell your own gun." But Carver knew the man was

probably telling the truth. It would be difficult with a high-powered handgun even to hit the car from this distance.

They stood there in the hot morning for a while, neither man moving. Gulls screeched about some difference of opinions on the beach. A jet plane tracked past out over the ocean, very high.

When the trailing thunder of the plane had faded, along with some of the tension of the moment, the man with the beard sighed loudly through his nose—the sound Carver had first heard—and said, "Mind if I dip something out of my pocket?"

"Depends on what."

"My identification. I'm a police officer."

For some reason, Carver wasn't surprised. "Orlando?"

"Fort Lauderdale," the man said. "Name's Gibbons. I'm McGregor's man."

"That's not moving you any further away from getting shot," Carver said.

The man smiled wider. Such a charmer.

Carver said, "You been following me in a white Ford?"

"Yep. It's parked down the highway. McGregor wants me to keep a loose tail on you, let him know if you're doing the job. Looks like you could use a bodyguard, while we're at it. I scared off somebody when I heard the shot and saw you duck down. I ran hell-for-leather up here, but whoever plinked at you drove away. There's tire tracks over there, and the dust was still settling when I arrived."

Plinked, Carver thought. "Get a look at the gunman?"

"I told you, I heard the shot and saw nothing but dust. I don't even know which way the guy went. I'm pretty sure he used a rifle, though. You can tell from the sound."

"I was too busy to reason all that out," Carver said. "Let's see your shield."

Gibbons fished in a hip pocket and drew out a wallet-size leather folder with his Fort Lauderdale I.D. He moved a few steps toward Carver and held it far out in front of him. Carver scanned it but didn't really need to look. Gibbons had flashed the I.D. in the smooth, practiced manner of a longtime cop. McGregor's man, all right. In on the deal and looking out for his future. His wagon hitched to a dark star that might soon be on the rise. Politics and justice, in bed together like the old lovers they were.

Carver tucked the gun back in his belt beneath his shirt.

"Gonna thank me?" Gibbons asked, grinning.

"No. Maybe you left your rifle in the brush."

"You'll look around for it later and won't find it," Gibbons said. "Cops don't shoot at other cops, even at private ones like you, Carver."

"Usually that's true, but this is kind of an unorthodox investigation."

"That's what McGregor said, but he didn't give me all the details."

"Me either, it turns out," Carver said. Something big, a truck or bus, whined past on the nearby highway. "He and I need to talk about that."

Gibbons shrugged. "Want a ride back to your place?"

"I'll walk."

"Thought you might. Mind if I leave now, or are you planning to Mirandize me?"

Carver raised the Colt level. "You have the right to get the hell out of here," he said.

Gibbons did, without looking back.

Carver decided not to search for the rifle that wouldn't be there. He'd done enough scrambling around in the rough.

He slapped at and missed a mosquito about to sting his left arm, then he stood still until he heard Gibbons's car start and drive off. The sound of the white Ford's engine wavered and died as it headed south toward Fort Lauderdale.

Then the only sounds were the gulls screaming, and the drag of Carver's footsteps and cane as he made his way down to the cottage.

After draining a cold Budweiser, he called McGregor.

"I been expecting to hear from you," McGregor said. "I just got done talking on the phone with Gibbons."

"There's a man I don't want to see again," Carver said.

"Shouldn't talk that way about him. He's a nice fella,

though he does give the impression he's on his way someplace to hijack an airliner. All he's really doing is the job I sent him on.''

"I want you to give him another job instead of having him shadow me. Gotta be some traffic somewhere needs directing. Aren't I always hearing how you guys are short of manpower?''

"Don't act like such a vigilante jackoff, Carver. Maybe you hadn't noticed, but Paul Kave went on the attack today. You oughta be glad to have Gibbons in the background. He might have saved your bacon this morning. You better keep in mind you're looking for a guy even crazier than you.''

"I do the job my way or I don't do it,'' Carver said.

"We both know you don't mean that, sweetheart. You're just zapping me with this late-night movie talk to scare me. We need each other like Bogie and Bacall. Gotta work together in concert, you might say.''

"You sound confident,'' Carver said. "You shouldn't be. I can chuck this arrangement, tell everything to the media, and take another approach.''

"Not an approach that'd net you the guy french-fried your son.''

Carver felt an almost palpable loathing for McGregor. The Fort Lauderdale lieutenant saw only opportunity in death, not the justice he talked about to rationalize his actions outside the rules. "You said it, though: I'm emotional about this investigation. I'm not thinking any more clearly than Paul Kave. He's running scared, I'm running hot. Hell, I might do just about anything; it doesn't have to make sense.''

"I know your history, Carver. You're too good a cop to do something stupid.''

"I wasn't a good cop last night at the Mermaid Motel.''

McGregor was silent for a long time. Then he laughed but it sounded hollow.

"Okay, Carver, no more Gibbons. You're a solo act the rest of the way. And I hope to Jesus for both our sakes you got this thing figured out so it happens the way we planned.''

Carver hung up. He knew McGregor was probably lying. He wondered how deeply Gibbons was involved with McGregor, and if McGregor was careful and ruthless enough to snip any loose ends after Paul Kave was killed.

That was how people like McGregor climbed to eminence, over the graves of people like Carver. It was the kind of world where anything might happen. Anything.

He drank another beer, then went outside and moved the Olds so he could change the tire with his back to the ocean.

CHAPTER 21

Joel Dewitt's car and motorcycle dealership was on a bend on Haven Avenue in Fort Lauderdale. It was flanked by two used-car lots, each with strings of red, white, and blue vinyl pennants draped above the front row of cars that were facing the street with headlights and grilles shining and eager, like puppies vying for adoption. About half the businesses in the block had American flags flying, or suspended in display windows. Patriotism for sale; Commie kisser if you didn't buy. Most of the cars on the lots were Japanese or European. The pennants fluttered and flapped like crazy when the wind barely breathed.

There were no pennants at Dewitt Motors. It was a neat, square brick building squatting on a blacktop lot. Late-model used cars were arranged in two rows in front of it, with an aisle wide enough so that the small showroom was visible from the street. Some of the cars had prices soaped on their windshields, along with *Cream Puff, Virgin,* or *Low, Low Miles.* The offices, where deals were consummated, were in back of the showroom, in which half a dozen new motorcycles were displayed. Besides Honda cycles there were a few larger and heavier American-made Harley-Davidsons. Apparently Dewitt didn't sell used cycles.

When Carver entered the cool showroom he saw Dewitt immediately. Nadine's fiancé was standing by a Coke machine, sipping from a red-and-white can and talking to a short, dark woman with bangs that almost completely concealed her eyes. He had on a pastel green shirt, striped aquamarine tie, and pleated blue slacks; he looked like an animated Picasso from his Day-Glo period. For neutrals he was wearing a white belt and white loafers. Carver thought a checked sportcoat would make it an ideal outfit for selling used cars. Maybe Elana Kave disliked Dewitt because of the way he dressed. Or maybe he had a few toned-down outfits especially for wearing to the Kave estate.

He noticed Carver, excused himself from his conversation with the woman with bangs, and walked across the showroom. The machine-gun chatter of an air wrench popped off out of sight behind him. Must be a service bay out back.

Dark green opaque plastic shades had been strategically lowered so that the sun was blocked everywhere but where it was needed to make the chrome on the motorcycles glitter. Dewitt squinted as he crossed a sunny patch and smiled. He extended his hand. He was quintessential salesman here in his showroom, a creature of his environs. Possibly the flashy clothes were his work uniform.

Carver shook the hand, glanced around at the empty showroom, and asked how business was.

"Most of our customers come in evenings," Dewitt said, "when they're off work and looking for ways to spend their money. You here because you're interested in that cycle we talked about? I can put you on that big Harley at a better-than-fair price." He pointed to a sleek silver-and-black machine that looked capable of creating sonic booms.

"I'm past the age for cycles," Carver said.

Dewitt smiled handsomely and his alert blue eyes flicked up and down Carver as if he were sizing up a trade-in. "Some guys hit forty and they get paunchy and soft. For some reason, others get tough. You could still handle a big cycle, despite the bad leg. Bet you'd enjoy hell out of it."

"Maybe someday when I've got something to outrun," Carver said. "I thought I'd drop by and ask you about the Kave family when we were alone and you could talk."

Dewitt rested a hand on the chrome handlebar of a Honda. "What about the Kaves?"

"Why's Elana so set against you marrying Nadine?"

Dewitt laughed and waved his free hand to encompass the showroom. "Maybe she doesn't consider this a respectable way to turn a buck. Not like getting rich selling hot dogs pumped full of chemicals." He suddenly got serious. "Sometimes I catch Elana looking at me oddlike, Carver. I mean odd for her. Like Nadine looks at me. So maybe she likes me a little after all."

Carver put that one down to male ego. "Is Nadine concerned about her mother's resistance to the marriage?"

"Sure. But it isn't going to stop us. Nadine's a girl with her own stubborn streak. I'll tell you, a kind of bullhead-edness seems to run strong in the Kave family."

"Hard not to notice. Would she marry you *because* of her family's disapproval?"

"Not a fair question, Carver. But the answer is no. Anyway, Adam doesn't really disapprove of me. One entre-preneur respects another. Maybe eventually there'll be as many Dewitt Motors as there are Adam's Inns." Dewitt stood away from the cycle and crossed his arms, smug in his vision of grandeur. Carver got the impression he thought a lot about that projected golden future. "But what's all this got to do with you looking for Paul?"

"I'm wondering if Nadine would tell you if Paul contacted her."

Dewitt thought about that, shifting his weight from leg to leg. "If I asked her to she'd tell me. But that doesn't mean she'd volunteer the information *without* my asking. Nadine and Paul are close. They gotta be, the shitty way Adam treats them. Especially the way he treats Paul. Letting him know one way or another all the time how useless he is. Wouldn't surprise me if Paul's innocent of those murders and just made up his mind to get the hell away from the family."

"Was Adam really that hard on him?"

"Any dog in its right mind would run away from Adam."

"What did Elana think of Adam's treatment of their kids?"

"She doesn't live in the real world, Carver. She's got her

own problems. Way Nadine describes it, that's how Elana always was, even before the cancer.'' Dewitt glanced to the side, as if to make sure no one had wandered into the showroom to overhear. ''You know about Elana's cancer, Carver?''

''Yeah, I was told.''

''Well, I'm not supposed to know. Nadine told me anyway. She's not supposed to know how serious it is, but she does. Keep quiet I mentioned it, okay?''

''Sure.'' Carver wondered if the cancer was why Dewitt didn't particularly care whether Elana approved of his engagement to Nadine. In another year or so, how she felt wouldn't matter.

''I feel sorry for Elana,'' Dewitt said, ''though she'd never believe it if I told her.''

''Would Paul run away without telling Nadine where he is?'' Carver asked.

''No, that doesn't ring right.''

Carver hadn't thought it would. He noticed the short woman with the bangs seated at a desk in a small office with the door open, talking on the phone and jotting something on a note pad with a long yellow pencil. Talking, erasing, talking, jotting. A salesperson making it all possible for someone with a dream of new paint and chrome. Out on the lot a man in a blue suit, with a skinny teen-age boy wearing a black sleeveless muscle shirt, was looking over the cars. The boy yanked on a door handle and found it locked. The man kicked a tire. Actually kicked a tire.

''How close to the family is Nick Fanning?'' Carver asked.

''Not close to the family at all, but close to Adam. Fanning's the guy who makes the day-to-day decisions for Adam's Inns. He's a damned sharp executive. Brains up the ass. Adam trusts him.''

''Think he should?''

Dewitt shrugged. ''Sure. Don't see why not. And Adam isn't the sort to trust anyone without good reason.''

''He might have something on Fanning?''

''He might. But that's not what I meant. I was only

saying Adam's nobody's fool. He couldn't be, to have made it the way he has.''

"He doesn't seem to have been very bright where his children are concerned.''

"True enough. But Nadine turned out all right. Paul . . . well, he's a nice enough guy but kinda odd. A genuine loner. I guess somebody like me doesn't really understand that, huh? Maybe Nadine doesn't really understand it either. Tell you, Carver, Nadine's the cream of that clan.''

"*Will* you ask her?'' Carver said.

Dewitt grinned. "Already did. She said yes.''

"I mean, every once in a while, will you ask her if she's talked with Paul? Find out for me where he is?''

"No, I can't do that,'' Dewitt said, shaking his head. "Sorry.''

"Don't be. Your decision.'' A loyalty point for Dewitt. "But anything you do feel you can tell me,'' Carver said, "I'd appreciate it.''

"All right,'' Dewitt said, "that's a deal. But Nadine's gotta know.''

"We're talking about murder,'' Carver told him, pressing again.

"Nadine's gotta know,'' Dewitt repeated, unmoved.

Carver nodded. "Okay, if that's how it has to be.''

"That's it. I guess I'm a little bit stubborn like Nadine.''

"No,'' Carver said, "not like Nadine.'' He limped across the neat square showroom toward the glass doors to the lot, thinking Elana should get to know Dewitt better. Nadine could do worse.

As he pushed out into the sun he glanced back. Dewitt was watching him and held out his hands palms down and fingers curled, as if he were riding a motorcycle. He twisted his right hand, the throttle hand, and said, "Vroom! Vroom! Sure you're not interested?''

"You ride a cycle?'' Carver asked.

"Not me,'' Dewitt said. "I got too much to lose.''

CHAPTER 22

Carver drove to Edwina's house but she wasn't home. A call to Quill Realty established that she was out selling real estate. She was holding open a house on the good side of town; going for a big commission. The job Edwina had originally taken as therapy after a disastrous marriage continued to lend sustenance to flesh and mind. All Carver really knew for sure about her former husband was that his name was Larry and he'd beaten her on a regular basis. Every few weeks, usually after making love with Edwina, thoughts about Larry disturbed Carver's sleep.

He helped himself to cold cuts with sliced olives in them, and lettuce from the refrigerator. Then he laid two slices of wheat bread on a paper towel, and put together a sandwich with too much Miracle Whip, the way he liked sandwiches. He'd never tasted a cold slab of processed meat that wasn't stomach-turning anyway, so why not overpower the loathsome stuff with condiments? Make assuaging his hunger bearable as well as quick.

Eat to live, he told himself, not the other way around. The sandwich was gone in four or five bites; that oughta hold him for a while. He suspected the strange meat might have been tasty if he'd taken time to notice.

He washed down the sandwich with a glass of ice water, then went out on the veranda and sat in a webbed lounge chair, looking out to sea and smoking a Swisher Sweet cigar. Though the sky was blue in the direction he was facing, there were low, dark cumulus clouds creeping in behind him, lead-colored and laden with rain. The kind of clouds weather forecasters loved because they were so obvious.

The seabirds had already found cover, and small boats were making for shore into the brunt of the wind. Carver watched a tiny sailboat sporting black-and-yellow canvas tack laboriously toward the marina on the other side of Del Moray. The craft described a slow, zigzagging pattern, using the wind to propel it at angles toward its destination. The boat's dogged antics reminded him of his progress in finding Paul Kave.

Where was Paul now and what was he thinking? Planning? Where had he gotten the rifle to take a shot at Carver? Was he driving a stolen car? Was that how the police would trace him before Carver could get to him? And was Joel Dewitt leveling? Was a barbecue-sauerkraut hot dog really as scrumptious as Adam Kave implied?

The last was the only question Carver could easily answer to his satisfaction, and the one that provoked the least curiosity.

Suddenly the veranda was in shadow and a few cool raindrops struck his bare forearms. He looked down at the moisture glistening like dew among the dark hairs above his wrist.

The veranda stonework was spotted with rain now, and the wind was kicking up feisty and cool at Carver's back. It was pleasant sitting outside and observing the increasing number of whitecaps among the blue-gray incoming waves, but the rain would get serious within a matter of seconds. The long fringe on the umbrella over the table by the swimming pool swayed seaward. The water in the pool rippled and danced like a miniature ocean. He could hear it lapping like laughter at the sides of the pool.

Carver felt his back getting wet as the rain gradually fell harder. He stayed outside until the little sailboat had tacked out of sight to safety, then he stubbed out the unsmoked half of his cigar in an ashtray with a tiny puddle in it. The wind quickly carried the acrid scent of the wet, smoldering tobacco out to sea. He stood still for a moment, relishing the coolness of the storm, then he limped into the house.

He removed his wet shirt and his shoes and stretched out on the sofa. The rain was beating on the west windows now, and wind was playing a comfortable low tune on the tile roof. The inside of the house smelled musty and close but not unpleasant. Cozy, in fact. Shelter from life's bad weather.

Carver glanced at his watch. Three-fifteen. This was the usual July late-afternoon Florida storm that blew in suddenly from the Gulf and would just as abruptly bluster out into the Atlantic. Edwina would probably be home before long. Carver's car was in the garage, out of sight and dry with its canvas top down. If Gibbons had been at least temporarily pulled from the task of shadowing him, no one knew he was here. The world was on hold, and without Muzak.

Something metal was snatched by the wind and clanked across the veranda or driveway. Outside; nothing to do with Carver. What was happening beyond the walls didn't concern him.

He closed his eyes and allowed himself to sleep.

He awoke to Edwina's kiss on his lips. His body jerked and she leaned back where she was kneeling beside him. Then she smiled and kissed him again, taking her time about it. He had an erection. How long had she been there and what had she been doing?

Carver blinked. Not a bad way to wake up. The room was dim.

"Whazza time?" he asked.

"Seven-thirty."

"How come it's so dark out?"

"Still storming. The rough weather turned around and drifted back to shore. There are tornado alerts all over central Florida. People in mobile homes have been advised to put on their lead shoes."

Carver sat up. He heard a drumroll of thunder that suggested trumpets might follow. Close. Lightning illuminated the living room like a dozen flashbulbs going off. More thunder, much louder this time. Something glass sang on a hard surface.

"I'm afraid of tornadoes," Edwina said, but there was no fear in her voice. "They pick up people and put them down somewhere else. And I don't want to be anywhere else."

"Then we better get under those heavy beams in the bedroom ceiling," Carver said.

The beams in the bedroom were probably no heavier than in the rest of the house, but Edwina nodded agreement to his suggestion.

They both stood up and she took his hand and walked ahead of him, going slowly as he supported himself with the cane. He was still a little woozy from sleep. The air seemed heavy and charged with static electricity. He could hear the rhythmic swishing of Edwina's nyloned thighs brushing together beneath her dress, and her damp hair smelled fresh from the rain.

He loved storms.

They both loved storms.

Thunder shook the house.

Neither of them noticed when the rain stopped.

At eleven o'clock Carver left Edwina sleeping and drove up the coast to his cottage. It would be wise to be there if anyone was looking for him, for any reason. And wise not to be with Edwina.

He entered the cottage cautiously. Within a few seconds he assured himself that he was alone; there weren't many places to hide. He locked the doors and windows, switched the air-conditioner on low so he might hear any unusual sound, and slept with his cane and Colt automatic within easy reach.

He thought he'd sleep fitfully, but instead he was unaware of dreams or time until he opened his eyes to daylight.

And noise.

Loud noise.

The phone was jangling.

Carver sat up on the mattress, fumbled for his cane, then managed to stand and limp toward the phone. He didn't know how long it had been ringing before he'd awakened, but he'd counted five rings; whoever was calling was patient. Sunlight was angling in low from just above the horizon. No wonder. Carver's watch read ten minutes after six. He ran his dry tongue over his teeth so he'd be able to speak; they seemed huge and coated with Velcro.

"*Amigo*," Desoto said, when Carver had picked up the phone and mumbled a hello. "Edwina's okay."

Carver was still half asleep, and caught off guard by the cold thrust of alarm in the pit of his stomach. "Okay? Why shouldn't she be?"

"There was a fire at her house last night. I got it on the telex from Del Moray."

Carver's mind jumped all the way to a hundred and ten percent wakefulness, thoughts a wild jumble. *A fire!* Where he'd left her so she'd be safely out of his presence! If there was going to be an attempt at murder by arson, it should have been here, at the cottage. He told himself to slow down, not to speculate. Coincidences did happen, even in the lives of cynics and the people they loved. "Is she hurt at all?"

"No. I phoned there and was told a smoke alarm woke her up and she crawled out of the house completely unharmed. Damned fine little gadgets to have around, eh? Like watchdogs that don't eat."

"Where is she now?"

"Her place. Hey, I told you, she's all right. The emergency's over, my friend."

Over for now, Carver thought. Fire had been introduced into his life like hell on earth, maiming him in body and then mind. First fire from the barrel of a sadistic holdup man's gun, then from the mind of a maniac. As if he'd done something to piss off a supreme being that liked to play with matches.

"I'm driving to Del Moray," Carver said.

"Thought you'd want to, *amigo*. That's why I called."

"Was the fire an accident?"

"Could be. Lots of lightning in that area last night. But it's too early to tell. Thinking about Paul Kave?"

"I can't stop thinking about him."

''And maybe now, *amigo*, he can't stop thinking about you.''

The eastern horizon was still smeared with orange-tinted pink, like an art student's garish first attempt at a sunrise, when Carver reached the highway and pointed the long hood of the Olds toward Del Moray.

Last night's storm had left the air clear and sweet-scented, and he had the top lowered. Large flying insects smacked off the windshield to abrupt oblivion. A sea gull soared gracefully along parallel to the car for a while, as if blatantly observing Carver, then veered sharply to the south, maybe on its way to report to McGregor.

Carver felt as if he were in deep water that was beginning to swirl and draw him toward the black vortex of a whirlpool. He cursed and goosed the Olds another five miles per hour faster.

If he drowned—or burned—he wanted to do it alone. Not with Edwina.

As if death came with options.

CHAPTER 23

As Carver braked the Olds to turn into the driveway of Edwina's home, a yellow-orange fire engine gave a shattering blast of its air horn, flashed more different-colored lights than Carver could remember seeing even at Christmas, and bounced from the drive onto the highway. The jackhammer roar of its powerful diesel engine reverberated as it disappeared into the bright morning like a chimera.

Carver expected to see more fire-fighting equipment when he topped the crest of the driveway, but there were only Edwina's red Mercedes, parked well away from the garage, and a yellow Plymouth with a cherry light on its roof and the seal of the Del Moray Fire Department on its door. The garage itself was blackened, and half the roof had either collapsed or been axed in by the fire fighters. He noticed that the front end of the Mercedes was also blackened, and both front tires were flat and melted like modernistic soft sculpture.

Edwina and a short, dark-haired man in a bright white shirt weren't looking at the car, though; they were staring up at the house as if assessing damage. The white shirt looked incredibly clean and pure, contrasted with the charred areas from the fire. When they heard Carver's car parking near the yellow Plymouth, they turned and looked in his direction. Edwina seemed relieved to see him and leaned slightly toward him. White Shirt stood his ground and gave Carver the flat, disinterested but appraising stare of officialdom everywhere. Carver saw now that there were epaulets on the man's pristine shirt, and a gold insignia

149

sewn above the left breast pocket. He wondered if firemen saluted.

Carver hugged Edwina and listened to her assurances that she was all right. She seemed calm and unafraid. He sensed a vibrant anger in her, held in check beneath her surface but seething.

White Shirt stood patiently waiting for the scene to run down, glancing only once at Carver's cane. Edwina stepped away from Carver; her eyes were puffy, as if still irritated by smoke. She said, "This is Chief Belmont of the Del Moray Fire Department. Chief, Fred Carver."

"Nice to meet you, Mr. Carver," Belmont said, not moving to shake hands. He spoke in a slow Georgia drawl that probably led people to underestimate him. He was in his fifties, starting to go to fat, and had pale, doughy features, what was either a burn scar or a birthmark high on his forehead, and murky green eyes the color of martini olives. His black, probably dyed hair, was swept back but mussed, as if combs were for pansies and he'd raked his head with his fingers. He looked as if he needed sleep. "Miss Talbot here tells me you mighta been the target of this."

"You mean the fire was deliberately set?" Carver had never really doubted it.

"Oh, it's sure-enough arson. Damage is mostly to the garage. Flames got to the insulation in the wall and smoke curled over the ceiling and set off one of those five-dollar alarms. It saved Miss Talbot's life, most likely. Don't take long for smoke to work its way down and fill a burning house. Sneaky stuff. Kill you while you sleep."

Carver had once almost died himself in a late-night fire. He knew the danger of slumber and smoke. For an instant he relived the panic he'd felt on awakening and realizing what was happening. Suffocation in the dark. Still real. Still scary.

"Maybe you'd better stay somewhere else for a while," he told Edwina.

Her smooth chin was thrust forward like that of an amateur boxer with too much heart and too little skill, begging to be hit to show she could take it. "I'm not leaving my home because of this. Besides, whoever set the fire must have thought you were still here."

"My car was gone," Carver pointed out.

"Maybe he thought it was still in the garage. That's where you had it parked. He might have seen you drive in but not out."

Carver didn't answer. Edwina had given this some thought. He looked at the chief, who seemed puzzled.

"You saying you know who mighta done this?" Belmont asked. He asked it lazily, almost as if inquiring about whether Carver thought it might rain today.

"I have some idea," Carver said. "I'm a private investigator working on a case involving fire."

"Arson case?"

"Murder."

Comprehension transformed the chief's pale features. The murky olive eyes narrowed and gained intensity. "That screwball that torches folks, huh?"

"That's the one," Carver said.

"Well, the law's gonna want to talk with you about this anyway, the way it was so damned obviously arson. Young lady here's lucky to be still amongst the living."

"How was it done?" Carver asked.

"Show you," Belmont said, and waved an arm a few inches in a signal to follow. He was a man comfortable in his authority and took for granted compliance with his orders.

The three of them walked around to the back of the garage. The ground was soggy there; Carver had to prod gingerly with the cane. Belmont pointed to a buckled and charred area of wall near where the garage joined the rear of the house. There were blackened chunks of debris scattered around, and pieces of roof tile. It looked like the scene of a pyromaniac's wild party.

"That wall's stucco," Carver said. "Stucco doesn't burn."

"Does if you pour a flammable substance on it. Which was done here, I'm sure. Burned long enough to catch the

wooden eaves, then the flames walked across the roof
timbers of the garage. Good thing we got here before it got
a hold on the house. We'd have had to create some real
water and smoke damage inside to put this thing out.
Sometimes we gotta make a helluva mess dousing a fire, but
there's no other way.''

"The house is all right," Edwina said. "It smells like
burned rubber but it's relatively undamaged. I can live in
it. I *will* live in it."

"You don't have to," Carver said.

"Sure I do." Her voice was low and unyielding, the
mind behind it made up. Carver remembered her telling him
she would never again run from trouble and create a past
that haunted. She'd meant it. "I'm not letting Paul Kave
influence my life," she said, "any more than you would.
You should understand that."

"You're acting stubborn."

"As you are. But is yours an act?"

"No."

"A little empathy then, huh?"

"I think Paul might have tried to kill you as a way of
taunting me," he said.

"Even if that's so, he isn't likely to try again. I'm
staying."

"Why isn't he likely to try again?"

"I'd say he's made his point."

"Maybe he doesn't think so."

"I'm staying, Carver. Nobody like that is pulling my
strings and making me walk."

If she'd had a stick, she'd have used it to draw a line in
the mud and dared him to cross it. Carver knew it was no
good arguing with her when she got this way.

But Belmont didn't know her and couldn't keep his mouth
shut. "Mr. Carver seems to make good sense, ma'am."

She showed him what real fire was in her glance and
stalked away toward the front of the house, her blue Nikes
making squishing sounds with each step.

Belmont looked at Carver and shrugged. Then they
followed Edwina. Carver noticed that the swimming pool

was only half full; the fire-department pumpers had used it
as a source of water to fight the blaze.

The chief left and a lieutenant named Braddock from the
Del Moray Police Department arrived and questioned Carver
briefly. He agreed with the chief and Carver that Edwina
should stay somewhere else until Paul Kave was appre-
hended. He tried to persuade her with horror stories of fire
victims, then with official bluff, now and then turning to
Carver, who nodded agreement to everything the lieutenant
said. Edwina finally got angry and told them both to fuck
off. The lieutenant left shortly thereafter, obviously
wondering why Carver wasn't leaving with him. The man
didn't understand the territorial imperative as it related to
wild animals and to Edwina.

Carver and Edwina stood near the fire-damaged Mercedes
and watched the lieutenant's car disappear down the
driveway. The last of the official vehicles was gone; the
ordeal was ended. The sea was pounding on the beach
below, sounding like a ponderous heartbeat, and the sun was
high enough now to have gained leverage and bore down
with heat that weighed and withered and would dominate
the day. Carver glanced toward the vast sparkling sea and
his eyes ached from the glare. He limped toward the front
door.

"Where are you going?" Edwina asked.

"Gonna make a call, if the phone still works."

"It works," she said, walking beside him. Her head was
bowed and she was trying to come to terms with what had
happened. This was damned personal, this setting fire to a
woman's home while she slept. "Who you going to call?"
she asked, as they reached the door.

"Lloyd Van Meter at Van Meter Investigations. I'm
going to get some manpower assigned to watch you in case
Paul Kave tries something like this again. Here or
somewhere else, like maybe a display home you're holding
open." He paused by the phone and looked hard at her.
"We going to argue about this?"

"No," she said. She crossed the room to the sofa and
plopped into it like a loose-limbed teen-ager. It was more

a gesture of weariness than of defiance. "You make sense, actually. I'm being unreasonable, but then people should be unreasonable at times." She crossed her long legs. She was wearing shorts, and there was a clump of mud smeared on her right calf. She twined her legs as if she felt cold, and some of the mud smudged her left calf. Her expression was placid and thoughtful. Carver wondered if she had ever lost her poise, even as an infant when she got ticked off over having to eat strained vegetables. "You're right, I'm wrong," she said, "about everything. I should leave, but I'm staying."

"I don't know," Carver said. "Maybe this really is one of those times to ignore reason. You're the only one who can judge, I guess." He punched out the Van Meter number and waited while the phone at the other end of the connection rang. "But I still wish you'd leave."

He noticed Edwina was right about one thing: the house did smell like burned rubber.

So much better than burned flesh.

CHAPTER 24

What a piece of work was Lloyd Van Meter. Carver had met him when he was an Orlando police officer and Van Meter was searching for the wayward lover of a wealthy New York woman. Carver had arrested the man on a burglary charge, and Van Meter had appeared in a flurry of sound and confusion at police headquarters with a local, high-powered attorney and had the man sprung and back in Manhattan within hours. Red tape ensued, miles of it, and as far as Carver knew the man had never returned to Florida and been tried for breaking and entering. Carver had figured at the time that Lloyd Van Meter had unique talents as a private investigator.

He'd been right. The woman in Manhattan had been a wealthy socialite who ran an expensive and exclusive call-girl operation from her mansion on Long Island. She'd rewarded Lloyd Van Meter bountifully for finding her lover and expediting his escape from legal consequences.

And now Van Meter had one of the largest investigative agencies in Florida, with offices in Miami, Orlando, and Tampa. Carver liked Van Meter, who claimed to be the illegitimate son of a notorious Prohibition-era gangster, Homer Van Meter. The present Van Meter, more or less on the right side of the law, was an obese man in his fifties, with a head of thick, flowing white hair, sharply defined features despite his weight, and a white beard that, though not all that long, lent him a distinctly biblical air. It was as if Moses had discovered pasta. He wore round glasses with gold wire frames, and he looked younger than he was until he removed the glasses and revealed the deep crow's-feet at the corners of his shrewd blue eyes. He was always sloppily and peculiarly dressed, as if he bought his clothes at an awning company and settled for bargain fabrics that weren't moving well. Today he had on a beige suit with darker tan vertical stripes. Van Meter's tie was gold with brown stripes running diagonally. He was color-coordinated but the effect was dizzying.

He and his operatives had been watching over Edwina and observing members of the Kave family for three days now. Van Meter had phoned Carver and asked him to drop by Van Meter Investigations' offices for a report.

"We came up zip," he told Carver, leaning so far back in his creaking desk chair Carver thought the big man might wind up on the floor. But then it was Van Meter's office, his chair; he should know how far he could stretch things. Leaning backward just far enough was his specialty.

Carver was in a comfortable walnut-and-leather chair near the desk. The office was large and furnished in Danish modern; an atmosphere of comfort and efficiency. He waited for Van Meter to continue, watching the sun's defeat as it tried to beat its way in through the tinted triple-pane glass and heavy fishnet draperies behind Van Meter's huge desk. Like many very fat people, Van Meter loathed heat. The office was about sixty-five degrees and might as well have been in Finland as in Florida. From an outer room came the muted chattering and intermittent screeching of a superspeed computer printer, as if a high-strung typist had gone mad.

"Paul Kave didn't make any attempt to contact his family," Van Meter said, his blunt fingers toying with the corner of a yellow file folder. There was a massive silver-and-turquoise pinkie ring on his left hand, the kind of jewelry Indians slapped together for twenty dollars and sold for two hundred, gaining some small revenge on white America. "Or vice versa."

"Might he have phoned?"

Van Meter smiled. "No."

Carver didn't ask how he knew that. There were all sorts

of wiretap gizmos and electronic listening devices, some of them legal, some of them not.

"Here it all is," Van Meter said, handing the file folder across the desk to Carver, "but what it says essentially is that Nadine spent most of her time with Joel Dewitt, away from the estate. She did have an argument one night with a young fella named Mel Bingham, about the aforementioned Dewitt. Adam Kave spent his hours involved in business. The wife, Elana, seemed to stay cooped up in her room like a recluse; woman lives in seclusion. Emmett Kave's the only one that was any fun; he drove to a motel out near the Orlando airport and met an elderly woman registered as Mary Jones. They spent two hours in the room. Hans, my operative who observed all this, says he checked with the maid and the bed had been used, though this was the middle of the day. It was a prostitute-client arrangement, most likely. 'Jones,' no less! A lotta Joneses register at that motel; it's a favorite place with the local pimps and their ladies of all ages." Van Meter shook his head. "These old folks in Florida never fail to amaze, Carver. Dr. Ruth should be tuned in on what goes on down here; she'd learn something. Hans said the old gal was still a looker, too. Wouldn't have minded knocking off some of it himself. I gotta talk to Hans."

"Emmett Kave doesn't seem the type to visit a hooker," Carver said. But on second thought, Emmett did. One of those "simple pleasures" he'd mentioned. It was just another difference between Emmett and Adam Kave; Adam would probably consider it a point of honor and business acumen to talk a prostitute into paying *him*. One brother was all too human, the other not human enough.

"Know anything about Dewitt?" Carver asked. "He's got a motorcycle-and-car dealership down in Fort Lauderdale."

"He's a car dealer, so he's probably a crook," Van Meter said.

"Now, now. You're thinking like Elana Kave."

"Show me one dealer doesn't roll back odometers or put on phony promotions. Sell you a car for thousands more than it's worth, then finance it for you at two percent instead of ten. Bastards!''

"This sounds personal," Carver said, amused by the big man's ire.

"I got one of them little foreign piles of crap out there only runs half the time," he growled. "Tilted sideways and stayed that way the day after I drove it out of the dealer's. When it ain't running, I drive a rental. When it *is* running, I'm usually waiting for some part or other from Southeast Asia so I can keep it running. Got a whale of a deal on it, though. It was whispered to me in confidence that the sales manager hated letting it go for what I paid.''

"So count yourself shrewd.''

"You're a bastard, too, Carver.''

"I know.''

Van Meter gulped down a deep breath, calmed himself, even grinned. He had a gold-rimmed tooth in front. "Some guy named Nick Fanning spent a lot of time at the Kave estate. Funny-looking little dude with a mop of curly black hair. Reminded me of a chimp dressed up in an expensive suit.''

"He's the CEO for Adam's Inns," Carver said.

"I eat there now and then," Van Meter said. "They got a helluva barbecued kraut dog.''

Carver had heard enough. He hadn't expected much other than what Van Meter had told him, but he couldn't help feeling deeply disappointed. He set the cane in the thick carpet and stood up.

"Want us to stay on the job?" Van Meter asked. "Help you out on this?''

"For another few days," Carver said. "I don't think Paul Kave's the type that can stand pressure for long. He'll try to contact somebody. And the kid's a loner; family's all he's got.''

"They always say that about a serial killer,'' Van Meter said. " 'Guy's a loner. Never caused any trouble, but he's a loner.' ''

"They usually are. Paul Kave fits the psychological

profile like he was the model. He'll keep killing, more and more frequently.''

"Sounds so classic," Van Meter said.

"Maybe it is."

"I mean, everything fits so snug."

"That's what classic's all about."

Van Meter adjusted his glasses on the bridge of his nose. "You want this one a lot, don't you, Carver?"

"Worst way, I guess."

"I can understand that. I mean, with your son and all. But you gotta watch yourself in a situation like this, use good judgment instead of thinking with your gut."

"You been talking to Desoto?"

"Sure. He and I get together all the time. He said you were all saddled up and charging like the cavalry on this one. He's worried about you. Guess he remembers General Custer."

"He oughta remember Cortez," Carver said. "Incidentally, you know a lieutenant over in Fort Lauderdale name of McGregor?"

Van Meter's fleshy face writhed in a grimace. He smoothed his Old Testament beard with his hand. "McGregor's a scumball, Carver." Then he shrugged, his massive shoulders heaving beneath the tentlike suitcoat. "An efficient cop, though, and one that plays a clever game with the higher-ups. Not a guy you want to butt heads with. Desoto told me your son's murder was his case. Thing about McGregor is he can be a relentless bastard, make the Mounties look like wimps when it comes to tracking down the man on the run. Especially if it means a possible promotion. He'll get Paul Kave, Carver, any way he can, no matter what it costs other people. Kind of guy he is; it's in his chromosomes. He'll probably be police chief of the world someday."

"The world won't be a better place when that happens," Carver said.

"Oh, I don't know. Maybe society needs people like McGregor, like it needs spiders to eat the flies. But that don't stop spiders from giving you the creeps."

Van Meter stood up to show him out. The vast expanse of striped brown material was startling, a towering mountain of wool and polyester that needed pressing.

"There's something else in that report," he said, stepping out from behind the desk. He moved with great smoothness and coordination for such a fat man; somewhere in there was an athlete. "A woman named Laura Nelson visited Edwina last night."

Carver stood still for a moment, trying to figure what that could be about. "Laura Nelson's my former wife," he said.

"Yep," Van Meter said, studying him. "She's staying at the Andrew Johnson Motel not far from your cottage. Been there two days and spends most of her time in her room or moping around the pool. She went to your place twice yesterday and once this morning, but you weren't there. My man latched on to her and followed to find out who she was. I had him nose around awhile. She made a couple of phone calls to a fella named Sam Devine in Saint Louis. She's taken all her meals at the motel restaurant." Van Meter hitched up his giant's pants, giving a glimpse of yellow suspenders. "No charge for the additional shadow, Carver; a personal favor. You got real serious woman trouble, pal, on top of your other problems."

"What makes you say that, other than the obvious?"

"Long time ago I took part in some parapsychology tests at Duke University. You know, ESP. I could guess cards that were facedown on a much higher percentage basis than any of the other student volunteers. I'd have made a terrific professional gambler, Carver."

"So why aren't you betting in Vegas?"

" 'Cause I had a hunch I'd make an even better detective. My hunches are like my guesses at cards: hardly ever wrong."

Carver limped toward the door. "I suppose I'd better find Laura and see what she wants."

"Don't trip over her," Van Meter said.

CHAPTER 25

Laura was on the porch of his cottage waiting for Carver. Score one for Duke University. She was sitting in the aluminum lawn chair facing the ocean, wearing white thigh-length shorts, straw sandals, and a bright flower-print blouse. She had on a wide-brimmed straw hat with a blue ribbon around it tied in a big bow. The upper half of her was in the deep shade of the porch roof, the sun beating on her tanned calves and emphasizing the neat turn of her ankles. She was shorter than Edwina and not as leggy, but her body was still attractive in a lithe, compact way reminiscent of cheerleaders. And of youth. Carver's youth.

She didn't move when he stepped up on the porch. "I was by here earlier looking for you," she said. She crossed her legs and one brown calf began a rhythmic pendulum motion.

"I know. A psychic told me. How are you?"

She smiled beneath the wide brim. "Your psychic didn't tell you that?"

"No. He's limited."

"I'm as good as you can be two weeks after the death of a son. Probably better than you are."

"Well, you always had more spring to your soul."

A large fly lit on the plastic arm of her chair. She didn't try to brush it away, but watched it until, of its own accord, it spiraled away into the sunlight. "I've been every day to the county library in Saint Louis to read the Florida papers," she said, "so I could follow the hunt for Chipper's killer. I read that a young man named Paul Kave is the leading suspect, and the family hired you to help find him. Is that how it is?''

"That's it,'' Carver said.

"Does the family know who you really are?''

"Of course not. They think I'm trying to find him so I can protect him from overzealous law officers with itchy trigger fingers. They go to the movies, watch television; they understand what can happen.''

"But you want him to die. You want to kill him.''

"He should pay with his life,'' Carver said. He considered telling Laura about that night outside the Mermaid Motel, but he decided it was something he didn't want to share with her. "Paul Kave's a threat to kill again any time or place. I want him found and stopped. He'll keep on burning people. People like him can't help what they're doing even if they try.''

"People like him, huh?''

Carver wondered what she meant by that, but he didn't ask.

"The police don't need you to find him,'' Laura said.

"They think they do.'' The surf hissed on the beach.

"I talked to Alfonso Desoto. He told me about the arrangement you have with that Fort Lauderdale policeman. Jesus, Fred, what are you thinking of?''

"Desoto should have kept quiet.''

"No. He's your friend. So am I.''

Carver thumped across the porch so he'd be in the shade, too. The sun was vicious, glancing blindingly off the sand. "You also talked with Edwina Talbot,'' he said. He couldn't see Laura's eyes beneath the hat's wide straw brim, but her lips drew tight, shadowed at the corners.

"Sure. I didn't know how else to go about trying to find you as soon as possible. But she wouldn't tell me where you were. The loyalty of love. She's an attractive woman, in her way, though there seems to be some ice floating in her blood.''

"There is,'' Carver said.

Now Laura's lips arced in a smile. She'd acquired permanent lines, indentations where he thought he'd seen shadows. "I suppose you know how to melt that occasion-ally."

Carver didn't acknowledge that one. "Why are you here, Laura?"

"To stop you from finding and killing Paul Kave."

"I don't understand. He murdered our son."

"Of course you don't understand. You don't see much beyond your own personal wants. Never did." Anger now, lips drawn back from strong white teeth perfect for ripping meat. Sexy, Carver realized. Middle-aged, like him, but still as sexy as she'd been years ago. *Don't think it, not for a second!* "I don't want our daughter to suffer the loss of her brother *and* her father within weeks of each other," Laura said. "Or doesn't her welfare enter into your calculations?"

Carver stood sweating, squinting out at the surf. She had him; how *would* it affect Ann if he were killed by Paul or taken into custody for murder? There was an angle he hadn't considered.

"It's something I'll think about," he said. It sounded weak even to him.

"Thanks so much," Laura said wryly. "That makes it worth the trip." She stood up and moved close to him. "I came here because I don't want you hurt any further, either, Fred. And that's the way it's headed. Sam tells me the legal ramifications of what you're doing are a tangle that might snarl you up and maybe send you to prison."

Carver was uncomfortable with her so near. He could smell her perspiration and perfume; it wasn't unpleasant. Something tightened at the core of him. *Christ!* "Sam, huh? How are you and Sam getting along?"

"Getting along," she said. "That pretty well sums it up." She looked out at the sea again. "This is peaceful, with the ocean and the boats and gulls. Are you at peace here, Fred?"

"No."

"At peace when you're with Edwina?"

"Sometimes."

"You going to ask me inside where it's cool?"

"I'd better not, Laura."

She gave him a slow, silky smile. She knew, all right. She said, "Worried about those statistics concerning sex after divorce?"

"What statistics? Where'd you see them?"

She waved a hand. "*People. Cosmopolitan.* Someplace or other." Baiting him. "Anyway, one in three couples sleeps together at least once after the divorce. Worried about that?"

"I'm not sure," he said. Why not be honest with her? She was being disturbingly honest with him.

"I won't try to convince you that way to stop searching for Paul Kave," she assured him. "But I want you to stop. If you won't, I'll go to the Kave family and tell them who you are and what you're doing."

He gripped her upper arm and squeezed. "I want you to promise you won't do that, Laura."

Anger flared in her eyes. "Trying to make my arm like your leg?"

"Why did you come here? The entire reason."

She locked stares with him; didn't blink. "I told you, I want you to stop hunting Paul Kave. Remember what Sam said, about how some things should be left alone."

"You didn't tell me everything."

"You hear what you want to hear. Always did."

He released her and moved back, leaning on his cane and breathing heavily. He wouldn't have minded crippling Laura just then, for coming here taunting and threatening. As if she were in control of things and he weren't. Her hand moved toward her reddened bicep, then withdrew. She wouldn't give him the satisfaction of letting him see her rub where he'd hurt her.

"You're sick with this thing," she told him. "Edwina told me about the fire. You need someone to save you from yourself. She won't, apparently."

"You don't understand how it is between us."

"Somebody doesn't."

"I don't want you talking to the Kaves. I mean that."

She gave him a long, careful look. Her entire face

trembled slightly, as if she were about to cry or scream. Or bolt into the ocean.

Then she whirled and stepped down off the porch. ''I can't promise I won't!'' she said, not looking back as she strode to her rental car parked in the sparse shade of the palms. Tiny clouds of dust kicked up behind her as her straw slip-ons flapped against her bare soles.

Carver watched her drive away, spinning the little car's tires on the sandy earth, raising more dust.

God damn her! She was complicating his life again, multiplying his worries and making him feel like a fool.

Hurling the truth in his face like a custard pie and then grinding it.

He struck his cane against the wooden porch railing hard enough to make a sound like a pistol shot, then he limped inside, slamming the screen door behind him like return fire.

CHAPTER 26

When Carver awoke in the dark cottage he thought he smelled smoke. He lay for the moment where he was, very still, the side of his face mashed into the sweat-damp pillow, his exposed eye bulged open. The clock by the bed read 5:00 A.M. The sea was pounding and smacking at the beach: high tide. It sounded as if it were all happening two feet outside the cottage, just on the other side of the wall.

The telephone rang, and he groggily fought toward greater awareness and realized it had been ringing for a while and its persistent jangle was what had drawn him from his dream of fire. A dream; that's all it had been.

He sucked in clean sea air from the open window; no smoke. Then he picked up the receiver and quieted the pesky phone. When he tried to say hello, his mouth was so dry and the taste on his tongue so sour that no sound came out. The smoke-filled dream he could barely remember had really worked him over, kicked around the old subconscious.

"This is Van Meter," the voice on the phone said. "You awake, Carver?"

"Yumph."

"Means yes, I suppose. Well, what I called about, my man watching the Kave estate said he saw Nadine return home fifteen minutes ago."

Carver swallowed. Licked his lips. They were coated with mucus that felt and tasted like glue. "Return from where?" His voice was a cross between a whisper and a croak. He swallowed again. It hurt his throat.

"That's the problem," Van Meter said. "She snuck out without being seen. We don't know where she went. My man figures, though, that she left sometime after midnight. He saw her at the house about then."

"She drive?"

"No, she came home in a cab."

"Why would she take a cab when the family's got three cars sitting around getting dusty?"

"Maybe she suspects the place is being watched. She's no dummy, if she's Adam Kave's daughter. Only thing my man can figure is she left the house by a side window and made her way down to the road, where she walked to a phone booth and called a taxi. That little red sports car of hers never moved; she probably parked it out where it was visible so her folks'd think she was home."

"Or so your man'd think so."

"Naw. He's good. She didn't know he was there; she was being careful in general. Maybe she went to meet Dewitt to go play house somewhere. Girl and Boy Stuff."

"She'd drive to see him," Carver said. "No need for secrecy there. Hell, they're supposed to be engaged, and Nadine's not the type to worry about whether people think she's a virgin. It's the late-twentieth century, Van Meter; I'm surprised at you. Girl and Boy Stuff goes on right under your nose all the time."

"Not under my nose," Van Meter said. "Not so much anymore."

"Point is," Carver said, "she wouldn't worry about her reputation or family if she went to meet Dewitt in the early morning hours. Not Nadine Kave."

Van Meter sighed into the phone. "Yeah. That attitude went the way of fins on cars. Looks like she might have gone someplace to meet her brother."

"Your guy get the cab number?"

" 'Fraid not," Van Meter said. "He was too far away, and it all happened fast. The cab let her out at the base of the drive and she walked to the house. I can check with the cab companies, though, and probably find out where she went. Don't know how much that'll tell us. My guess is she'd meet Paul Kave someplace other than where he's holed up. Some bar or all-night restaurant, maybe.''

"Better check anyway," Carver said. "She and Paul might set up another meeting at the same place—if that's who she went to see.''

"Yeah. Listen, I'm sorry we fucked up, Carver.''

"S'okay.''

"It's not, but that's how it goes sometimes. Imperfect world. Sorry I had to wake you, but I thought you'd want to know about this as soon as possible. In case you wanted to act on it right away.''

"Right now, I'm too tired to act on anything short of an alligator chewing on my good leg.''

"Get back to bed, why don't you?''

"I will," Carver said, and hung up.

But he was finished sleeping. He lay awake and watched the black patch of the window, waiting for the sun.

He'd decided not to tell Nadine he knew about her night-time excursion, but he wanted to talk with her anyway, in case she might volunteer information.

A part-time maid, in for the day from Fort Lauderdale, answered Carver's ring at the Kave estate. He waited just inside the door amid mock-Spanish splendor while she disappeared down the hall to announce his presence. Her footfalls made no noise.

A few minutes later she returned and showed him to the large room off the veranda. As they approached the closed door, Carver heard loud, argumentive voices. He glanced at the maid, a middle-aged Latin with a closed stone face. She might have smiled—but no, that was simply the cast of her features. She had a great face for a maid, with a permanent wry expression perfect for deflecting trouble.

She knocked lightly on the door, and the voices were abruptly stilled. She pushed the door open and shuffled soundlessly aside for Carver to enter.

The entire family was there. Adam Kave was standing near open French doors, holding a ceramic coffee mug. Elana, looking pale and distraught, was curled on the sofa, also gripping a coffee mug. She'd spilled coffee on her pink robe, leaving two small but distinct wet spots on her lap. Nadine was standing next to Joel Dewitt, her expression tight and stormy. Dewitt looked mad, but not as mad as the red-haired Mel Bingham, who was standing a few feet from him on the other side of Nadine. Not many people could look as angry as Bingham. He resembled a skinny modern-day Viking consumed by the red rage. A berserker with wild eyes and clenched fists. A large vein pulsed and writhed like a blue worm trapped beneath the taut flesh of his forehead. Ugly, ugly.

Adam Kave cleared his throat loudly; he was embarrassed. He nodded and said, "Carver." Nadine glared at Carver. Elana regarded him remotely, as if from behind soundproof glass. Dewitt and Bingham hardly noticed him; they were glaring at each other. Carver felt like a servant in a British movie: part of the scene yet not a part, existing in a lower-level universe of manner and meaning. He wished just then that he had a face like the maid's.

"We were discussing where Nadine went last night," Adam said. "I happened to hear her leave a few minutes after two and then return several hours later. She refuses to tell us why she sneaked out in the middle of the night or where she was going under cover of darkness."

"I don't see why I should have to tell," Nadine said. She was wearing yellow shorts and a sleeveless white top. Her thick, tennis player's thighs flexed powerfully as she shifted her weight. Her black hair was skinned back and braided with a yellow ribbon. A healthy and vigorous girl who looked ready to play time to a draw and always have her own teeth and live to be two hundred.

"We assumed you went to meet Joel," Elana told her. "Since you and he are seeing each other anyway, we simply wondered why you felt the need to sneak away behind our backs." She talked as if they weren't engaged and were merely casually dating. There was something about her daughter's involvement with Dewitt she couldn't even come close to acknowledging as reality. Or maybe she figured that, with her limited time left alive, she could accept or reject whatever she pleased and ultimately it wouldn't matter whether it had been fantasy or fact.

"But when it was mentioned this morning at breakfast in Joel's presence," Adam said, "it was obvious he knew nothing about it."

If either of them suspected Nadine had sneaked off to meet her brother, they weren't saying so.

"I think she went to meet this turd," Dewitt said, pointing at the seething Bingham, "but she's afraid to admit it, and so is he. Why's he always hanging around the house, anyway? He's got no business here."

"I come to see Nadine," Bingham said, "whether you like it or not. We've been friends since childhood, and I've come and gone here whenever I wanted for years."

"Only to see Nadine?"

"Of course."

"Well, that'll soon be over."

Bingham fumed and Elana smiled. It was as if she were pleased at seeing Dewitt's true personality exposed under stress. Will the real sleazy seller of doctored engines and tired transmissions please stand up? Yet there was a kind of regret in her eyes.

"If you want to think I met Mel, fine," Nadine said. "There's no way either of us can convince you otherwise, so fuck you."

Dewitt said, "I notice our friend Mel's not trying very hard to convince me that it wasn't him you sneaked out to meet."

"I wish she *had* met me last night," Bingham said in a strained but controlled voice. "Or met anybody else but you. She'd have been doing herself a favor. And who needs to convince you of anything?"

The tension level in the room was electric, tickling the nape of Carver's neck. It must feel that way where lightning was about to strike.

Nadine said, "Hey, calm down, Mel," and moved closer to him and gently rested a hand on his shoulder.

That seemed to burn Dewitt's fuse all the way down. He reached around her and grabbed the taller but thinner

Bingham by the shirtfront. Nadine ducked low as Bingham pulled back, popping buttons. "For God's sake!" Nadine said. Bingham raised an arm, elbow crooked, and awkwardly angled a punch over her head at Dewitt. Not with much force. Dewitt blocked it and yanked Bingham around Nadine, who took two off-balance steps and dropped hard to her hands and knees, jarring the room.

"Joel! Stop it!" Adam Kave yelled.

But it was Bingham bringing the fight to Dewitt. The lanky redhead was hurling windmill punches, landing one in four. Not a lot of skill, and too much righteous fury. Each time he threw a punch he grunted with effort and the mindless joy of combat. Forward was the only direction he knew.

Dewitt was all icy determination now, infuriated but calm, slipping punches and weaving and conserving his energy and waiting for Bingham to wear himself out. His blue eyes never blinked, even when Bingham landed a punch.

Finally Bingham stepped back, his scrawny chest heaving. He'd had enough action, worked away his rage. Reason had returned.

Dewitt smiled and said, "My turn," and neatly kicked him in the groin. A short, economic flight of the foot. Must have had karate lessons somewhere along the line.

Bingham went white and dropped in a hunched position on the floor, his hands cupped between his legs. He rocked forward until his nose touched the thick rug. Dewitt, still with that nasty calm smile, began systematically kicking him, starting with the ribs and working toward the head.

Carver knew Bingham would soon be hurt seriously, if he didn't already have some broken ribs or bruised internal organs. Dewitt was wearing pointy-toed leather loafers that could do genuine harm; Italian-import Mafia shoes.

Reaching out with the cane, Carver hooked Dewitt's arm and pulled him away from Bingham. Dewitt whirled and tried to wrest the cane from Carver's grip. It took him only a second to realize Carver's superior strength; a man's upper body developed powerfully from pushing around with a cane, from hours of swimming against strong ocean current.

"You're gonna hurt him in a way you'll regret," Carver said, holding the cane tight and leaning into Dewitt to keep from falling. If he went down, he knew he'd have to drag Dewitt with him; he didn't want to be kicked like Bingham.

Dewitt let out a long, trailing breath and released the cane. He looked around, his eyes dull and his mouth slack. Blood was dripping from the point of his chin onto the floor. Carver listened to it *plup! plup! plup!* onto the rug. One drop sounded different; it had landed on the toe of Dewitt's right shoe.

He stepped over Bingham and stalked out.

"Joel!" Nadine cried, and ran after him, leaving Bingham whimpering on the floor. "Dammit, come back, Joel! Please, honey!" Not hard to see where her loyalty lay. Carver knew she hadn't met Bingham last night. Or Joel Dewitt.

He and Adam Kave helped Bingham to his feet.

"You hurt bad?" Adam asked.

Bingham, still pale, shook his head. ". . . Be okay," he mumbled. "Pain going away. A little sick to my stomach."

Adam helped him walk to the sofa. Bingham slumped down on the cushions, clasping his right side where Dewitt had scored with some well-placed kicks. Pain was bending his body forward in a tight coil.

Elana stood up slowly, almost as if she were bored, and without speaking left the room. The lilac scent of her perfume followed her.

"You should get upstairs and rest, dear," Adam called after her unnecessarily. "Try not to worry about all this." She didn't answer. He turned toward Carver. "She seems calm, but inside she's upset, sucked dry of energy. This kind of scene can . . . well, it takes a toll on her."

"I imagine," Carver said.

"The bastard!" Bingham groaned, feeling better and getting mad again. "He kicked me in the balls!" As if mayhem were a sport and there were rules.

Carver limped over to the sofa. "I'll drive you to get those ribs X-rayed," he said.

"I can drive," Bingham snapped, acting as though Carver had insulted him. He struggled to his feet. His tall, lanky body swayed, then steadied. His long face was still pinched with pain. He couldn't quite believe what had happened. The good guys were supposed to win. This was an aberration and an outrage.

"Mel, you need help," Adam told him. "Go have yourself looked at by a doctor. Promise to do that?"

"A doctor and a lawyer," Bingham said. Man of the eighties. He hobbled bent-over out the door.

Carver and Adam said nothing while they waited, then they listened to the sound of his Jeep starting and screeching away. Tires counted for nothing in his budget.

"Shit!" Adam said, uncomfortable with this new silence and what had gone before it. "For something like this to happen . . ." He glanced up at the beamed ceiling, as if suddenly he'd heard thunder and remembered there was a storm in the forecast. "You'll have to excuse me, Carver; I better go upstairs and see to Elana."

"You should. We can talk later."

Adam clenched and unclenched his fists, as if exercising with invisible devices to strengthen his grip. His spring-trap jaw moved silently; he wanted to say more but couldn't formulate adequate words to direct Carver's way. He gave up and shambled from the room with his head bowed.

Carver put weight on the cane and moved out to the veranda; he needed fresh and less vibrant air.

Nadine was seated at the glass-topped table that was still cluttered with dishes and flatware and wadded napkins from breakfast. She was staring at the mess as if it were the remnants of her ruined young life. When she heard the clack of Carver's cane she looked up at him, and then away. Her eyes were black with a nameless fear. "How's Mel?"

"I think he'll be all right," Carver told her. The steady pulse of the ocean and the vastness of the sky made everything seem more placid out here. Eternity close by. Waiting.

"God, I thought Joel was gonna kill him!"

"He might have."

Far out at sea hundreds of gulls were circling in the wake of a fishing boat, like a cloud of fleas following an indifferent dog.

"Joel's in the bathroom washing blood off his shirt," she said. "Mel hit him and cut his lip." She talked as if a split lip were as serious as a cracked rib or ruptured spleen. "Despite what Mother says, Joel's an honest and honorable man. I mean, just because he's in a business where there are some crooks . . ."

"I know," Carver said. "In fact, I sympathize. Private investigators suffer from an unfair stereotype just like used-car dealers."

"A couple of times I've driven down to Miami with Joel to pay back money his grandfather lent him. That old man's Joel's only relative; his mother deserted him when he was an infant. Joel's always repaid the loans, and on time. That's how he's kept his business going through rough times, not by stealing people's money like Elana or Mel Bingham would have you believe. His grandfather himself told me that. Joel's a man who feels the responsibility of his debts."

And Nadine was a woman who knew how to avoid an uncomfortable subject. Carver leaned with both hands cupped over his cane and looked deep into her dark eyes, trying to understand what was staring back at him and making him uneasy. "You met Paul last night, didn't you, Nadine?"

She'd been waiting for him to ask. She pushed away from the table and stood up, not realizing her arm had brushed crumbs from the smooth glass onto her pale yellow shorts, where they clung like tiny insects.

She said, "Let's go down to the beach, Mr. Carver. We need to talk where no one can overhear us but the fishes."

CHAPTER 27

Carver was having difficulty walking with the cane on the damp sand, near where the surf foamed on the beach. Nadine looked over at him and stopped. He turned, and supported himself gingerly with the cane, facing her. She was wearing white Reebok jogging shoes that were wet from waves that had crawled far enough up on the sand to reach them. She didn't seem to care that her shoes were wet. The mind was where she lived.

"I didn't meet Mel Bingham last night," she said. "I did meet Paul."

Surprise, surprise, Carver thought. "Where?"

"At a marina in Fort Lauderdale. And if you're thinking of trying to figure out which one, forget it. We won't meet there again." Her voice was taunting, as if she were playing a game and had gone one up on Carver.

"How'd you know where to go?"

"Paul swam to the boathouse here and left a note for me where we used to hide things when we were kids. It told me where and when to meet him. We talked for over an hour, Mr. Carver. I mean talked about everything, really deep. The way we used to confide in each other when we were in grade school. Nothing but the truth." Her strong Kave features, half in bright sunlight, became serious. "Paul didn't kill anyone."

"Paul would say that."

"Of course. Because he's innocent."

"The evidence says he's guilty."

She tilted her head to the side and stared at him with the

175

mocking tolerance of youth. Wisdom time. "Isn't that for a judge or jury to say?"

Carver matched her trite for trite. "I'd like to help Paul so he'll stand in front of a jury instead of police guns."

"That's bullshit and we both know it." Really, she was grown-up. At times, anyway.

Carver wasn't sure how much she knew. He let her remark go by. He guessed she was letting her emotions talk for her. Like every other kind of love, sibling affection had a flip side that could cause pain. She'd learned, like everyone else; vulnerability was part of love's bargain.

Then she said, "Paul didn't kill your son."

Carver felt his stomach dive.

Nadine had found him out and knew who he was and what he was doing, and there was nothing below him but space and a haunted future. Haunted by things interrupted. Incomplete. His son's life. Justice and balance after death. Even simple revenge. He wondered with dismal detachment if he could live with that.

"How did Paul know one of his victims was my son?" he asked. His own voice sounded unfamiliar, muted by the sibilant roll of the surf.

Nadine spread her feet wide and propped her fists on her ample hips. Long-legged and sturdy, she stood as if nothing in the universe could budge her. She was a female colossus in complete charge of the conversation now. Or thought so. Information could do that to people. "He first knew you were . . . stalking him when he learned you were asking about his car at Scuba Dan's. You were all over the beach, asking about the murders, so he followed you and learned your identity and your relationship to the boy who was burned to death in Fort Lauderdale. He read in the papers that you were working for the family, trying to locate him, and he knew you must have lied to us about who you were."

"Where's Paul now?" Carver asked.

Her dark eyes were level, calm yet defiantly candid, as if it were only Carver who should fear the truth. Strength through naïveté. ''I don't know. He doesn't want me to know. It has to be that way.''

Carver believed her. Paul Kave was turning out to be wilier than he'd anticipated. Not to mention more persuasive. But then, Paul was supposed to possess a stratospheric I.Q. It would be easy for someone like him to take advantage of a sister's unquestioning, simple love. To sense weakness and exploit it.

''He wanted to meet with me,'' Nadine said, ''to assure me he was okay, and to convey to you that he's innocent.''

''And to ask you to bring him some of his antidepressant medicine?''

Nadine jerked her head high and held it there, staring down at Carver. ''You've been talking to Dr. Elsing.'' This wasn't fair; Carver had been caught cheating at whatever game they were playing. Seeing Dr. Elsing had been against the rules, maybe even off the board.

''The police know Paul was on medication to control his schizophrenia, Nadine.''

A wave made it far enough up the beach to lick at the toe of one of her already wet shoes. She didn't move. Foam sloshed around Carver's cane planted in the sand. ''There's no way I can get any of those pills,'' Nadine said. ''They're strong stuff, prescription medicine. Only a doctor can help Paul that way.''

''You tell Paul that?''

''Of course.''

''Did you take him pills he already had in his room?''

She shot a dark look at Carver. ''How did you know that?''

''A guess. You're his only sister, and a devoted one.''

''You got that part right, Mr. Carver.''

''If Paul's innocent, why's he running?''

''Stupid question. He found out you and the police were looking for him, and read in the newspapers he was the chief suspect. He had no choice other than to run.''

''Smart answer. But has it occurred to you that the reason all the evidence points to him and he's running is that he's guilty? Despite what he told you.''

She gazed out at a large incoming wave and laughed hopelessly, shaking her head. "I told Paul you wouldn't believe. You're on a revenge mission; it's as obvious as if it were stamped on your forehead like some kind of biblical mark. You want Paul's blood."

"I don't equate what I'm doing with religion."

"You should. It's ages old and twisted, even if it's fresh in you. It controls you. You're lost in it. You must be, to have done what you did. Vengeance can be a religion, don't you think?"

She was grown-up, all right. But not quite far enough to realize how badly people needed their faith, twisted or otherwise.

"Explain away the evidence," Carver said, "and I'll try to believe Paul."

"I can't explain it away. Neither can Paul. If he could, he wouldn't be running." Quite logical, in its fashion.

"I guess you're going to tell the rest of the family about me?" Carver said.

"No. Paul made me promise not to. He sees you as his only hope. The only one who can help him."

Stunned, Carver lifted the tip of his cane a few inches, then drove it back into the sand, as if trying to spear something elusive out of sight below the surface. "He knows who I am, and he expects me to *help* him?"

"He thinks you're a better bet than the police to get at the truth."

"He told you that?"

"Sure."

"He's even craftier than I thought."

"Or else he's innocent."

Carver looked beyond Nadine at a figure descending the wooden steps by the boathouse. Joel Dewitt. Nadine noticed something had grabbed Carver's attention and turned her head to look.

Dewitt was striding toward them along the beach now, five feet beyond where the surf was spreading like white lace and then reluctantly backwashing to the sea. He was walking heavily, heels kicking up the sand. His shallow footprints seemed insubstantial, at the mercy of the stiff breeze off the endless Atlantic.

"He'll want to know what we're talking about," Carver said.

Nadine nodded. "I suppose he will. I'm planning on telling him. You object?"

"Would it make a difference?"

"Sure. It might make it more fun."

Carver didn't shoot back. He couldn't blame her for not liking the man who was after her brother.

When Dewitt reached them, he tried a grin but it quickly rearranged itself into a grimace. His lower lip was swollen and split, and not for smiling. He touched a knuckle lightly to the lip, then drew it away and examined a speck of blood on it. He looked at Carver and wiped the blood from the knuckle with his other hand, rubbing his fist tightly, the way a pitcher rubs a baseball before launching it toward home plate. If he rubbed hard enough, it would be as if the blood had never been there and his lip was all right.

"Hope I didn't hurt the idiot," he said. "How'd he seem after I left?"

"You might have cracked some of his ribs," Carver said. "Maybe he's hurt worse than that."

Dewitt looked miserable and shrugged. "Lost my temper. It doesn't happen very often."

"You looked in control to me," Carver said.

"Yeah. That's how it is when I really get mad. I get kinda calm at the same time." The ocean breeze plastered his pale blue shirt to his body. The front of the shirt was bloodstained. Drips. Spatters. Unlikely bold patterns that reminded Carver of abstract art. Dewitt glanced at Nadine, back at Carver. "What's going on here? More secrets?"

Nadine explained to him that she'd met Paul last night, and told him of Paul's claim of innocence. She didn't tell him that one of Paul's victims was Carver's son, and that Carver had conned the family into hiring him.

Dewitt dabbed at his split lip again with a knuckle. "Paul might be using you, Nadine, making you an accessory to murder. That's major trouble, babe. Sorta thing can mess up your life. I think, for Paul's sake as well as yours, you oughta tell Carver where he is.'' The extended stretch of talking caused fresh blood to ooze from the lip.

"But I don't know where Paul is. He was afraid I might be pressured into revealing his whereabouts, so he kept that a secret from me."

Dewitt shuffled his pointy black loafers on the damp sand, staring down at the odd indentations the smooth leather soles were leaving on the beach. More surreal artwork, indecipherable and temporary. "Okay, don't tell even if you know. You love the guy. He's lucky." He managed a painful smile. "Hell, I'm lucky, too. For the same reason, even if it's a different kinda love."

Nadine, the reason, lit up like neon and leaned over and kissed him on the cheek.

"Would you know how to get in touch with Paul again?" Carver asked.

"No," Nadine said. "He said he'd contact me if he wanted to talk again. He's being careful; you can't blame him for that."

Carver felt like telling her that mass murderers usually were careful, until near the end when they killed more and more often, riding their relentless compulsion to oblivion. Which maybe was what they yearned for all along. He knew it would be useless to point this out to Nadine, to tell her about the woman in Orlando and what her death might signify. Paul, with or without his medication, was probably going to take more lives, with less time between murders. He was losing control.

"Think Paul would meet with me?" Carver asked Nadine.

"Maybe. Under certain, safe circumstances."

"If he contacts you again, will you tell him I want a meeting? Only to talk, to get his side. He can arrange it so he's safe."

"Sure, I'll tell him. *If* I talk to him again."

The waves were building higher, curling in on themselves as they met the undertow from shore—"tubing," as the surfers called it. Maybe it meant a storm was moving in, though the sky was blue except for a couple of broken white slashes very high. They might have been clinging vapor from a jet plane, marring the heavens like scrawls from a giant hand.

"Want to go back up to the house?" Nadine asked, staring at Dewitt intensely and deliberately excluding Carver.

"No," Dewitt said. "Fanning's up there with your father. Let's walk the beach awhile and talk."

Nick Fanning again. Carver wondered just how Fanning fit into the Kave family equation in matters other than business. How much did he know? How much did he pretend not to know?

Carver left Nadine and Joel Dewitt prowling the angry edge of the sea. Then he drove to a roadside phone and called Emmett Kave in Kissimmee.

He asked the same promise of Emmett: If Paul contacted him again, would he try to set up a meeting with Carver? In a safe place where they would talk and nothing more.

Emmett agreed, but he skeptically asked Carver why he wanted the meeting, if it was for a reason other than tricking Paul into getting caught. Wary Emmett; a survivor of the jungle.

Carver told him he was having doubts about Paul's guilt. It would help if he could talk face-to-face with Paul, and straighten out some problems regarding the evidence. A plausible lie.

When he hung up the phone and got back in the baking Olds, he sat for a while perspiring, staring without focus through the insect-dashed windshield and seeing nothing but opaque swimming patterns of heat.

CHAPTER 28

Carver met Edwina for lunch at The Happy Lobster on the coast highway. They sat at a table near the long curved window that looked out on the sea. Far offshore, half a dozen sailboats resembled brightly colored shark fins cutting the glittering surface in rough formation. They appeared to be racing, describing a circular course that would deliver them across an invisible finish line at the point where they'd started. How the world worked, perhaps.

Edwina had ordered the seafood salad, Carver the broiled shrimp. They were sipping drinks and munching fried zucchini appetizers dipped in horseradish sauce.

Carver had called Van Meter and had him pull everyone off surveillance except for a man to continue watching over Edwina. It was up to Paul Kave now to contact Nadine or Emmett. And up to Nadine or Emmett to arrange a meeting and call Carver. It all seemed so easy that it was bound to turn into trouble.

"So what did Laura say to you?" Carver asked. He dipped a zucchini slice and popped it into his mouth, chewed and washed it down with a sip of Budweiser. He hadn't had much breakfast and it tasted terrific.

"Awkward small talk at first," Edwina said, "then she got around to saying she didn't understand how I could let you get caught up in a vendetta without trying to stop you."

"What did you tell her?"

"Nothing. She's right; she doesn't understand. Pass the horseradish."

Carver slid the small plate the necessary few inches across

the white tablecloth. Edwina delicately dipped and ate two zucchini slices. She seemed absorbed in the task. The scent of the cheese sprinkled over the hot zucchini mingled with that of the tangy sauce. Watching her savor the stuff made Carver even hungrier. They were both starving and where was food they could really attack?

He said, "Laura's worried about how it will affect Ann if something happens to me. She wants this all to end for Ann, for both of them. It makes sense."

"It does if you love your daughter more than your former husband."

He took another long pull of beer, then set the damp glass down precisely on its cork coaster. Outside, in the hazy distance, seabirds were circling high over the slanted colorful sails. Nearer to shore a man in white shorts and shirt was jockeying an outboard runabout down the coast, standing staunchly at the wheel to peer over the boat's Plexiglas windscreen. The waves were giving him a wild ride; probably that was what he wanted.

"Laura's threatening to tell the Kave family who I am," Carver said. "I think she means it."

"Bet on it," Edwina said. She craned her neck, anticipating the arrival of their waiter. He was across the room, leisurely taking the orders of a table of executive types; he knew an expense-account-size tip shaping up when he saw one.

"She'll be hanging around this part of Florida till this thing's resolved," Carver said. "She might talk to you again, try to get to me through you."

"I doubt it. I told her you were compelled to do what you thought needed doing. She said it was a mistake. I told her maybe it was, but it was your mistake and neither of us had the right to keep you from making it. I asked her if she wanted to see her son's killer caught. She said she didn't care, it wouldn't make any difference to her or to him. I told her if you were fucked-up, so was she. I'm starving; where's the food?"

Carver grinned. "I wish I'd overheard that conversation."

"No you don't," Edwina said. "There was more." But she didn't elaborate. Her green-flecked eyes were unemotional. She said, "Laura's interested in more than your daughter's welfare. You do know that, don't you?"

He looked out again at the distant sails. "Maybe she is. A child dies, it does something to both parents that draws them toward each other, I guess. They're the only ones who understand the depth of the grief, the pain. It's a lonely place to be."

"I know. And I can't be there with you."

"Yeah. But Laura coming down here and trying to talk me out of looking for Paul Kave, it might be the pain and loneliness that made her do it. I suppose I feel sorry for her. And she feels sorry for me. Some things develop between people and they can't help it."

Edwina said, "I'm going to eat this last zucchini." And did.

The waiter finally glided over with their food, and Carver and Edwina asked for fresh drinks. He slowly made note of that in a leather-covered order pad.

"I'd like mine before the ice melts," Edwina told him. Feisty today. The waiter let it bounce off and coasted away at half speed. A professional.

"Get the insurance claim in on the house?" Carver asked.

"This morning. I think the place might always smell like burned tires, though. Compliments of Paul Kave." She tore a roll in half and buttered it.

"I put you in danger," Carver said. "I'm sorry."

"Don't be. That's what life comes down to sometimes, putting other people in danger and them willing. Nothing you can do that won't make ripples that might become waves. Or might swamp boats."

"Two members of the Kave family already know who I am," Carver said. He told Edwina about his oceanside conversation with Nadine.

"Was there ever anything between Nick Fanning and Nadine?" Edwina asked.

He thought that was a curious reaction to his story. He'd

hardly mentioned Fanning in his recounting of what had happened at the estate that morning.

Edwina must have read the puzzlement on his face, though her gaze was fixed higher, on his tanned, bald head, as if his thoughts might be printed there. "From what you've told me about him, and her, it seems a real possibility. The virile friend and business subordinate of the father, the rebellious daughter, the frequency of Fanning's visits to the house. The setup might seem like a sexual challenge to a man like Fanning. Or to a girl like Nadine. Kind of thing you see on soap operas every day."

"That's what's wrong with the notion," Carver said. "Anyway, whatever might have happened, it's irrelevant now. Nadine's too in love with Dewitt to see a wart on him."

"Lucky Nadine."

"You mean Dewitt."

"No, Nadine."

Carver slid his plate of shrimp nearer to him. The smooth white china was warm. He couldn't imagine Nadine involved with Fanning.

"So how do you feel?" Edwina asked, forking a bite of salad into her mouth.

"About what?"

"Laura."

"I told you, I feel sorry for her. Probably pity is all she feels for me. Hell, we got a divorce, Edwina; we thought it all out years ago and called off living together."

"Numph," Edwina said, around another bite of salad.

"Meaning?"

"I'm not sure she has it all thought out as thoroughly as you say. What love's about is two people making a long-term investment in each other's happiness, willing to go to the wall for each other. That's what Laura doesn't seem to understand. Maybe what you don't quite understand."

"That's a lot for one 'numph,' " Carver said.

"It only seems that way. Love's actually a simple, one-syllable emotion."

The sea smell of the shrimp and Edwina's salad was

suddenly too much. Carver's appetite left him, but the hollowness in his stomach made him queasy.

He wasn't sure how he felt about Laura. Or about Edwina, or Chipper, or Paul Kave, or about the wilderness he'd charged into and that had absorbed him.

He sat back and stared out at the waves, rolling in murky, ever-changing patterns and darkened by sudden low clouds. It all kept kaleidoscoping in his mind: Laura, Edwina, Paul, Nadine, Adam, McGregor, and the dark, sad corpse of his only son.

The ocean, vast and implacable, exerted a primal pull that was frightening.

CHAPTER 29

After leaving Edwina, Carver returned to the cottage and checked his answering machine. He'd received a call from Laura, and she'd left a number where she could be reached. Carver dragged out his dog-eared directory and looked up the phone number of the Andrew Johnson Motel. It was the number on Laura's recorded message. He imagined her sitting in her room, staring at vapid afternoon television and wondering where some oversized roulette wheel would stop. Or lounging by the motel pool, sweating and not really liking the sun, waiting for his return call. She was far from home, from where she belonged.

Carver decided not to return her call. Edwina was right about Laura's renewed interest in him, and that scared him. He'd gone around the course once with Laura and didn't want to again. Yet he knew that a mutually dependent attraction had been engendered by their son's death, embryonic now, waiting to grow. She needed him, her fellow voyager through the mourning process. Carver didn't want to need her.

He punched the Play button again on the answering machine and listened to a wrong number, a pitch to buy into a time-share project in Clearwater before his rare opportunity was gone forever, and a reminder from his insurance agent that the premium was due on the Olds.

Nothing from Emmett or Nadine Kave.

Carver had barely eaten at lunch, but he was feeling better now and figured he'd soon be hungry. He clomped with his cane into the kitchenette and opened the refrigerator.

187

Not an inspiring sight. Only two cans of beer, a small steak he'd allowed to go bad, and a container of yogurt that never had a chance. Edwina had bought the yogurt weeks ago. Carver loathed the stuff; it looked like cream trying to be something else.

Plan ahead, he thought. Resolving to eat an early dinner out this evening and then do some elemental grocery shopping, he pulled the tab on one of the beer cans, shoved the refrigerator door shut, and carried the can out onto the porch.

It was hot outside, even in the deep shade beneath the porch roof. But there was a breeze off the ocean that now and then evaporated perspiration on his arms and face and cooled. He settled into the webbed aluminum lawn chair, propped his good leg up on the wooden porch rail, and watched a tan and shapely woman in a red bikini dashing in and out of the surf far down the beach. She was animated and loud; she swayed her hips in exaggerated motion when she ran, and her shrill, desperately happy screams carried to Carver on the breeze. Some great time she was having, everything about her shouted. Trying to impress someone Carver couldn't see. Her hair was long and dark and flew wildly with each foray into the waves. Carver enjoyed watching her.

One of the woman's shrieks trailed off, then was continued by the phone inside the cottage.

Carver lowered his leg, pushed himself up out of the light-weight chair, and limped inside with his cane. Because he was in a hurry, he allowed the screen door to shut too fast and it nipped him on the right heel. Hurt like crazy for a second or two. He didn't need another bad leg.

He snatched up the receiver and snarled a hello, still mad at the door.

"Carver?"

"Yeah." He recognized McGregor's voice. Wished he hadn't picked up the phone.

"Whazza matter? You sound outa sorts and outa breath."

"Just giving the place a quick coat of paint; you interrupted me."

"Nice you can still joke," McGregor said. "Now here's something to cheer you down: your ex-wife's been by to see me and threatened to tell Adam Kave you're the father of one of his son's victims. The poop'd hit the propeller then, hey? I thought she lived in Saint Louis; how the hell she even know you were on the case?"

"She's been reading the Florida papers to keep track of the hunt for Paul Kave. When she read I'd been hired by the Kave family, she figured out the rest."

"Well, I got her promise to stay clear of the case for a while. Scared shit out of her with the official-police-business line, then played nice cop and asked for her cooperation. It won't last long, though; she's too smart to buy it. I was very impressed. You seem to attract smart women, Carver. And good-lookers. Guess it's that opposites thing. Anyway, you're gonna have to talk to her, see she keeps her mouth shut."

"I've already talked to her."

"So talk again. Fast and hard. Do whatever you got to fast and hard. Damn it, she's *your* ex, Carver; you oughta be able to control her."

"Yeah, that's logical."

"You're the only one's got a chance, pal. I could tell that after spending fifteen minutes with the lady. She's worried all to hell about her daughter."

"My daughter, too," Carver said.

"Sure. What's happening with the all-American Kave family? Not exactly Ward and June Cleaver and the kids, hey?"

Carver told him about Dewitt's fight with Mel Bingham, and Nadine talking with Paul. He didn't mention he was trying to set up a meeting with Paul through Nadine or Emmett Kave.

"Sounds like an ordinary tiff over pussy," McGregor said. "We checked Bingham. He's a senior at Florida State, going back soon for the fall semester. Working toward a degree in biochemistry. Normal asshole college kid. Drives a Jeep and thinks he's living a beer commercial. Family's well off, but not like the Kaves. Maybe he's chasing the daughter for her money. Seems he dated Nadine all through high school and for awhile when she went to college, but the past several years she's been spreading it around. Kind of wild, but no legal trouble. A minor drug charge two years ago, but it was dropped. One fella after another for her, though. Until Joel Dewitt. You'd think a girl like that, her money and looks, could do better than a guy like Dewitt. I can see why her mother wishes Dewitt would get run over by one of his used cars.''

''Could be they're in love.''

''Uh-huh. I was younger, I'd try to move on that Nadine. Put it to her like one of her daddy's jumbo hot dogs and change both our lives for the better. Hey, maybe you oughta try getting to her, Carver.''

''You're twisted in a lot of ways,'' Carver said.

''It's the world made me that way,'' McGregor said, agreeing and not caring. ''What I am's a realist. Better for you if you were one too. If you'd spent another five years on the force as a real detective, you'd *be* one. Then you'd see life the way it is: damned yeast pile, Carver, and it'll fester till the planet quits spinning.''

It scared Carver to think McGregor might be right. And it bothered him that he'd developed a modicum of compassion for Paul Kave, and a loathing for the police lieutenant stalking him. What had started out so simply had become a horrendous tangle of emotions and confusion, thanks mainly to McGregor, who seemed to care about nothing so much as McGregor.

''Buncha hypocrites out there in the world, Carver,'' McGregor said. ''Specially here in Florida. It's all that fundamental religion bullshit; them people won't fuck standing up 'cause somebody might see 'em and think they're dancing. At least I know what I am and accept it. Tell you the truth, kinda enjoy it now and then. Like this gamble I'm taking on you.''

''I admire your honesty,'' Carver said. Damned if he didn't.

A car drove up outside and parked, its tires grinding on the sandy soil alongside the cottage. Carver heard its engine race, then die. Dust from its arrival drifted like a heat-spawned apparition across his field of vision outside the window.

He moved a few feet to the left and saw Laura's tiny blue rental car. The driver-side door opened and she climbed out, glanced at the ocean and perhaps the young woman romping in the surf, then strode toward the cottage. She was wearing a plain navy blue dress today, and dark high heels. The wind grabbed at her hair and ruffled it, like the hair of the girl down the beach. She touched it lightly with spread fingers and smiled absently, as if luxuriating in the breeze's caress. Something in Carver moved.

"Thing is," McGregor said, "you gotta corner that ex-wife of yours and work on her. Tell her any fuckin' thing, but keep her away from Adam Kave. Will you do that?"

"If I can find her," Carver said.

As he hung up, she was peering into the dimness through the screen. She knocked on the door. Wanted in.

"I phoned you earlier," she said, when he'd called for Laura to enter and she stood a few feet inside the door.

"Did you? I just got here, haven't had time to check my calls."

"It's warm in here."

"It doesn't have to be. Switch on that air-conditioner."

She walked to the window unit, studied the controls for a second, then turned it on High. The compressor clunked on and the blower began a wavering, powerful hum. She closed her eyes and sucked in some of the cool, filtered air, then moved away from it. She seemed instantly refreshed, oddly invigorated. Or had she been that way since she'd entered?

Some of the cool air found its way across the room to Carver. "Why'd you call?" he asked.

"We need to talk."

"About Ann?"

"About what you're doing. About you. I talked to Lieutenant McGregor in Fort Lauderdale. I don't like him. Or trust him. Being around him makes my flesh creep."

"And he thinks he won you over."

She walked to the water-stained chair Carver usually sat in after swimming and lowered herself onto it, then folded her hands in the lap of the blue dress. As if she were planning on staying awhile.

"What's Sam Devine think about you coming to Florida?" Carver asked.

Her hands tightened on each other, fingertips whitening around pink-enameled nails. "We argued about it. He tried to talk me out of it. Then he wanted to come with me. I think he would have, but he's wrapped up in a case with the Highway Department. Something about land acquisition."

"And you came anyway."

"I had to. I told you why."

"I guess you did," Carver said.

She looked out past the dead plants hanging in the window. The rush of surf was still audible over the hum of the air-conditioner. The place was cooling off fast.

"Edwina Talbot's more than pretty," she said. "She's beautiful."

"Yeah, she's that." Carver thought of Edwina, and, for some reason, of the woman down on the beach.

Laura tilted her head to the side and sighed, then stood up and walked over to stand near him. She moved as if she had no choice in the matter, as if some celestial puppet master were skillfully working her strings. "She can't give you what you need right now. Sam can't give me what I need."

"Maybe not," Carver said, somehow not surprised by her direct approach. It was all so clear to her, as she must think it was to him. Or would be to him if only he'd open his mind and let the light in. If only he'd read that survey in *People*. Or was it *Cosmopolitan?*

He hadn't wanted this, but then he hadn't counted on Laura's candidness, and the effect she'd have on him standing close and looking so honestly, so yearningly, into his eyes. Years hadn't passed. Acid hadn't spilled. Fire hadn't burned. Their son was still alive.

No, he was dead.

Dead forever.

Carver's throat tightened. He felt his eyes well with tears.

Laura said, "We can give each other what we need. Only you and me. That's how it is, I'm afraid."

Carver reached for her before he knew what he was doing and was pressing her to him, feeling her body vibrate as if she were trembling on the edge of an endless drop. Her forehead and cheek were crushed against his chest and her tears saturated his shirt like warm blood. "Oh, Christ! . . ." she moaned, and clung to him as if he alone and not Christ could save her. This was shared self-pity, he realized. Maudlin. A staged catharsis. But she was right: they needed it.

On the bed they twisted grief into desperation and desire, and hid from death in the ultimate act of life.

Her sharp cries were still lodged like shards of pain in his mind when Carver rolled exhausted from her, dragging his bad leg across her perspiration-slick thigh. The heated scent of their lovemaking lay over them.

He let his eyes slide sideways to study the sweat-gleaming plane of her stomach and the faintly quivering swell of pale breast. Her breathing was shallow and ragged, as if just enough to sustain life. There were distinct dividing lines where her swimming suit had shielded flesh from sun at the Andrew Johnson Motel.

Carver realized he was parched and thirsty. He felt like a man suddenly awakened after sleeping off a long drunk. Hair of the dog, he thought, and said, "There's a beer in the refrigerator. Want to share it?"

"Sure." Her voice was slow and drained of feeling. Cold beer time. Cold logic time. The way it had been years ago. He wondered what she was thinking now, lying among the ruins.

He got up and considered leaving the cane and using walls and furniture for support to cross the floor to the kitchen. But his good leg felt rubbery, and he didn't like the idea of possibly falling in front of Laura. He grabbed the cane, and, barefoot, he padded and thumped across the plank floor.

She was sitting up when he returned behind the folding screen that partitioned off the sleeping area. His bedroom. With Laura in it. Her breasts were bare and seemed larger and more pendulous now as she leaned her back against the oak headboard. She seemed relaxed.

She said, "Don't worry, I'm up to date on my pills."

"I should have asked," Carver said. "Didn't even think about it." Or maybe some part of him had thought about it and he hadn't wanted to ask. But he didn't want her to be pregnant; God, he didn't want that!

He took a long swallow of beer, feeling some of it dribble coldly onto his chin, then handed her the can. She tilted back her head and drank deeply. A few drops of beer or condensation from the can rained onto her right breast, and she absently lifted her left hand and rubbed away the glistening dampness without lowering the can. He waited, watching her drink.

Finally she handed the half-empty can back to him.

He placed it on the table by the bed and sat down on the mattress, twisting his body so he could face her. She smiled and said, "So how do you feel?"

"Relieved," he said. "Not good, though. Not at ease."

"Why not?"

Carver wasn't sure he could crystallize the reasons in his mind so he could analyze them and frame an answer for her. Guilt was in there. And Edwina. A part of him felt like a wayward teen who'd cheated on his steady. But it was more than that. It involved so many things, some of them indefinable right now and maybe forever. Uncertainty seemed to be a permanent facet of life. His life, anyway.

He groped in his mind for what he was sure of, found it, and said, "I don't want you to talk to Adam Kave, Laura."

She stared at him and something deep in her eyes changed. She seemed to retreat from him without changing position propped against the headboard. As if she were diminishing in the small end of a telescope. Soon she'd be too far away for them to hear each other. "Is that what this was about? An exercise in persuasion?"

It hadn't occurred to him that she'd think that; he knew it should have. "No! For God's sake, Laura!" It hurt him physically that she believed that about him, a heavy ache in the pit of his stomach.

She got up, stepped into her shoes, and raised her dress above her head and wriggled into it. Fumbling, she buttoned it up the front, missing half the buttons, and yanked its belt tight. Then she snatched up her underwear and pantyhose from the floor and stood angrily holding them bunched tightly in her right hand, as if they were something dead that she'd loved. She glared at him as if he were responsible for the death.

Carver braced himself on the headboard and stood up, tried to reason calmly with her. "Laura, listen . . ."

But she turned and stalked out. He didn't follow. Instead he stood listening to the *tap, tap* of her high heels across the cottage floor. Then the reverberating slam of the screen door. The solid thunk of her car door. And the sound of her driving away. He didn't know what he would have told her if he *had* managed to stop her and make her stand and listen.

Still nude, he stretched out on his back on the bed, laced his fingers behind his head, and studied the ceiling.

Maybe he'd had nothing to say to her, no words to stop her, because she was right. Maybe dissuading her from talking to the Kave family before he had a chance to find Paul *had* been what the last few hours were about. Lately he'd come to realize how little he knew about the man he'd become. As if a stranger were wearing his skin.

He began to perspire, beads of sweat trickling from his armpits to play over his ribs and down to the already damp sheet that still smelled of his and Laura's physical reunion.

Apparently it was only their bodies that had met and merged. The old distance was back.

He reached over, found the warming Budweiser can, and drained the last few ounces of beer. It tasted flat and sour. Yummy, he thought, and tossed the empty can away and listened to it bounce clattering into a corner. Empty.

CHAPTER 30

Between Emmett and Nadine, Carver thought it was Nadine who was less likely to notify him if Paul contacted her. He decided to watch her, and periodically check to see if Emmett had phoned him.

He borrowed Edwina's incredibly complicated, many-knobbed answering machine, which had a beeperless remote feature that allowed him to phone his number and punch in a code that would command the machine to play back messages. The microchip was a hell of an invention, he thought. He'd be able to call from any phone to check for messages while he was following Nadine. He wondered if this technology was an off-shoot of the space program, all those tons of metal and flesh and fire hurled from a point on the coast, out of Earth's grace and gravity, and now Carver could hear from a distance people who wanted to sell him time shares and vinyl siding.

Nadine spent most of her days at the Ray and Racquet Tennis Club on the coast highway, a sprawling white stucco complex interspersed with palm trees, angled concrete walkways, and neatly laid-out green asphalt tennis courts. There was a sunwashed symmetry about the place that hurt the eye.

Carver didn't attempt to get past the gate, which was guarded by uniformed security in the person of a small, white-haired man toting a large, black-holstered sidearm. He looked like an ex-cop past retirement age but still willing and capable. Police work could be an occupation that got in the blood and eventually took over the entire organism.

There was only one way in and out, so Carver found a shaded, secluded spot off the highway to park the Olds. From there he could both observe the tennis-club entrance and sometimes with binoculars see Nadine seated at an outdoor table in the lounge, sipping drinks with her friends. One of the friends frequently near her at the crowded table was Mel Bingham. A lot of animated conversation went on among that group, tanned waving arms, glinting jewelry, perfect white smiles, and very sincere expressions above designer tennis shirts and gold chains. The rich at play, aimless but with style.

Occasionally Nadine would wander out to one of the courts for a singles match, and Carver would watch her through the binoculars as she destroyed her opponent with her powerful base-line game. To him she looked good enough to be a pro, and he envied as well as admired her two strong legs and the fluid mobility she took for granted. She was an intimidating figure with a racket, in a white-and-yellow tennis outfit that might have made a smaller woman seem more feminine but on her was almost a parody. A strapping, athletic girl with a firm bite on life.

In the evenings she'd usually drive into Fort Lauderdale and meet Joel Dewitt at his car lot. They did a lot of handholding and kissing. Dewitt liked to sneak up behind her, cup her breasts in his hands, and buss her on the nape of the neck. Looked like fun to Carver, too.

Sometimes they'd go out to dinner, or to a movie. They liked comedies. Almost always they returned to Dewitt's apartment on Low Citrus Drive, where Nadine would stay until well past midnight.

Dewitt's apartment was in a three-story sandstone building with a lighted pool whose water looked as if it needed filtering, though it wasn't as bad as the pool at the Mermaid Motel. Red iron steps led to the upper-floor apartments, where railed balconies overlooked the pool and a row of ratty-looking, flood-lighted palm trees. A flower bed along a low stone wall was colorful with azaleas and marigolds but wildly overgrown. The place could have used a caretaker who actually cared.

The building had a ground-level garage where tenants' cars were kept out of the sun and safe from vandalism. Carver would sit in the parked Olds where he could keep an eye on the garage exit, as well as on the windows of Dewitt's apartment. Usually, around eleven o'clock, the lights in the apartment would wink out and Carver's imagination would switch on. He couldn't stop flashing back to his night with Laura. All movement and softness and warmth, familiar yet strange. A new beginning and an end all packaged in a few hours; something personal yet independent of both of them that had to try its wings, and soared and fell.

Sometimes Nadine's low-slung red Datsun would screech like a thing in agony from the garage and make a sharp turn onto the street, taking Carver by surprise. He'd have to hurriedly start the Olds and catch up to tail her. She knew no way to drive other than fast.

The Datsun had metal louvers across the rear window to keep the sun out, like exterior venetian blinds, and it was difficult for him to know if Nadine was alone. At times she and Dewitt would leave the apartment, and Carver would think she was by herself in the car. He'd follow her several blocks, encouraged by the fact that she wasn't heading home. Maybe she was on her way to a secret rendezvous with Paul. Then, at a traffic signal or in a brightly lighted area, he'd discover that Dewitt was with her and they were only going out for drinks or a pizza and would return to the apartment later and probably do things he didn't want to envision.

Occasionally, when he knew she and Dewitt were set in one place for a while, Carver would phone his cottage number, key-in the answering machine for messages, and listen in the hope that he'd hear Emmett Kave's voice, or possibly Nadine's. He was always disappointed.

But one afternoon, when Nadine and Dewitt were at lunch, Carver finally did receive a phone message from one member of the Kave family: Adam, who wanted to see him as soon as possible and sounded disgusted and angry.

Carver was sure he knew what Adam wanted with him.

He thought he should get back in the Olds and drive straight to the estate and level with Adam Kave. Tell him about Chipper, about McGregor, the entire convoluted tangle of lies and deception. Get everything out in the open and make his quest for vengeance burn hot and pure again. There was nothing Adam or McGregor could do now to stop him from finding Paul Kave and the truth. And nothing anyone could do to protect Paul, or Carver, from the fire of that truth.

But Carver didn't leave right away for the Kave estate. He stayed in the stifling phone booth near the tennis club and called McGregor first.

After a series of switches from one headquarters line to another, there was a muted clatter on the other end of the connection, and McGregor came to the phone.

"I think Laura talked to Adam Kave," Carver told him.

"Balls! How sure are you?"

"Very. She stormed out of my place last week furious with me. Did everything but yell back that she was going to the Kave family. And just now I got a message on my answering machine: Adam Kave wants to see me as soon as I can get to the estate. He sounded hot as one of his barbecued kraut dogs."

"Used all your charm on your ex-wife, did you?" McGregor said nastily.

"Charmed her about like you did. She gave me the impression she didn't like or trust you. Mentioned something about her skin crawling."

"Ah, she's being coy." But McGregor was wisecracking absently; there was an edge of intense concern in his voice. He was the type who calmed himself or bought time with his own inane patter while he got his balance. It didn't take him long to regain equilibrium. "Hey, Carver, why don't you avoid old Adam for a while?"

"No. I'm driving out now to talk to him."

"Why meet trouble halfway?"

"Because it's trouble I caused."

"Find ethics or something?"

"Never could shake them, I guess."

"It's people like you cause most of the problems in this world."

"Doesn't some of the evidence against Paul Kave make you stop and think?" Carver asked.

"Stop and think and you're lost," McGregor said. "Trick is to keep moving and thinking at the same time."

"If Paul—"

McGregor interrupted. "Don't lay this bullshit on me, Carver. I don't wanna hear it. I mean it!"

"What *do* you want?"

"For you to stay away from Adam Kave."

"Sorry," Carver said, "can't do that. However bent the arrangement is, he's still my client. I should talk to him, tell him what he oughta know."

McGregor lost his patience. "Why the fuck call me if you're gonna do what you want anyway? No, wait a goddamned minute! It's not that you shouldn't have phoned, come to think of it. I got something to say in this matter, way I see it."

"We don't see it the same way. Can't you get it straight Adam Kave's on to us? I thought I owed you enough to inform you what's happening, so you don't get caught by surprise."

"You mean when the chief struts in here and rips my rank off? Chews my poor cop's ass and puts me back in a uniform and a patrol car?"

"It'll be more than that, and you know it."

"Don't ever bet on me taking a fall, stranger. You'd lose the farm on that one."

Carver felt his features alter in a slight smile. "You're such a survivor."

"Way I figure it, too. I'm still here; there are plenty who ain't."

"You set this up with the Kave family, remember? You recommended me."

"Nope. Don't remember a thing about that. Somebody record that conversation? For that matter, who the hell is this? Do I know you? Do I? Hey, let's have a look at your American Express card, see if I recognize the name."

This new tack didn't really surprise Carver. It was possible, he realized; McGregor could play dumb, toss out angry denials, and slip through unscathed in his quest for job and rank retention and even promotion. He was a convincing guy in his sick way. And his arrangement with Carver couldn't be proved. People like McGregor learned early how to obscure their tracks, and got better at it as life wore on. Takers who were also keepers.

"I won't mention to Adam that you know who I really am," Carver said.

"I *don't* know who you really are, pal. Know your name, is all. Heard you was a troublemaker. Maybe went a little whacky after your son got baked. Hell, can't blame you for that. But I tell you, it gets thin. Time passes, you gotta try and forget instead of getting snagged on what happened. Attempting to stir up some shit is all you're doing."

"What do you think, the phones are bugged there at police headquarters?" Carver said. "Jesus, can't you talk straight?"

"It's your hearing ain't quite straight," McGregor said. "I got work to do now, pal, so call somebody else and tell 'em your smoke-dreams. You on booze or drugs, fella? You talk like your brain's lost some circuits." He was rolling now, laying out grounds for denial and letting Carver know the new rules. That's what this conversation had become about, letting Carver know.

"Listen, McGregor—"

"Sorry, dumb fuck, I'm not so lonely I gotta pass the time with a crank caller."

"You must be. You've got no friends."

But McGregor had hung up. The first step in taking on a new and innocent attitude. Blending back into the bureaucracy. He'd be good at it.

Carver left the cramped, ovenlike phone booth and limped across the pavement toward his car, which by now would also be sizzling in the sun. In each direction on the highway, heat vapor rose shimmering and gave the illusion of wetness on the flat concrete. As he neared the Olds, a small lizard regarded him warily, then darted into green-tinted shadows and became instantly invisible.

Carver wished he were as adaptable. But then, what kind of life was it if you were a reptile?

Ask McGregor.

CHAPTER 31

Adam Kave himself appeared at the door and wordlessly ushered Carver through pseudo-Spain and into the large room where Mel Bingham and Dewitt had fought. The place was messy; apparently the maid hadn't come in today from Fort Lauderdale. There were still a few drops of Dewitt's blood on the rug; they were dark brown now.

Adam walked to the French doors and carefully closed and latched them, as if someone might be lurking on the grounds and overhear the conversation. Maybe he had something there; the Kave family seemed to attract the bizarre. Such as an investigator working for and against them.

Carver was surprised to see that Adam looked as if he'd been drinking heavily. The flesh of his face was sagging. Even his intense dark eyes seemed oddly elongated. They were also very bloodshot. His black hair was slicked back carelessly and stood out in oily tufts behind his ears. He was wearing blue pinstripe suit pants, a wrinkled white shirt, and a red silk tie that looked as if it had been knotted in the dark. There was a tremulous quality to his wide, steel-trap jaw that evoked in Carver the special pity reserved for the strong gone weak.

Adam knew how to drive to the point, however. He faced Carver and said, "You're a deceitful bastard." His voice was even huskier than usual but it was somewhat slurred, lacking its customary force.

Carver moved to the black leather sofa and sat down. The cushions hissed beneath him as he settled in. He sank lower

than he'd anticipated and felt constricted and immobilized
by the soft upholstery. He waited for Adam to talk out the
emotion that was obviously pulsating and pressuring within
him. On the credenza were an empty bottle of Cutty Sark
and a clear glass with half-melted ice floating in diluted
amber liquid. The room was quiet. The ocean breaking
rhythmically on the beach outside sounded like labored
breathing.

Adam paced three steps to his left, three to his right,
almost as in a ritualistic dance, and squared off again at
Carver. "Your former wife came to see me. She told me
about the way you tricked me. About the shitty deal you
made with that police detective, McGregor. He knew who
you were all along." Kave slammed his right fist into his
left palm so hard it had to bruise, but he gave no indication
of pain; the effects of expensive Scotch. "By God, I'll have
his ass for this! Both your asses!"

"You'll find McGregor's covered his," Carver said.

"And you haven't?"

"No. I guess, under the circumstances, I don't care
enough about it."

Adam was wringing his powerful hands now, flexing and
unflexing them. He felt strong. He could wrench the lid off
any stuck jar. "You want revenge," he said, staring down
at the floor. "That's all you were after from the beginning.
That was the plan. Eye-for-an-eye fanaticism. So appeal-
ingly simple, it must seem to you. You want to kill Paul,
the way you think he killed your son."

"It began that way," Carver admitted.

"Ah! But now you have your doubts?"

"Some."

"Of course! You think he's innocent and you want to
help him!" The slurred voice was thick with irony. Adam
shook his head slowly. "More lies. Ha! Know what,
Carver! I think you're wriggling on the hook and trying to
keep your investigator's license. What passes for your
professional reputation."

"I don't care about that," Carver said. "It's just that
certain things I learned while searching for Paul don't fit

tight. Never really have, only I was too blind and deaf to realize it. Pieces from some other puzzle have accumulated.''

Interested despite his anger, Adam relaxed somewhat and dropped his hands to his sides. ''Example?'' he snapped, some of the old command back in his bullfrog voice.

''The accelerant—what was used to start the fires and keep them burning. Why this mixture of naphtha and chemicals, when plain old gasoline or kerosene would have been just as deadly? And if the object was to cause maximum suffering, there must be other, less traceable ways to make flammable liquid gelatinous, ways using common, over-the-counter products. I think an amateur chemist like Paul would have known them. Why a homemade flame-thrower in the first place? It'd be easy and effective enough simply to throw a can or jar of flammable liquid on a victim, then follow it with a lighted match. And would Paul be careless enough to use his car for the murders, and later leave evidence of his involvement to be found in the trunk? A schizophrenic operating under delusions of persecution isn't necessarily illogical in every way. Especially one as intelligent as Paul. And his symptoms were under control; he was rational enough to request his medicine, and Nadine took it to him.''

Adam removed his squarish, silver-rimmed glasses from his shirt pocket, polished them absently with his tie, then slipped them back in the pocket instead of placing them on the bridge of his nose. As if he'd decided not to look closely at Carver after all. ''You're right,'' he said, ''Paul isn't stupid or careless, whatever his frame of mind.''

''You don't have to be either of those things to be set up.''

Adam rubbed his wide jaw and squinted dubiously at Carver. He had a straw to clutch. And how he wanted to believe! But he knew the potential pain of false hope. He was reluctant to embrace what couldn't be proved, and Carver didn't blame him. This affair had already produced enough agony. What had Jerry Gepman said at his door in

Chattanooga? *Some families, tragedy just haunts them. Won't let up.*

"The murders were more elaborate than was necessary," Carver said.

"Do you seriously think someone burned those people to death just so Paul would be blamed?" Adam asked. More of a challenge than a question. *Prove it,* the blood-rimmed dark eyes pleaded, while the curbstone jaw remained unyielding.

"I don't know. Who'd have reason to do this to him?"

Adam thought for a moment, then shrugged. "No one, I'm sure. Oh, he inspired some petty grudges with his occasional temper tantrums, but not to the degree anyone would want to do *this*. It would take an insane person to commit murder so Paul could be blamed. No, no, it doesn't make sense strategically at all. Even to someone with a sick mind."

A sick mind, Carver thought, remembering his conversation with McGregor. "Maybe there's a strategy at work neither of us understands," he said.

"Whether there is or not," Adam said, "I want you to stay out of the matter. I can't and won't accept what you've done. I'm going to do everything possible to see to it you never practice your sorry profession in Florida again. Or anywhere else where I can stop you. You've got my solemn promise."

"I don't suppose you could understand how it feels to lose your only son to a maniac with a makeshift flame-thrower," Carver said. But he wondered. Nick Fanning had said Adam loved his son; it was proving true.

"It's *my* son I'm thinking about. And my daughter. I want you to stop following her."

"Huh? Nadine thinks I'm watching her?"

"Mel Bingham saw you spying on her at the tennis club and told her about it."

"How much do you actually know about Bingham?"

"Enough to believe him."

"What about Nick Fanning? How long's he been with your company?"

"What significance does any of this have?" Adam asked.

"Maybe none, maybe a lot."

"It doesn't matter to you," Adam said. "You're off the case. And I'll see that it was your last."

There was nothing more to say. At least nothing to which Adam would respond. He was staring down cold-eyed at Carver, waiting for him to leave. He seemed to have recovered most of his sobriety and was plainly glad the unpleasant conversation was ended.

Carver levered himself to a standing position with the cane, then turned and started for the door.

"You should have listened to your former wife," Adam said. "She had your best interest at heart."

Without moving his legs or the cane, Carver twisted his torso and glared back at Adam. Then he limped from the room.

Outside, in the shade of the portico, he was about to lower himself into the Olds when a soft voice called his name.

He looked up to see Elana Kave beneath the palm trees near the house. She was wearing a silky gray flowing robe and was barefoot. She glided lightly through brilliant sun and into shadow to stand beside Carver. He couldn't hear her feet on the driveway. The top was down on the Olds; he took the strain off his good leg and finished lowering his body in behind the steering wheel. He closed the door slowly, with only a muted double-click, and stared at Elana. She looked haggard and very sad. It deepened her fragile beauty into something soul-wrenching. There was a burning in her eyes smaller but brighter than the sun.

"Paul's innocent," she said quietly. "I know it."

"How do you know?" Carver asked. He found it difficult to look directly at her, sensing that he was seeing the uncanny flare of life preceding imminent death. She was suffering in soul and flesh, and he felt guilty and soiled at being a part of it.

"I'm his mother," she said simply. "I'm—" She stopped

herself from saying more, as if the words once uttered would deflate the will that kept her alive.

"What is it?" Carver asked gently. "What?"

"I can't tell you. I'm sorry, but I can't."

He felt sweat bead on his forehead though it was cool there in the shadows.

She sensed the sudden compassion in him and smiled eerily. Maybe winning him over at least temporarily was all she'd wanted. It suggested hope, and she existed on hope and not much more. She turned and floated back across the patch of bright sunlight and into the shadows of the palm trees. Then she disappeared around the corner of the house without glancing back.

He sat transfixed, staring at the empty space she'd occupied.

Then birds started nattering again and crickets resumed chirping. The sea continued sighing on the beach. A gull screamed in the endless blue distance beyond the house. The world back to normal.

His encounter with Elana had been so brief and unsettling, Carver drove away wondering if it had been something he'd imagined in the heat.

"How did Adam Kave find out about you?" Edwina asked that night in their dark bedroom in Del Moray.

Carver lay beside her and stared at the blue-black rectangle of the window, watching the curtains swaying in the ocean breeze. The scent of the sea was in the room. "Laura told him."

Edwina didn't ask the questions she might have. She could live not knowing the answers.

She said, "I don't like Laura."

"Laura did what she thought she had to. Can't blame her for that."

"That's not what I blame her for. Anyway, she was wrong in going to Adam Kave."

"She was," Carver agreed.

"You have this sick streak of moderation where Laura's

concerned. I'd have thought you'd be mad enough to choke her.''

''I was, for a while.''

''Uh-huh. Then you got all philosophical.'' She stared off to the side in the dimness. The ocean was loud in its timeless assault on the beach. ''Goddamned ex-wives!''

''You're one, and you're kinda nice.''

''Are you planning to sit back now and wait for the ax to drop on your neck?'' Edwina asked.

''No. I'll finish what I began.''

''Good. That's what life's about, finishing what we start.''

''Sometimes.''

The bedsprings groaned. She rolled onto her side, close to him, and rested a cool hand on his chest. ''Begin something now and finish it,'' she suggested.

He did.

CHAPTER 32

The next night, Carver found a different vantage point to watch the garage exit of Dewitt's apartment building.

He sat sipping bitter black coffee from McDonald's and listening to soft music on the Olds's radio. Sade was sighing her bluesy, velvet version of love. The car's canvas top was up, but he had both front windows cranked down so a breeze pressed through the interior. It was 11:00 P.M. It had rained that afternoon, and though the temperature was still in the eighties the air smelled fresh, carrying the scent of the untended flower bed bordering the low stone wall around the apartment grounds. In the swimming pool a lone teen-age girl frolicked like a carefree mermaid, splashing and submerging, then surfacing to tread water with her head and shoulders above the rippling surface. Now and then she'd shake her long hair and hurl drops of water glistening in the pale and shimmering artificial light bouncing off the pool. Carver hoped someone had cleaned the water and added chemicals, or the mermaid might contract anything from athlete's foot to trench mouth.

Nadine and Dewitt had eaten supper at a steakhouse downtown, then stopped for a while at something called Roll-the-Dice Corner Lounge. There was a mural of a huge pair of dice showing snake eyes painted on the front brick wall near the entrance. The place seemed to be one huge speaker cabinet from which hard rock music pulsed. It made Carver's head hurt even where he was parked halfway down the block.

Dewitt had finally driven Nadine back to where her car

was parked at his dealership, and she'd followed him in her sleek red Datsun to his apartment. There was no indication that either of them had been drinking; they both drove straight and true.

They'd been inside the apartment since just after ten, maybe trying to recover their hearing. The lights were still burning, lessening the likelihood that any of what Lloyd Van Meter called Girl and Boy Stuff was going on.

Occasionally Carver chanced leaving his parking space to drive to the McDonald's two blocks away, either to relieve his bladder or to get another cup of coffee to help keep him alert. The two things seemed to be related.

He was on his third cup, and the inside of his mouth tasted flat and stale. The coffee itself was beginning to taste flat and stale. It made his teeth ache.

The garage's wide door twitched and then started to roll up, tugged by an automatic opener. Pale fluorescent light spilled out onto Low Citrus Drive. Carver placed his foam cup of coffee in a plastic holder he had stuck with adhesive on the dashboard. He waited to see what would emerge from the garage.

It was a gray Cadillac, with the darkly tinted windows that seemed almost mandatory for luxury cars in Florida. Carver had learned a lot about the building and its tenants, and he knew the car belonged to the gem dealer on the second floor.

He relaxed and watched the overhead door glide down as the Caddy made a smooth left turn and drove past him. The last glimmer of light disappeared from the pavement in front of the door. The street was dark and quiet again. He reached for his coffee.

At eleven-thirty the garage door rose again. Carver glanced up and saw that the lights were still on in Dewitt's apartment, but he wedged his half-full coffee cup in the plastic holder and sat ready.

Dewitt's dark blue Jaguar four-door sedan pulled slowly from the garage and picked up speed as it rolled toward the corner. In the wash of illumination from the streetlight, Carver could see only one figure in the car's front seat.

The right side of the seat!

Then he remembered the Jag was imported from England, and the steering wheel was on the right. Dewitt was alone. The smooth snarl of the car's turbo-charged engine drifted back to him as Dewitt played the accelerator.

Nadine was in the apartment by herself. Maybe she and Dewitt had had an argument. Maybe Dewitt was driving to pick up Paul and bring him back to see Nadine. Maybe Dewitt was going out for ice. Carver cautioned himself; it was easy to make much of nothing.

He settled back again to wait. The breeze picked up, bringing more fragrance of flowers, mingled with the noxious residue of the departed Jag's exhaust fumes.

Fifteen minutes later the gleaming gray Cadillac came back and disappeared down the shallow ramp into the garage, like an exotic craft returning to its mother ship.

The garage door stayed open. Nadine's red Datsun darted out and screeched into a sharp left turn, following the course of the Jaguar.

Carver sloshed warm coffee onto his hand as he jammed the cup into the plastic holder. He started the Olds, crammed the shift lever into Drive, and fell in behind the Datsun, hanging well back.

Nadine knew she'd been watched, and even if she'd talked with Adam and gotten the impression Carver was off the case, she might be warier than usual. Paul possessed an I.Q. of over 140, but Nadine might be ahead of him. It was difficult to know; youth had a way of overriding intelligence.

Through the Datsun's rear louvers Carver saw that Nadine was alone. On the left side of the car this time. He smiled. No momentary surprises.

Keeping several cars between them, Carver followed her out of town. The Datsun had a dim left taillight and was easy to track from a distance. Nadine turned north on Highway 95.

He thought she might be going home, but she soared past the Hillsboro turnoff, holding a steady seventy-five. The

Olds, with its prehistoric powerful V-8 engine, kept pace easily a quarter of a mile back.

There was very little traffic on the wide highway. The car's tires whined on still-warm pavement. Carver relaxed and rested an arm on the metal window frame, feeling the cool wind pound at his bare, crooked elbow. The rush of air whirled in the Olds, ballooning the canvas top and howling out the unzipped back window. The speedometer needle might as well have been painted on seventy-five. The Olds slipped into that automotive high-speed trance that only big cars can achieve.

Nadine drove for about an hour, then cut west at Palm Beach Gardens and got on Florida's Turnpike. An uneasy feeling started at the nape of Carver's neck and spread coldly. This wasn't Nadine's normal behavior. She was on her way somewhere out of the ordinary tonight, in a hurry even for her, and that could spell Paul Kave. Paul Kave, the kid the odds and the law said suffered from a compulsion to burn people to death.

And the odds and the law might be right. Carver still wasn't sure about Paul, despite what he'd told Adam to try to get Adam to back off and give him room and time to operate. Paul was still the number one possibility as the killer of Carver's son.

Carver reached over and pulled his old Colt automatic from the glove compartment and checked the action. He placed a hand over the top of the gun and yanked backward on smooth steel; a round snapped from the clip into the chamber.

Just below Orlando, Nadine exited the turnpike at 192 and drove west toward Kissimmee. The sensation on the back of Carver's neck grew colder. He was beginning to suspect where she was going, and it didn't figure. Why would Nadine drive to see family black sheep Emmett Kave?

Unless Paul was at Emmett's place and wanted to talk with both of them before deciding on a meeting with Carver.

That was it, Carver figured. *Must* be it!

The low red Datsun veered onto an off-ramp, geared and

growled neatly through a series of turns, and Carver found himself in Emmett Kave's neighborhood. Oddly, the area was even more depressing at night. Flat streets, low houses, rusted cars and pickup trucks. The occasional glint of a discarded beer can glaring like a weary eye from the weeds. Glimpses of poverty caused the imagination to conjure up exaggerated pictures of despair.

Then he was on Jupiter Avenue, Emmett's street.

Carver braked the Olds and pulled to the curb half a block from Emmett's run-down house. He watched as the Datsun's brake lights flared, and it slowed and right-turned into Emmett's driveway, bouncing as it rolled over the bump at the sidewalk. It edged up near the front porch and stopped, then its headlights winked out.

The driver's-side door opened.

Joel Dewitt stood up out of the car, raised his arms, and stretched.

Carver reached for the cold cup of coffee, fumbled it, and dropped it to the Olds's floor. He felt some of the cool liquid splash onto his right sock at the line of his shoe. He ignored the spilled coffee and kept his gaze nailed on Joel Dewitt, even though the inside of the Olds reeked of the stuff. Hot night air closed in on the motionless car.

Damn Nadine! he thought. She'd fooled him, taken Dewitt's car to meet Paul, while Dewitt, in her car, had deliberately misled Carver.

And Carver had snapped at the bait and devoured it and half the line in his eagerness.

But no. Dewitt had left the apartment too long after Nadine to be a decoy. He would, in fact, have left *first* if he'd wanted to trick Carver. Nadine had simply borrowed the Jaguar to throw Carver off the trail; possibly Dewitt hadn't even given her permission or known about it until it was too late to stop her. Dewitt, even without a key, would have had no trouble starting Nadine's car; every dealer knew how to hot-wire an ignition. Nadine was an independent girl.

One who might be anywhere tonight. With her brother.

As Carver watched, Emmett's yellow porch light came

on, flickering as if the bulb were loose. Dewitt slowly
strolled around to the Datsun's trunk, or what passed for a
trunk, and raised the rear deck. He bent low and pulled
something out of the trunk, then slammed the deck lid back
down and carried the object toward the front porch, where
Emmett was waiting now beneath the yellow light with the
door open. The light had attracted a large moth that was
flitting zanily around the porch. Though it was late, Emmett
was fully dressed in bib overalls and a plaid work shirt with
the sleeves rolled above the elbows.

And suddenly Carver knew for sure that, while Nadine
might have taken Dewitt's car to get past him, Dewitt hadn't
realized what she was doing or had an inkling of her
purpose. The fact that his car instead of hers was missing
from the garage had surprised him. He didn't suspect that
Carver had followed the Datsun from Fort Lauderdale,
thinking the driver was Nadine.

And Nadine wouldn't dream where Dewitt had gone after
she'd left the apartment. Or why.

In the unsteady stream of light from the house, even from
half a block's distance, Carver recognized the bulky, cylindrical object cradled in Dewitt's arms.

A scuba diver's air tank.

Dominoes fell one after another in Carver's mind,
arranging themselves in a comprehensible pattern, revealing
the landscape behind them.

Making clear what should have been obvious to him long
before now.

He snatched up the Colt from beside him on the seat and
tucked it beneath his belt. Then he quietly slid out of the
car.

He limped toward Emmett Kave's house, keeping his
cane's rubber tip on firm concrete in the dark. His shadow,
a twisted, potent thing, writhed grotesquely before him like
a tentative yet eager advance scout.

CHAPTER 33

Carver stayed away from the pool of light cast by the yellow porch bulb and made his way around the side of the house. He checked the windows, but Emmett had all the shades drawn. The blank glass panes gave back only the night. From inside came the drone of voices, but he couldn't make out what they were saying.

For several minutes he crouched beneath the window where the voices were loudest. Then he gave up trying to interpret them and, as quietly as possible, moved along the dirt-and-gravel driveway toward the dilapidated garage with the swaybacked roof. Ahead of him a black cat with white paws, and gleaming eyes like mysterious twin moons, glanced at him and then padded silently into the bushes.

Ivy had climbed wildly up the near side of the garage, clinging to checked paint and bare, rotted wood. Carver could smell the age and the dry corruption. There was a stone path to a bulky and crooked side door with a thick piece of rough plywood nailed over what once had been a window. The persistent vines had been cleared away from the area of the door, and moonlight gleamed off new metal—a heavy hasp and large brass padlock.

Carver limped around to the garage's wide front doors and discovered a similar hasp and lock. Heavy-duty hardware.

He moved along the far side of the garage to the back and found a spot where the wood was particularly rotted. Stooping on his good leg, he inserted the cane into the space between two boards and pried back and forth. He had help from termites; the two boards gave like cardboard and crumbled rather than splintered. Carver wedged his fingers between them, yanked once, and rusted nails creaked and gave way and a board pulled free.

He pressed his face close and peered into the musty garage, and was hit by the stench of cat urine. He remembered the feline prowler with the pale paws.

There was enough moonlight filtering through the cracks in the garage to reveal an old but shiny blue Lincoln sedan with a white top; a jewel in an unlikely setting.

"So what's inside?" a voice whispered behind him.

Carver's head jerked around so quickly it hurt his neck.

He knew immediately the identity of the youth crouched behind him. The long, sensitive face. The mussed blond hair. The firm jaw contrasting with unfocused dark eyes. Poet's eyes. Frightened eyes. Eyes of the hunted.

Paul Kave.

Carver's heart was slamming hard and he was having difficulty breathing. He planted the cane and pulled himself to his feet.

"What's inside?" Paul repeated in a voice more curious than demanding.

"Look for yourself," Carver growled. He wasn't quite sure how to treat his longtime quarry's sudden presence. This was something Carver hadn't figured on, this three-dimensional Paul so close to him; not separated from him by a thick pane of glass or the distance of deception, but here, speaking to him, as human as Carver himself. It was goddamned unsettling. Almost paralyzing.

Paul bent down easily and peered through the space left by the pried-out board. He was wearing faded jeans and a blue or green T-shirt that said *Buccaneers* across the chest in black letters. He might have been any kid roaming the Florida resort areas looking for girls. That was the thing about Paul that threw Carver—the boy's apparent normalcy. Except for the lost look in his eyes, and the faint but unmistakable scent of desperation that clung to him the way it lingered on junkies and drifters.

He glanced up at Carver and stood, not seeming surprised

at finding a near-duplicate of his car in the garage. Carver knew Paul was finally ahead of the game. It had to happen, given that he'd survived this long. Paul had access to most of the knowledge Carver had, plus what Nadine had told him. He'd analyzed the same information and reached the same general conclusion. That lofty I.Q. at work. But what did he have in mind now?

"Why are you here, Paul?"

"When I talked to Nadine earlier tonight things clicked in my mind. She told me what you'd said to my dad, about how some of what's happened didn't fit. I decided someone was trying to set me up. Uncle Emmett had to have told you about my being at the Mermaid Motel in Orlando; he was the only one who knew I was there. And I remembered how he felt about my father. And mother."

"Your mother?"

"Years ago Uncle Emmett tried to rape her. Didn't anyone tell you about that?"

"No," Carver said. "Not the sort of dirty linen a family's likely to air out." He understood now the depth of Adam's hatred for his brother. And Emmett's intense jealousy of Adam.

"Uncle Emmett said it was all a big mistake, that my mom and dad misunderstood what had happened and he was the one who was wronged. I believed him. Up till now."

Carver thought about a younger Emmett. And a younger Elana. What must she have been before age and illness had worn her down? The wife that was her possessive husband's treasure.

"Why did my father hire you, Mr. Carver?"

"To find you before the police did. To protect you from harm."

"That's not easy to believe."

"Doesn't make it less true. Where's Nadine?"

"Where I left her, I guess. Where I sneaked away from her with Dewitt's car in Fort Lauderdale. Hated to trick her like that, but I needed a car. I thought I should drive here and talk to Uncle Emmett about this. I was surprised to see your car parked down the block. I turned off my headlights and stopped across the street, and got a glimpse of you sneaking up the driveway. But what's Nadine's car doing parked out front?''

"Joel Dewitt drove it here. He went inside the house about twenty minutes ago—carrying a scuba diver's air tank.''

Paul was quick, all right. He put out a palm and leaned hard against the garage, as if he needed support to stand. Carver thought he saw the old garage sway. He waited while Paul assembled all the available pieces and got most of the picture. Insects droned nearby and racketed in the field beyond the back fence. Something tiny and brittle that flew very fast bounced off Carver's forehead and buzzed angrily into the night.

When Paul pushed away from the rotted wood and stood up straight, he said, "Why, Mr. Carver?" He didn't mean, why was Dewitt here with the scuba tank? Why was the old Lincoln hidden in the garage? He meant, why was Dewitt involved in this at all?

"I'm not sure. Emmett or Dewitt can tell us that.''

Paul's jaw was thrust forward. He looked as fierce as Nadine in the final set of a tennis match, and at the same time he resembled Emmett and Adam in a way that was uncanny. Reaction had set in. The Kave blood was up. "Damn it, Mr. Carver, let's go ask!''

He dug in a heel and took a long stride toward the driveway.

Carver hooked his arm with the crook of the cane and dragged him back. "Think it out first," he said. "Do this my way, Paul.''

"They tried to make me out a murderer!'' Paul sputtered, knocking the cane away with such force that Carver almost lost his grip on it. The kid was powerful. He'd become strong the way Carver had—all that swimming in choppy water.

"They killed my son," Carver reminded him.

That calmed Paul somewhat. He squared his shoulders and let out a long breath, managed to unclench his teeth.

"Yeah, I know they did. Your way, then, Mr. Carver. Time for the cops, I guess."

Carver knew it was, but he said, "Not just yet."

Paul looked closely at him and understood. A balance had shifted and their roles had changed. They both sensed it; they'd spent so much time trying to think each other's thoughts that a subtle telepathy had developed. It was Paul now who must be the moderating influence. And Paul knew it.

"I think I oughta call the law, Mr. Carver."

"Sure," Carver said. "You can drive to a phone and do that while I keep watch on things here." A breeze whispered through the yard, molding his sweat-soaked shirt to his back. Unexpectedly cool, but for only a moment. Then the heat enfolded him again like an unwelcome lover with its suffocating embrace.

Paul squinted at him. "You're not going into the house, are you?"

Carver asked himself the same question and wasn't sure of the answer. But he said, "No, Paul, I'll just make sure Dewitt and Emmett don't leave."

Paul didn't know whether to believe him, but had little choice. Carver watched him wrestle with the idea of driving away to find a phone. A car passed on Jupiter Avenue, making a swishing sound as its headlights ghosted through the night. A lonely sound.

"You're supposed to be the head case here," Carver reminded him with a tight smile, "not me."

"So I've been reading and hearing on the news."

"Get to a phone, Paul. It'll be all right."

"Okay. Sure." Still dubious.

Carver nodded toward the street, a signal to move, and they started down the driveway.

When they'd almost reached the rear corner of the house, a light came on in a basement window, spilling faint light outside.

In silent agreement, Carver and Paul both crept to the window and peered in through its dirty glass.

It was a half-basement of the type developers once sold

as tornado shelters. During the hurricane season, tornadoes often ripped through central Florida, amazing in their unpredictability and destruction. The walls were thick poured concrete, stained by cloudlike patterns of dampness.

Dewitt and Emmett were standing near an ancient wooden workbench with a bare light bulb dangling on a cord above it. A cylindrical tank, and a tangle of hoses and gauges, rested on the workbench. Emmett had the scuba tank valve unscrewed and was fitting a brass hose connection to it. The hose led to what looked like an ordinary cleaning-fluid can. Beside the bench were a number of glass jugs and square, gallon-size cans bearing chemical symbols and naphtha-based household-solvent labels.

Carver realized Dewitt and Emmett were charging the scuba tank with propellant and homemade napalm to commit another murder. To burn someone the way they'd killed his son.

He thought about the searing pain that must seem to last forever, and then the endlessness of death. He *felt* the pain!

Comprehension, and a rage he never dreamed would be so overwhelming, wrested control of him. It was as if something silently exploded within him, wiping out reason. Obliterating almost everything except his desire to strike back at the people who'd scorched the flesh he'd created. Images of death and horror tumbled through his mind. But even through his consuming emotion he was recalling the layout of the house, acting the good cop, the one Desoto and McGregor had described.

Beside him, Paul felt the heat of his building fury. Carver pulled the automatic from his belt, aware of the front sight snagging for a moment on the leather. Paul's hand was on his shoulder, clutching desperately. The boy was afraid now, like any twenty-year-old staring at the front end of violence and death, unable to comprehend something terrible and imminent that had taken on its own will and couldn't be stopped. "Mr. Carver, for God's sake, don't—"

Carver shoved Paul away so violently that the boy stumbled back and went sprawling into the hedge on the other side of the driveway. He saw Paul struggle to get up, catch the look Carver gave him, then settle back down on his elbows. Paul's dark eyes were huge pools of helpless resignation and horror.

Too much noise might have been made already; Carver turned and limped fast toward the rickety back porch.

When his cane thumped on the porch boards he gave up any thought of silence and opted for suddenness and surprise. He used the crook of the cane to smash in a back-door window, reached through and yanked a bolt lock free, then flung the door open and charged through the kitchen toward the basement stairs.

He knew Emmett and Dewitt would hear his cane clattering on the linoleum above them and be ready.

He didn't care.

CHAPTER 34

The door to the basement stairs was hanging open. Carver hurled himself through it and half fell down the steep wooden steps. His knuckles hit the banister and his cane bounced and racketed down the stairs ahead of him.

Dewitt had a revolver and was firing at him, blue eyes not startled but wide and cold and calm; for some reason Carver couldn't hear the shots. Then something snapped past the side of his head. He saw the banister miraculously splinter beside him. His own arm and hand, holding the Colt automatic, were extended, acting of their own volition. He was returning fire, feeling the solid kick of the gun and watching his arm jerk upward and settle back with each squeeze of the trigger.

Something exploded behind Carver's right ear. He thought he'd been shot, but he fell to the side and saw a grim-faced McGregor crouched on the steps above him, gun drawn and blasting away at Emmett and Dewitt—McGregor, who must have been keeping tabs on Carver personally in the absence of Gibbons. Like the goddamned O.K. Corral, Carver thought inanely. He glimpsed more dark, tumultuous figures behind McGregor. On the stairs. Above them, in the kitchen outside the basement door. Everything seemed to be moving unnaturally fast but with vivid clarity. Someone was screaming; a man's voice. Not in pain, but to fill the lungs and heart with something other than fear.

The basement lights blinked out, but the firing continued. Glass shattered. Carver felt McGregor shove past him. He bumped the stairwell wall hard, feeling a shock tingle up from his elbow. The heavy report of a riot gun sounded from farther up the stairs. Pellets roared past startlingly close; Carver thought he felt one pluck at his sleeve, like someone trying to get his attention.

"Jesus!" McGregor screamed. "Cut that out!"

There was a *whump!* of flame at the far basement wall. Another burst—this time a large fireball. One of the bullets had sparked something flammable. The naphtha compound.

In the eerie orange glow, Carver saw Emmett scampering toward a corner, on fire, slapping at his clothes, moving with the agility of a teen-ager. Even his hair was burning. What was happening couldn't be real; special effects like in a movie, right? Had to be! Dewitt was crawling toward the stairs, shouting something Carver couldn't understand. *Real—it was real!*

Finally McGregor's voice pierced the semidarkness and the acrid stench of smoke. "Out! Everybody fuckin' out!"

Carver let himself bounce down the stairs, beneath the lowering pall of dark smoke, and grabbed Dewitt's arm. With his free hand he slammed a fist into Dewitt, who merely whined and coughed and went limp. No fight left. Nothing. There was a clamor of footfalls on the stairs. McGregor suddenly had Dewitt's other arm. Without speaking, he and Carver dragged Dewitt toward the steps. The flames were crackling now and the smoke was soup thick. Emmett was no longer visible.

Carver somehow found his cane in the flickering glare. He clutched Dewitt's shirt in his right hand, and with his left he extended the cane and hooked it over the back edge of a wooden step and pulled while he propelled himself upward with his good leg. McGregor had a hand under Dewitt's armpit and was working frantically to get out of the basement. Carver was remotely aware of sirens screaming outside, some of them deafening, some growling to silence nearby so that other shrill, singsong cries could cut through the night.

He was ahead of Dewitt now, pulling desperately, ripping Dewitt's shirt, tearing his own fingernails. McGregor was snarling up at him like a mindless rabid animal, pushing both Dewitt and Carver forward. Carver felt Dewitt's body mash his good leg against a step, bruising bone just below the knee. Then the leg was free, digging for leverage. Right now the sharp pain was a reminder of life, a spur to action.

The black smoke rolled thicker and started up the stairs behind them, as if suddenly it had taken on malevolence and purpose and sensed a dark victory.

Then they were on the smooth, hard linoleum. Carver was surprised to find that the kitchen floor was warm.

Legs and feet surrounded them. Scuffed shoes, shiny shoes. Someone grabbed Carver beneath the arms and lifted, shoved and bullied him toward the gaping back door. Carver resisted, though he didn't understand why. There were multicolored lights outside, flashing, revolving, casting dancing, strangely hued shadows from another dimension, another life where nothing had depth or weight or solid meaning. But it was the real world out there—not here in the burning house.

Carver sucked in smoke, retched and spat. The whole house must be blazing to create so much smoke. There was a thick, sweet stench in the haze that he recognized. Nausea almost doubled him over. He started to retch again, then controlled it and refused to breathe, holding what little air he'd retained in his straining lungs. He didn't want to pull in any more smoke, any more of Uncle Emmett burning. His chest heaved and his heart smashed in on itself, slower but more powerfully with each beat. He absolutely refused to breathe; he was finished breathing, forever! A voice, far away, called, "Dad, Dad, Dad, Daddy, Daddy!" He was aware of his mouth involuntarily gaping wider and wider, like the house's back door to the night outside. He heard a high, rasping shriek, a harsh intake of air—Carver fighting for oxygen and life.

And suddenly he was in the clear night, slumped against the rough bark of a thick tree and breathing. Eating the air as if it were spun sugar at a carnival. Sweet, sweet breathing.

Stronger now than he'd ever been, he shoved away from the tree.

He was standing in a whirling, dizzying world that had gained substance and reality. Standing straight and tall again without his cane.

No, he was falling . . .

Oh God, how far?

CHAPTER 35

The tugging Carver had felt at his sleeve turned out to be three pellets from a twelve-gauge riot gun fired by a Kissimmee police officer behind him on Emmett's basement steps. The pellets had entered at an angle, two of them lodging just below the skin's surface, the other penetrating about an inch. The two near the surface the doctor had removed. The other one he was going to leave in Carver in the hope that infection wouldn't occur and the pellet would eventually work its way closer to the surface, where it could be removed easily and without complication. A nurse joked with Carver about his not being able to use a compass until the steel pellet was removed. Carver didn't think magnet jokes were funny.

After treatment at the hospital emergency room, he'd spent the night in Orlando in Desoto's spare bedroom. He lay now in the harsh morning light, listening to the hum and hustle of traffic outside, grateful for the prognosis that his arm would soon return to its full range of strength and mobility. The idea of a second useless limb had frightened him badly, colored his dreams, and made him think about being at the mercy of small boys who delighted in slowly pulling the legs from insects.

The syncopated beat of Latin music drifted into the room from another part of the condo unit. Desoto had left for work, Carver knew. Must have forgotten to turn off the radio. Or maybe he left the damned thing playing all the time. That would be like him.

Carver lay quietly until the hypnotic beat threatened to

lull him back to sleep. But it was ten o'clock, and he'd slept enough. Though he had no compelling reason to rise, he struggled up to sit on the edge of the mattress. A dull ache beat through his arm, in time with the music and his heart. It was a pain he'd endure rather than take the Percodan pills the doctor had prescribed. Carver preferred to be in slight pain, but awake and with his full mental facilities.

The room he was in was small and square, with a modern dresser and a high-riser that made into a comfortable bed. The draperies had come with the unit and were a dull gold color and not thick enough to block much sun. An unframed Delacroix print hung on the wall by the bed, a curiously flat French street scene. Somewhere Desoto had picked up an appreciation of art.

Carver found his cane, got up, and reached his pants where they were draped over the back of a chair. His wallet had dropped to the carpet behind the chair, and he used the cane to slide it over to where he could pick it up. He sat back down on the bed and struggled into the pants, then he stood up and limped from the room.

The rest of the place reflected the familiar Desoto. The carpet and drapes in the living room were deep red, the furniture black vinyl, stainless steel, and laminated wood that was lacquered to a high gloss. It was expensive furniture. Desoto spent most of his salary on clothes and on his environment. A Fisher stereo system took up most of a long shelf along one wall. There was a tiny red light glowing on it, and a series of needles on illuminated dials were twitching and bobbing in time with the rhythm that throbbed from the two big speakers at the ends of the shelf. It made Carver wish he could still dance. He crossed the thick carpet to the stereo and punched plastic buttons until he found the right one. The red light winked out.

The silence in the apartment seemed to pulsate after the tango music stopped, as if the beat had permeated the air and would die hard.

Carver made his way to the bedroom door to make sure Desoto was gone. He glanced into the room. Red carpet and drapes in there, too. Another print, a large one of a fleshy nude woman reclining among some flowers. There were two gigantic speakers that were probably wired to the stereo in the living room. The dresser and headboard were black and highly lacquered like some of the living-room furniture, in a simple art deco style. There was a round water bed large enough for the moon to affect with tides. It had some kind of white fuzzy spread over it. Carver looked up and was a little surprised to see no mirror on the ceiling. The closet ran along an entire wall and was no doubt full of Desoto's elegant suits and accessories. There were mirrors everywhere except above the bed.

In a sort of awe, Carver turned away and went to the kitchen to put some coffee on to brew while he tried to take a shower and keep the dressing on his arm dry.

When he'd located the coffee and got the electric percolator going, he returned to the living room and found that Desoto had come home.

There he sat on his black and silver sofa, wearing a tailored cream-colored suit, pale blue shirt, and lavender tie with a gold clip. The condo was coolly air-conditioned, but Desoto looked as if he didn't need it; he carried his cool with him.

He said, "Thought you'd be awake, *amigo,* and you'd want to be filled in on some facts. Didn't want you calling and aggravating me at headquarters, busy as I am and pesky as you are, so I came by here."

"Champion of you," Carver said. "Want some coffee?"

"Ah, such a genial host. Nice to see you've made yourself at home."

"Have to wait—it's perking."

"Yes, I can hear."

Even the coffeepot seemed to percolate with a Latin beat; maybe it was in some way hooked up to the elaborate stereo system.

Because of the dress-shop killing and the proximity of Orlando to Kissimmee, Desoto would have access to all official, and some unofficial, information. Carver lowered himself into an uncomfortable chair that consisted of leather

slung in the middle of a contorted stainless-steel creation
and waited to hear what the lieutenant had to say.

"Dewitt is talking beautifully," Desoto told him. "Can't
shut the man up, in fact. They tend to cooperate fully in a
state that executes people more frequently than it sprays for
mosquitoes."

"Now why don't *you* talk?" Carver said impatiently.

And Desoto did.

It pretty much confirmed what Carver had figured out.

"Emmett Kave served with Dewitt's father in Korea,"
Desoto said.

Carver had thought so. He told Desoto about the group
photo on the wall in Emmett's house, and how one of the
grinning young marines in the snapshot strongly resembled
Joel Dewitt.

"Dewitt's father was killed by enemy fire not long after
the photo was taken," Desoto went on. "After returning
home, Emmett became the lover of his slain buddy's
widow, Joel Dewitt's mother. He married her, and shortly
thereafter she abandoned him and her infant son. Emmett
gave little Joel to an elderly, childless couple who agreed
to pretend they were the child's grandparents. Dewitt's
mother used her maiden name, Jones, on the motel register
when she recently returned to Florida and met Emmett,
probably lured by his promise of prospective wealth."
Desoto smiled handsomely. "You following, *amigo?*"

"I think so. Keep leading."

"Emmett hated and envied brother Adam, schemed to
obtain his riches, and years ago even apparently tried to rape
Adam's wife Elana. Adam interrupted this brotherly act and
there were harsh words; if Adam and Emmett disliked each
other before, now they hated as only brothers can.

"Anyway, *amigo,* Emmett included young Joel Dewitt,
who'd grown up just the way Emmett would have wanted,
in his latest plans to even the scales with Adam. Joel was
to court and marry Nadine. Meanwhile, Paul would be made
out to be a serial killer. Then Emmett was going to murder
Adam so Paul would appear responsible. He knew Elana
Kave had terminal cancer and would probably be dead

within the year. That'd leave Nadine—and Joel—with the money. Joel would share it with Emmett. He'd have no choice, since Emmett knew about his part in the flame-thrower murders. Partners in the worst kind of crime."

Carver squirmed in the suspended leather, listening to it creak like a new saddle. "Christ, those people, my son, were killed only to establish that Paul was a murderer."

"I'm sorry, *amigo*, but that's the way of it. It was Joel Dewitt, deliberately being mistaken for Paul, who committed the murders by fire in a way that conformed to Paul's hobbies and known bouts of paranoia and aggression. The kid was a schizophrenic; ideal to be set up. Emmett and Dewitt planted evidence all over the place. Through his car dealership, Joel even went out-of-state and bought a Lincoln that was similar to Paul's. Then he dented the right front fender so it resembled the damage to Paul's car. He obscured the plate numbers, and kept the car out of sight in Emmett's garage except for use in the murders."

Desoto stopped talking and stood up. "Coffee's done perking, *amigo*. You look like you need some badly."

He deftly straightened the creases in his suit pants, then walked into the kitchen. A minute láter he returned with two cups of sharply aromatic coffee, handed one to Carver, then sat down again on the sofa. Just the scent wafting from the cups might be enough to keep someone up all night.

Carver sipped the scalding black coffee, then waited for the caffeine to kick in or for the stuff to cause an acid attack.

"Those are imported beans from Mexico," Desoto said proudly, holding up his cup and gazing at it. "Specially grown in the mountains. Good, eh?"

"A brisk waker-upper," Carver said.

Desoto looked at him dubiously, then continued describing the world according to Joel Dewitt: "Emmett and Joel learned someone independent of the police was trying to solve the murders; they were aware of your identity even before Adam Kave hired you. They decided to use you, Carver. They weren't trying to scare you off the case; they understood your blind determination and tried to fan your rage and drive for vengeance whenever it showed signs of losing intensity. Among other methods, they committed another murder—in the Orlando dress shop—and made an attempt on Edwina's life by torching her house. They wanted you to find and kill Paul, before the police located him and maybe somehow learned he really hadn't committed the murders. There was always that slight chance if the law caught up with him first. Emmett and Dewitt knew he'd have no chance with you.''

"And after I'd killed him?" Carver asked.

"Paul's death, or his arrest, would have been Emmett's signal to murder Adam immediately, burning him so severely with the adhesive, super-hot naphtha compound that the time of death would have been impossible to determine. If Elana got in the way, she would have been killed in the same manner. Paul would surely have been blamed for their deaths.'' Desoto sat back and crossed his legs at the ankles; his black leather loafers had long tassels and tapered toes. He looked ready to go to a dance instead of a crime scene. "That's the story, *amigo*. First Emmett and Dewitt committed murder, then they planted evidence pointing to Paul Kave. Then they seized opportunity and tried to use you to kill Paul so it could never be established that he was innocent of the killings before, and even slightly after, his own death.'' Desoto shook his head sadly. "Some family, the Kaves. Could be a curse runs in their blood." He solemnly crossed himself; Carver didn't know if he was kidding. "You had this all figured out?" Desoto asked.

"Most of it," Carver said.

"You're good at your work, *amigo;* always were. Emmett, Dewitt, and McGregor counted on that.''

"What's McGregor saying?"

"Oh, he's saying a lot. He's a hero, you know. Used you to find the killer, tricked you and then saved your life. Even saved Dewitt's life so he could stand trial and justice could be served. Some cop, McGregor. Gonna get a promotion, you can bet.''

"He had himself covered all the way," Carver said softly, regretting the admiration that crept into his voice.

"Of course," Desoto said. "Politics. Something you never understood, Carver, my friend."

"A lot I didn't understand."

"Well, it's not easy to comprehend the Kaves. All that money from wieners, it had to come to no good. Know what's in those hot dogs, *amigo?*"

"Don't want to know," Carver said.

"Damned additives," Desoto said. "Things'll kill you."

He finished his coffee in a gulp, somehow without dissolving his tongue and tonsils, then placed the cup on an end table and stood up. "I'm heading back to work, dutiful civil servant that I am. You rest, eh?"

"I can't rest," Carver said. He considered making a smart-ass remark about the coffee but thought better of it. Desoto was proud of the terrible stuff.

"Guess you can't," Desoto said. "Take care of the arm then, okay, *amigo?*"

"Sure," Carver said. He gripped the cane and worked himself to his feet. "You were right most of the way," he said. "Thanks for trying to make me listen. Thanks for . . . well, just thanks. I mean that."

Desoto smiled, shrugged, and went out.

Carver limped into the kitchen and poured the rest of his coffee into the sink, listening to it hiss and gurgle down the drain. Steam rose. That should take care of any clogged pipes.

He decided to shower and get dressed. He owed Adam Kave a final report and some explanation, regardless of his status as a former client.

How would Adam receive him, after Emmett's death and the arrest of Joel Dewitt?

And the return of Paul.

CHAPTER 36

No one answered Carver's ring at the Kave estate. He limped around the side of the house, calling Adam Kave's name, getting only silence for his effort. The hot weight of the sun bore down on his shoulders; the day was heating up to record temperatures, according to the sadistic forecast out of Fort Lauderdale. He unfastened the top button of his shirt.

Then he saw the figure on the beach, a man seated facing the wide ocean with his knees drawn up. An exceptionally large wave sent foaming surf fingers scrambling up the sand, getting the man's ankles wet. He didn't budge. There was something unnatural about his perfect stillness. He reminded Carver of one of those sculptures of people in repose that kept turning up in museums and shopping centers, appearing real even down to the color and texture of their clothes.

Carver gingerly took the steep wooden steps down to the beach, then started across the sand, moving tentatively as the tip of his cane sank into softness and lent little support. The cane left a pattern of deep depressions and narrow drag marks behind him.

As he neared the unmoving figure he recognized Adam Kave. Adam was dressed in a white shirt and dark pants. He had on polished black wing-tip shoes and black silk socks, waterlogged by the ocean. The back of his neck was flushed and his dark hair was matted with perspiration.

When Carver got close he called, "Adam?"

No answer. No movement.

Carver worked forward with the cane and stood a few feet

behind and to the side of Adam, who sat staring out at the sea and tightly hugging his knees. The surf slapped and spread high onto the beach again and foamed around his skinny black-clad ankles. He was clutching something white in his right hand. It looked like a crumpled envelope, but Carver couldn't be sure.

"Where's Paul?" Carver asked between crashes of surf.

Adam didn't look at him. "He and Nadine drove to Joel Dewitt's apartment to get some of Nadine's things. They left this morning." The husky voice was an odd monotone.

Carver started to crouch but found that he couldn't. The cane in the soft sand was too unstable. "What's wrong, Adam?"

Adam seemed to have forgotten Carver was there. Had he been so devastated by the news about Emmett and Dewitt? Or was his peculiar behavior in some way connected to Paul's recently established innocence? Paul the troubled son, back in the human race and the family fold.

Carver turned and stared up at the rambling house with its many windows looking out on the ocean. He studied the green and manicured lawn and shrubbery, broken here and there by colorful flower beds. The place looked postcard-plush and sterile. Unoccupied. No one was on the grounds, or at any of the windows. No one had answered Carver's ring. That could mean nothing. Elana might be asleep in her upstairs room, and Adam was here on the beach.

Sitting in the surf in his suit pants and wing-tip shoes. Not doing much talking.

A gull wheeled and soared delicately on an updraft, then arced in low off the sea and screamed. The sound pierced something in Carver's mind and sent a cold tingle up his spine.

"Adam, where's Elana?"

Adam said, "You did a fine job, Carver. Lying bastard that you are. You unearthed the truth. That's why I hired you. But I didn't know . . . The truth's a sonuvabitch, isn't it?"

"Too much of the time," Carver said. He watched a sailboat in the distance tack away from shore and disappear into low haze, as if it had never been there. Magic on bright water. "Where's Elana?" he repeated.

Adam was still staring out at the ocean, his head raised in a strained, attentive attitude, as if anxiously waiting for something to appear among the waves. "Elana?" he said vaguely. "Oh, she's in the boathouse."

Carver left him there and trudged with his cane toward the boathouse down the beach, near the base of the wooden steps. A miniature canal had been carved in the beach, lessening the impact of the waves, and the boathouse, a weathered old structure with a leaky roof and glassless windows, straddled the foot of the canal. It had been there for decades, and only a small boat could be docked in it out of the weather. The white-and-brown Kave pleasure yacht still rode at the dock on the beach beyond, clean and fresh and yearning for deep water.

Carver clomped with the cane across gray, weathered wood to the boathouse door. He could hear water lapping inside in rhythm with the surf. He saw the rusty padlock hanging sprung on its hasp, and he extended his cane and shoved the door open on screaming hinges. The scream sounded exactly like the gull that had circled in near where Adam was sitting on the beach.

Sun and water sent shimmering reflections over the old walls. A small, open boat with a rotted teakwood bow rose and fell with the rush and ebb of the sea. The inside of the boathouse was undulating with dancing shadows and brightness, all silent, glimmering motion.

The only still thing—so very still—was Elana Kave, hanging by her neck from a rope looped over a rafter. She was even stiller than her husband out on the beach.

She was nude, her wasted, pale body unblemished and suspended in frozen grace. Her face was grotesque, tongue protruding and eyes wide with the final surprise and comprehension. Death had diminished her, made her seem incredibly small; she was a perfect but ephemeral miniature with a gargoyle head. Ruined mortal beauty on the first leg of its journey to dust.

Glittering brilliance shafted and swirled through the old

structure and bounced broken off the water, a thousand brightly mocking things playing over her, somehow only emphasizing her waxlike stillness. She was no longer any part of the warmth and movement and suffering of life.

Adam must have found her like this.

Almost stumbling, Carver backed out of the boathouse. He didn't look away from Elana until he'd shut the squealing door.

He glanced down the beach at Adam, who was still seated as before and staring out to sea. Then he made his way toward the house and a phone.

An hour later Carver was sitting with McGregor on the screened veranda overlooking the beach and ocean. The police technicians had come and gone, and Elana had been removed in a black rubber body bag. Adam Kave had been taken inside and was being treated for shock. Nadine and Paul hadn't been located and still didn't know about their mother's death. They hadn't learned they were in a nightmare without end.

Carver sat at the glass-topped table where he'd seen the Kaves have breakfast. Not exactly amiable family meals. He tapped his cane lightly and rhythmically against a chair leg, trying to keep his mind from flashing to Elana dangling in the boathouse. It wasn't unusual for suicides to hang themselves nude, as if the act were a return to the moment of birth rather than chosen death. The sea wind was brisk, and the canvas awning, rolled out to shield from the sun, rustled and snapped overhead.

McGregor was standing with just his fingertips slid into his pants pockets, as if he liked to stay ready for action. He was chewing on something infinitesimal and hard, working it around with his long jaw, probing now and then with his tongue to find out how he was doing. Carver could hear a faint clicking as McGregor's eyeteeth slipped off the stubborn morsel and met with enough force to dismay a dentist.

"So, we know each other again," Carver said. He

watched McGregor turn his head and spit out whatever it was he'd been chewing, barely parting his lips.

"You betcha," McGregor said. "Pals, you and me, right down the line. We done okay in this thing, Carver. Might even call us heroes."

"Might," Carver said. He knew McGregor had read Elana's suicide note, which was in the white envelope the stricken Adam had clutched in his fist on the beach. "Why'd she hang herself?" Carver asked. "She'd just got her son back. Was it the cancer? She knew she wasn't going to recover."

"Wasn't that," McGregor said. He straightened his tall body awkwardly, as if his back were stiff, then walked over and sat down opposite Carver. He ran his tongue across the wide gap between his front teeth and folded his big hands. He seemed to consider not telling Carver about the note's contents, but only for a second; pals all the way. He said, "She was, in a manner of speaking, Emmett's accomplice."

Carver remembered Elana's beauty and gentleness and reacted instinctively, as Adam might have. Protecting her memory in Adam's stead. Carver's obligation. He'd done things to this family. "Bullshit! She hated Emmett. He tried to rape her."

"That's true," McGregor said. "Still, she had no choice but to cooperate with him. She married young, before she knew Adam Kave, and had a child. Her husband was killed in Korea. Afterward, while she was grieving, she fell in love with and married a guy who made her life pure hell and caused severe depression. She ran away from her new husband and her son, and probably herself. Years later she was penniless and in trouble, and she remembered things she'd heard about Adam Kave even though she'd never met him. She came to the Fort Lauderdale area and got to know him under an assumed identity, and ingratiated herself until he helped her financially and in other ways. It was a desperate kind of con she worked on him, but not an unusual one, what with all the unattached big-rich assholes in Florida. Then she unexpectedly fell in love and married him, and never could muster the guts to tell him the truth."

McGregor smiled nastily, loving the effect this was having on Carver. "Some juicy suicide note, hey?" he said. "Never know what you'll find when you kick over a gold rock and study these wealthy families. I seen it time and again."

Carver's mind was numb except for some far corner that was trying to fit all this together. Trying to accept it as truth. McGregor helped him.

"Elana had to stay silent or have Adam and the kids learn about her long-ago relationship with Emmett, and the blackmail money she'd been paying Emmett for years, in amounts small enough to escape Adam's notice. She was Emmett's former wife, Carver. Her maiden name was Jones. She was the woman who met Emmett Kave at the Orlando motel. Joel Dewitt's mother."

Carver said, "Sweet Christ!" And full realization rolled over him.

McGregor laughed. "Explains some things, don't it?"

"Some things. Other things can never be explained."

"Don't you believe it," McGregor said. "The guy doing the explaining just has to be convincing, is all. Way the world works, pardner."

"Did she actually think she could marry Adam without Emmett ever finding out her identity?"

"Sure. Remember, the brothers were estranged, hated each other, and never saw one another. There's so many rich jokers in this part of Florida, they get married and divorced all the time without anybody's picture getting on the society page—not that Emmett would read the society page. And she hadn't planned on love rearing its nasty head. Once she fell for Adam and didn't want to lose him, she had no choice. She was desperate."

"Did Dewitt know about all this?"

"I was interrogating him when you called and told me Elana was dead. He knew about everything. That was how Emmett got him to go along with the plan. Dewitt was getting even with the woman who abandoned him as a child, and he thought he had some kind of moral claim on the

Kave fortune. Once Elana died before Adam, Dewitt was out in the cold forever. Adam ain't the charitable type."

"Then Dewitt knew Paul was his brother."

"Hey, don't look so shocked, Carver. Cain did it to Abel. And these guys are only half brothers."

"But Nadine . . ."

"So Dewitt was plugging his sister—hell, there was a lotta money at stake."

Wind off the ocean whipped the canvas awning again, cracking it like a sail. The breeze felt cool on Carver's face and he realized he was perspiring. He was nauseated and wanted to get away from McGregor immediately. Didn't want to look at him or hear his voice ever again.

He stood up shakily with his cane and shoved his chair back, almost tipping it over. His mind still trying to assimilate what had happened, he limped toward the door to the house. He knew his way through the place and out.

Behind him McGregor said, "We oughta work together again sometime, tough guy. Ain't we a fuckin' team?"

CHAPTER 37

Carver wanted to attend Elana Kave's funeral, but he found out too late that she'd been cremated. There'd been only a brief, private memorial service. Adam Kave had wanted it that way.

Three months later Carver read in the *Orlando Sentinel* that Adam's Inns had been sold to a conglomerate that owned a series of chain restaurants. Adam would no longer be connected with the company he'd built with his life at the cost of his son. Nadine, Carver heard, had gone to Hawaii to finish college and do postgraduate work in anthropology. He thought that was exactly the field for her.

Lieutenant McGregor was now Captain McGregor and in charge of Internal Affairs, investigating reports of corruption within the Fort Lauderdale Police Department. Justice was blind, all right.

Carver spent his days at Edwina's, rising early and limping down to a flat stretch of beach. He'd leave his cane on the warm sand, slither awkwardly into the surf until he was floating free and graceful, and take long, therapeutic swims.

Occasionally Paul Kave would drive up A1A from Hillsboro and join him. They both loved the sea and liked to test themselves against it.

They'd roam far enough out from shore to worry Edwina. One man of maimed body and the other of maimed mind, struggling against the incoming waves.

Strong swimmers.

During unlikely moments, Carver would find himself

wondering whether Adam Kave had suspected all along that there'd been something between Elana and Emmett, and had held his silence to protect the possession he'd most treasured. But not even Adam could answer that one with certainty, Carver decided.

And it was something he never asked Paul.

Some things you left alone.